WE

By

EUGENE ZAMIATIN

Translated and with a Foreword by

GREGORY ZILBOORG

Introduction by PETER RUDY

Preface by MARC SLONIM

New York

E. P. DUTTON

Published in the United States by E. P. Dutton, a division of Penguin Books USA Inc., 2 Park Avenue, New York, N.Y. 10016.

ISBN: 0-525-48323-3

34 36 38 40 39 37 35

INTRODUCTION

It is pointless to see the tragedy of Soviet Russian literature, as some do, in the mere existence of great numbers of literary hacks, since even democratic societies are heavily burdened by inferior writers. The real tragedy of post-revolutionary Russian literature lies in what has happened to a small number of exceptional authors who, under normal circumstances, would have made us forget the mediocre crowd. Through unofficial and official pressures, these few talented men were forced into silence, into varying degrees of conformity, or into exile. The names of most of them are hardly known to their countrymen or to the world. One of these unusual men was Evgeni Ivanovich Zamiatin, who died in France as a voluntary exile in 1937.

Zamiatin was born in 1884 in the Central Russian town of Lebedian. While studying at the St. Petersburg Polytechnical Institute, he developed an interest in social and political problems, an interest that was to be strongly reflected in his literary work. He became actively involved in the revolutionary movement and suffered both imprisonment and banishment. A tale called "Provincial Life," which came out in 1911, was Zamiatin's first ambitious attempt at writing, and it showed him to be a meticulous craftsman with exceptionally acute analytical powers. Three years later these talents were again demonstrated in "At the End of the World," a story for which the government tried unsuccessfully to prosecute him on the grounds of antimilitarism. In 1917 Zamiatin published "The Islanders" and "The Fisher of Men," tales in which his satirical abilities were first given full play, with the English—

among whom he had lived briefly during the war—serving as the victims.

Zamiatin had worked and suffered so that the Revolution might take place. When it finally became a reality, he greeted it with enthusiasm and spent endless hours in lecture halls and conference rooms on its behalf. But he was quick to notice the alarming tendencies that were developing in the new society, and in his writing he boldly pointed out the impending dangers. "I Fear," an essay which appeared in 1920, warned against the insidious pressures for conformity: the new Russia would have no real literature until it cured itself of this illness; and if the illness proved incurable, then there would be only one future for Russian literature—its past. The novel *We*, written in the same year, treated the problem of conformity on a much broader scale. Although the book could not be published in the Soviet Union, it was not unknown to the critics there, since it was read in manuscript form and, during the twenties, appeared abroad in English, French, and Czech translations. In such short stories as "Draco," "The Cave," "Mamai," and "A Story about the Most Important Matter," Zamiatin stressed with satirical force the cruelty, the pettiness, and the futility characterizing Russia under the new order. His play, *The Fires of St. Dominic*, while ostensibly dealing with the Spanish Inquisition, was actually aimed at the activities of the Soviet security police. In criticism, fiction, and drama that showed his constantly maturing satirical and analytical abilities, Zamiatin fought to preserve his vision of the Revolution.

Antagonized by Zamiatin's insistence on telling the truth as he saw it, by his open disdain for anything that smacked of literary servility, Communist critics opened an offensive against him which reached an incredibly vituperative intensity after 1929, when a Russian version of *We* (allegedly retranslated from the Czech) was published abroad. Zamiatin, the self-styled "devil of Soviet literature," was thoroughly exorcised, and every effort was made to prevent any further contact between him and the public. Publishers and theaters were intimidated into ignoring him; libraries were forbidden to circulate his work. In June 1931 Zamiatin wrote a letter to Joseph Stalin. This letter was not the sort that dictators are accustomed to receive. Far from being an abject plea, it displayed an unruffled dignity underscored by an ironical tone. The author stated that he was no longer free to continue with his writing, that such a situation was for him tantamount to a death sentence, and that he was requesting permission to leave the Soviet Union. Permission was granted and, for all practical purposes, Zamiatin's career came to an end. Cut off from the immediate reality of Russia, he never again produced anything that equaled his earlier work.

Initially because of his time-consuming service in the revolutionary cause and later because of the frustrating pressures that gradually deprived him of access to editorial and theater offices, Zamiatin's quantitative contribution to Soviet Russian criticism, fiction, and drama was very slim. But if the Zamiatin chapter of Soviet Russian literature is necessarily brief, it is nevertheless brilliant, for here was a man who possessed the social and psychological perceptiveness, the courage, and the technical skill which identify the real creative artist. Such a man can produce work that is vitally significant in his own era and that retains this significance with the passage of time. This is true of Zamiatin's short stories, plays, and criticism. They were important for his day and have kept their freshness with the passage of time. But the writing of such a man can, in its basic conception, leap beyond immediacy. It may have a certain topical relevancy in his time, but its main impact will be saved for the future. The novel *We* belongs in this category. Today, in the problems it poses, it is even more important than it was thirty-nine years ago. It is an example of how man's imagination can intuitively grasp the essence of his own future problems.

In the first years of the twenties, *We* was simply another

variation on the utopian theme, a clever, stimulating, satirical fantasy that inspired speculation and debate. The ruling principle of the rigidly controlled society in *We* is that freedom and happiness are incompatible: men are congenitally incapable of using their freedom for constructive ends and merely make themselves miserable by their abuse of it; most of them yearn for a materialistic happiness and are eager to surrender their troublesome freedom and to be reduced to the status of lotus-eaters. This was hardly a new theory, except in its application. Zamiatin had obviously become intrigued by the guiding philosophy of the Grand Inquisitor in Dostoevsky's *Brothers Karamazov* and had skillfully adapted it to the needs of a modern technological state. But provocative as this restatement was, a stable society based on it was hardly credible within the context of those years. Although strange and ugly social and political theories were circulating and even being put into limited practice, it was still generally believed that man was not desperately committed to a goal of materialistic happiness and that he was a born rebel who, except during such emergencies as wartime, could not be forced to tolerate more than a minimal amount of regimentation for very long. What made *We* even less credible were the scientific advances which it predicted. At that time there was also an unintentionally comic note for most readers. Zamiatin was obviously thinking about future developments in the Soviet Union when he wrote *We*, and to any sensible person the implication that that backward country could ever build a successful interplanetary rocket was ludicrous.

When the modern totalitarian states proved how meticulously they could refine and organize the apparatus of control, then history finally began to catch up with *We*. The mathematical precision of life in Zamiatin's glass paradise was no longer an improbable nightmare. *We* seemed almost like an early blueprint for what was now happening in the world, an advanced textbook for the regimentation of mankind. In the novel there were unanimous elections which were unabashedly ritualistic in nature; prophylactic surveillance of private lives as well as torture were justified by reasoning that was as specious as it was pious; denunciations, even of those closest to one, were encouraged; children were considered the property of the state; and art was completely subservient to the aims of society. These and other characteristics of the state that Zamiatin had envisioned were now integral parts of a way of life in totalitarian countries. With respect to the most extreme practices outlined in *We*, the question was not *whether* but *when* they would be realized. It became plain that even if man is born a rebel at heart, his psychological make-up is so plastic that he can usually be effectively intimidated to the point where he will accept a rigidly controlled pattern of life for a long period of time. Since history proved Zamiatin right in this respect, the problems of the people in *We* who dared to think have lost their haze of unreality. In the light of what has been and is still occurring in totalitarian states, such problems have become fresh and compelling.

But the prophetic scope of *We* has not been fully exhausted. Totalitarianism has shown that Zamiatin's state was right about the practicability of intensive regimentation over long periods of time; however, there has been no broad proving ground for the theory on which Zamiatin's state is built, the theory that most men believe their freedom to be more than a fair exchange for a high level of materialistic happiness. It appears, though, that this theory will be put to a final test in the future. If the present rapid rate of technological development continues, both totalitarian and democratic societies will be involved in this test. When the material wants of the Soviet people are satisfied, will many of them continue to resent regimentation? As we ourselves pursue even higher goals of materialistic happiness, the complexity of our technological society will increase and exert even more intense pressures for efficiency through the regulation of our lives. What decision will we make under those circumstances? Mankind is rushing toward a final proof or refutation of Zamiatin's prophecy.

In this novel, Zamiatin tried to put into practice his belief that in its content a literary work should be heretical, refusing to accept reality at its face value and always posing those two "final, most terrifying, most fearless" questions: Why? And what lies ahead? He also attempted to carry out his conviction that form should keep up with ideas, that only a heretical form could adequately dramatize heretical ideas. Drawing on the techniques of Gogol, Dostoevsky, Andreev, and Blok, Zamiatin had created his own synthesis, and this was now adapted to the special needs of *We*.

The novel uses the notebook format, which is a particularly flexible medium for reflecting the varying moods of the narrator. A dynamic pace as well as a multidimensional characterization is obtained by techniques that are grounded in the principles of human psychology. As the narrator's emotional state changes, his perception moves between the extreme limits of objectivity and subjectivity. There is a dramatic running duel between the rational and irrational forces within him, a shifting between his conscious and unconscious powers of perception, and a constant association of ideas that forms elaborate networks. Accompanying this psychological method is a laconic language that frequently lapses into the provocatively elliptical and imparts a sensation of breathlessness. Compressed and startlingly strange similes and metaphors are used in a variety of sophisticated roles: they not only serve the conventional purpose of intensifying the description of a person or object, but they also sharply characterize the narrator and his environment; they are frequently linked to an individual through so much repetition that they attain an impressionistic force; and sometimes they are employed as a triggering mechanism to flood the reader's mind with impressions that were associated with these figures earlier in the narrative. The total effect of this imagery is to provide the novel with a strong inner unity.

Zamiatin once gave an apt metaphorical definition of good books, and this definition could well apply to *We*: "There are books of the same chemical composition as dynamite. The difference lies only in the fact that one stick of dynamite explodes once, but one book explodes thousands of times." It is very unfortunate that circumstances prevented Zamiatin from writing other books with such an explosive potential. The ability was there, but the opportunity was not.

PETER RUDY

NORTHWESTERN UNIVERSITY
1959

FOREWORD

In submitting this book to the American public the translator has this to say:

The artistic and psychological aspects of the novel are hardly to be discussed in a Foreword. Great as the art of the writer may be and profound as his psychological insight may seem to one, the impression is largely a matter of individual reactions, and this aspect must naturally be left to each individual's judgment and sensibilities.

There is, however, one side of the matter which deserves particular mention and even emphasis.

This is perhaps the first time in the history of the last few decades that a Russian book, inspired by Russian life, written in Russia and in the Russian language, should see its first light not in Russia but abroad, and not in the language in which it was originally written, but translated into a foreign tongue.[1] During the darkest years of Russian history, in the forties, sixties, eighties and nineties of the last century many Russian writers were forced by oppression and reaction to live abroad and to write abroad, yet their writings would reach Russia, as they were intended primarily for the Russian reader and Russian life. Most of Turgenev's novels were written while he was in France, and with the exception of his last short story, which he dictated on his deathbed, all his novels and stories were written in Russian. Hertzen, Kropotkin, and at one time Dostoevsky, were similarly obliged to write while away from their native land.

[1] History repeated itself recently in the case of Boris Pasternak's *Dr. Zhivago*. G.Z., 1959.

Here is a book written by an artist who lived and still lives in Russia, and whose intimate love for Russia and her suffering is so great that he finds it impossible to leave Russia even in these days of stress and sorrow. But his book may not appear in the country where it was written. It is a great tragedy—this spiritual loneliness of the artist who cannot speak to his own people. In bringing out this book in English, the author tries to address himself to the world without having the opportunity of being heard by his own people. This situation, however, is to a great extent symbolic of the spiritual mission of Zamiatin, for no matter what the language in which he writes originally, and no matter how typically national his artistic perception and intuition, he is essentially universal, and his vision transcends the boundaries of a purely national art. Moreover, is it not true that the more genuinely national a man's art, and the more sincerely national his personality, the more universal he becomes? Abraham Lincoln is much more than just an American national figure, and I doubt if the appeal of Lincoln's personality would be so universal if he were not so typically American. It would be difficult to find personalities more national than Tolstoi or Dostoevsky, and this is perhaps the reason why they stand out as two of the most universal minds with a universal appeal that the nineteenth century has given us.

Zamiatin is not so great as the men referred to above, but despite his youth, he has already proved to have that quality of greatness that characterizes a personality with a universal appeal.

We is, as Zamiatin himself calls it, the most jocular and the most earnest thing he has written thus far. It is a novel that puts before every thoughtful reader with great poignance and earnestness the most difficult problem that exists today in the civilized world—the problem of the preservation of the independent, original, creative personality. Our civilization depends upon the energetic movement of great masses of people. Wars, revolutions, general strikes—all these phenomena involve great masses, large groups, enormous mobs. Despite the fact that there is hardly a corner in the world where the average man does not make the trite complaint, "What we need is leadership," the world seems for a time, at least, to have lost its capacity to produce real leaders. For our great successes in mechanical civilization, our exceptional efforts in efficiency, tend to bring into play large masses rather than great individuals. What, under these conditions, is the lot of the creative personality? The tragedy of the independent spirit under present conditions is pointed out in a unique way in *We*. The problem of the creative individual versus the mob is not merely a Russian problem. It is as apparent in a Ford factory as under a Bolshevik dictatorship.

Of course, the sincere, honest, and frank treatment of this problem seems offensive to anyone who prefers to be a member of a mob or to keep this or that part of humanity in the state of a mob. That is why *We* could not be published in Russia, and will probably be disliked by those whose spiritual activities are reduced to the mechanical standards of a mechanical civilization which is devoid of original creative effort.

A few words should be said about the method by which Zamiatin tries to drive home his main ideas to the reader. It is the method of "laughter through tears," to use an old expression of Gogol's. It is the form that is dictated by a profound love for humanity, mixed with pity for and hatred of those factors which are the cause of the disindividualization of man today. It is the old emotion of ancient Catullus: "*Odi et amo.*" Zamiatin laughs in order to hide his tears; hence amusing as *We* may seem and really is, it barely conceals a profound human tragedy which is universal today.

The reader may be interested in knowing something about Zamiatin himself. Zamiatin does not like to talk about himself, and the translator does not think he has the right to tell more than to quote Zamiatin's own answer to a request addressed to him a couple of years ago to write his autobiography:

"I see you want my autobiography by all means, but I assure you that you will have to limit yourself only to an outside inspection and get but a glimpse, perhaps, into the dark windows. I seldom ask anybody to enter.

"As to the outside, you will see a lonely child without playmates, lying on a Turkish divan, hind-side up, reading a book, or under the grand piano while his mother plays Chopin. Two steps away from Chopin, just outside the window with the geraniums, in the middle of the street, there is a small pig tied to a stake and hens fluttering in the dust.

"If you are interested in the geography, here it is—Lebedian, in the most Russian Tambov province about which Tolstoi and Turgenev wrote so much. Chronology? The end of the eighties and early nineties, then Voronesh, the *Gymnasium pension,* boredom and rabid dogs on Main Street. One of these dogs-got me by the leg. At that time I loved to make different experiments on myself, and I decided to wait and see whether I would or would not get the rabies and, what is most important, I was very curious. What would I feel when the time would come for the rabies (about two weeks after the bite)? I felt a great many things, but two weeks later I did not get the rabies, therefore I announced to the inspector in the school that I got the rabies and must go at once to Moscow for vaccination.

"In the *Gymnasium* I would get A *plus* for composition and was not always on good terms with mathematics. Perhaps because of that (sheer stubbornness) I chose the most mathematical career—the shipbuilding department of the Petrograd Polytech.

"Thirteen years ago in the month of May—and that May was remarkable in that the snow covered the flowers—I simultaneously finished my work for my diploma and my first short story. The short story was published in the old *Obrazovanye*.

"Well, what else do you want? That meant that I was going to write short stories and was going to publish them. Therefore for the following three years I wrote about nothing but ice cutters, steam engines, refillers, and 'The Theoretical Exploration of the Works of Floating Steam Shovels.' I couldn't help myself. I was attached to the chair of Ship Architecture and busied myself with teaching in the shipbuilding faculty, where I teach until now.

"If I mean anything in Russian literature, I owe this completely to the Petrograd Secret Service. In 1911 this service exiled me from Petrograd and I was forced to spend two years in a non-populated place in Lachta. There, in the midst of the white winter silence and the green summer silence, I wrote my 'Provincial.' After that the late Ismaylov expressed in print his belief that I wore very high boots and was a long-haired provincial type, carrying a heavy stick, and he was later very much surprised that I 'didn't look a bit like that.' Incidentally, 'not a bit like that' I became in England where, during the war, I spent about two years, building ships and visiting the ruins of ancient castles. I listened to the banging of the German Zeppelin bombs and wrote a short novel 'The Islanders.'

"I regret immensely that I did not witness the Russian Revolution in February and know only the October Revolution, because it was in October, a life preserver around my body and all the lights out, passing German submarines, that I returned to Petrograd. Because of this I felt like one who never having been in love gets up one morning and finds himself married about ten years.

"Now I write little, perhaps because my requirements toward myself become greater. Three new volumes are in the hands of the publisher and begin to be published only now. The fourth will be my novel *We*, the funniest and most earnest thing I have written. However, the most serious and most interesting novels I never wrote. They happened to me in my life."

Zamiatin continues to live in Russia and continues to live with Russia, but such is the sarcasm of Fate that the first Russian novel giving a real psychological synthesis of the Russian Revolution and its greater universal meaning, this novel written by Zamiatin, should remain unknown to the Russian people.

GREGORY ZILBOORG

New York, N.Y.
1924

THIRTY-FIVE YEARS LATER

A generation has passed.

When *We* was first published, the Atlantic had not yet been spanned by an airplane. The survivors of World War I prayed and hoped for unity among nations and for the abolition of war. The Russian Revolution had taken the turn of "permanence," but there was hope that man would be spared the anguish of being lost.

World War II has come and gone. Millions were killed. Many hopes were drowned in blood, sweat, and tears. Today the Russian colossus stands stronger and firmer than it did thirty-five years ago, but man as an individual, not just as a statistical datum, seems to have lost his value. This, the truth must be told, is true not only of Russia but also in some degree of many other nations. If one stops to think of all the secret persuaders and the variety of effective and efficient modes of so-called communications—liminal and subliminal—one is bound to find in *We* the prophetic, heartrending picture and voice of the man who does not want to be stifled, but who wishes with all his heart and soul to stand erect and remain the master of his own fate in all the anguish and glory of his will to live as a person.

A little more than thirty-five years ago Marc Slonim, who contributes here some of his reminiscences of Zamiatin, and the translator, who now writes these lines, stood together in the dark of the night in a much-bombarded street in Kiev. We had "put to bed" the last issue of a paper that made the Germans angry and the Communists more angry and the Ukrainian separatists most impatient with us. Our time had run out, so to speak. So we shook hands, and each went off into his own darkness and into the unknown.

Here at the reissue of *We* we meet again (not for the first time, of course): Slonim an American college professor, myself an American psychiatrist, both still keenly aware of the horrors through which our generation has gone. We are both hopeful that the spiritual vibrancy and insight that Zamiatin offered us in the midst of the "red terror" will serve now as an inspiration to those who are still "naïve enough" to love the humanity of man, and who would stand up erect and fearless in the name of that humanity.

GREGORY ZILBOORG

New York, N.Y.
1959

PREFACE

> "Man ceased to be an ape and overcame the ape the day the first book was published. The ape had never forgotten this humiliation: just try to give him a book, and he will immediately spoil it, soil it, and tear it to pieces." (From Zamiatin's unpublished preface to a book)

In 1927, while serving as literary editor of *Volia Rossii,* an émigré monthly published in Prague, I got hold of the Russian manuscript of *We* by Eugene Zamiatin. The English version of this remarkable novel, the forerunner of works like *Brave New World* and *1984,* had come out at Dutton's in New York in 1924. Since it had never appeared in Russian, I jumped at the opportunity of offering *We* to our readers, but I was afraid that this might create trouble for the author who lived in Leningrad and obviously was not a favorite with Communist authorities. The novel was about to be translated into Czech, and I pretended that we were retranslating it from the Czech version. To give weight to this assertion, which was stated in the introductory note preceding the text in our magazine, I purposely changed or reworded quite a few passages of the original—and I must say that crippling and distorting Zamiatin's concise and beautiful prose made me feel like a criminal.

The subterfuge, however, did not work. As soon as *We* appeared in *Volia Rossii,* the Communist press in the U.S.S.R. opened a violent campaign against the author and indicted him for having given his novel, which was banned in Russia, to an émigré publication. Dubbed a counterrevolutionary and an enemy of the people, Zamiatin was vilified and ostracized. He was compelled to resign from professional organizations and could not publish a line in Soviet periodicals. As he said later, by 1931 he became "the Devil of Soviet literature, and since to spit on the Devil is considered a good deed, all the critics did nothing but spit on me as viciously as they could." His situation grew untenable, and he addressed a letter to Stalin asking for permission to go abroad, to "rest awhile from baiting and persecution." Zamiatin's request was backed by Gorky who loved and admired the creator of "The District Tale," "The Islanders," and many other stories which influenced a whole generation of Russian writers. To the general surprise, Zamiatin and his wife were granted passports for traveling in Europe. After a short sojourn in Germany and Czechoslovakia, they finally settled in Paris, where I was living at the time.

I must confess that I felt rather self-conscious about our first meeting. Was I not responsible, however indirectly, for what happened to Zamiatin in 1929? Had not the publication of *We* in *Volia Rossii* precipitated the attacks against him? But the moment I expressed my scruples to Zamiatin, he dismissed them with a smile. His sin, he explained to me, was not venial but cardinal—almost original—and the *Volia Rossii* incident served simply as a pretext to crucify a heretic and shut him up forever. He spoke in a calm, even voice, hardly changing his inflections when throwing out a sarcastic hint or an ironic allusion. Even after a short conversation with Zamiatin one could easily understand why Communist officials fought him so fiercely. His whole personality represented a threat to conformity and a challenge to accepted platitudes. Here was a man, a gentleman, an independent artist, and a fearless thinker. We soon became very good friends, and our close relationship confirmed and deepened my first impressions. In the course of the four years Zamiatin stayed in Paris I saw him very often; in the fall of 1935 he shared my apartment, and we had long, intimate talks almost every evening. To my admiration of the writer was now added my affection for the man.

He was lean, of medium height, clean shaven, with reddish-blond hair parted on the side. Then in his early fifties, he looked much younger, and the malicious twinkle of his gray eyes gave a boyish expression to his handsome face. Always wearing tweeds and with an "unextinguished" pipe in his wide, generous mouth, he resembled an Englishman. His whole appearance was neat and controlled. His manners were reserved, and to those who knew him but little he seemed all "buttoned up," a man who kept an "unmelting icicle" inside—some hard core of strong will, perfect self-mastery, and sharp intelligence. Naval engineer and professional technician, he was equally devoted to mathematics and to the arts, and united logic and imagination, precision and fantasy. In his conversation he used technological or theatrical terms indiscriminately, and would say: "At this time I was living in the town of Nikolaiev; I constructed there several bulldozers and a few short stories." During the Revolution he trained a whole group of young men who later became known as "Serapion Brothers"—and he told me with his usual grin: "I taught them the art of writing with ninety-proof ink." But this master of compact and lucid prose, this economic craftsman who preached "functional expressionism," was, despite his cold and balanced exterior, a man of passions and delicate sensitivity. Alexander Blok, the great Russian poet, called him, with friendly mockery: "The Englishman from Moscow." To all his friends the national traits of intensity and deep feelings, of profound inner life and idealistic aspirations, were apparent in Zamiatin. Like many people with a scientific background, he loved dreams and irrational flights and glorified man's desire to overcome all his limitations. The enemy of conventional rules, dogmatic strictures, and the letter of the law, he fought for the freedom of man in art and life. He told me with laughter how some petty Party officials in Leningrad gasped with horror when he unfolded in a public meeting his beloved theory of "the true revolution—the universal one, of which the social upheaval was but a minor aspect." "The most revolutionary process," stated Zamiatin, "was cosmic and it encompassed the conservation of energy or its expense, the transformation of matter or the reduction of movement to immobility. And dogma," he would add, "is the hard crust which imprisons the fiery magma, that molten material from which the hard rock is formed." Zamiatin had had a rich and varied life—filled with creation, work, and struggle. Exiled under the czarist regime, persecuted under the Bolshevik regime, he never ceased to be a social satirist and to lash at triviality and pettiness. He possessed a strong weapon—irony—and loved quoting Anatole France's slogan: "Teach men to laugh at the stupid and the angry lest we fall prey to the weakness of hating them." But often, telling me about the crimes and abuses committed in Russia in the name of mankind's emancipation, Zamiatin could not hide his indignation.

The more I knew him the more I respected his integrity, the strength of his convictions, his moral courage, and his sense of human dignity, which made him reject compromise or political surrender. One evening while describing the details of his departure from Russia, he read me the letter he addressed to Stalin in 1931. Its opening passage sounded like an excellent self-characterization: "I know," wrote Zamiatin, "that I have the very uncomfortable habit of saying not what is advantageous at a given moment but whatever I believe to be the truth. I never concealed what I think of literary servility, toadyism, and coat changing. I have always thought and I continue to think that such things are as degrading for the writer as they are to the revolution." Leaving his beloved Leningrad, he wrote: "I may come back home as soon as it is possible in our literature to express devotion to great ideas without crawling before small men, and as soon as our attitude toward the artist of the word changes."

This hope, however, never materialized. Nothing changed in the status of Russian writers while Zamiatin was working and struggling in Paris. His health, undermined by the privations of the revolutionary era and by the nervous tension in which he lived for years, declined rapidly. In the fall of 1936 I was summoned by his doctor, who told me that Zamiatin was incurably ill and that his days were numbered, a heart ailment, which kept him in bed for weeks, making his end imminent. Zamiatin became thin, almost transparent; he talked with difficulty, and his only joy was to listen to music, especially to Musorgski, whom he always admired as the greatest expression of Russian genius. He listened to *Boris Godunov* on the day of his death, in March 1937.

A small group of friends followed his coffin to the French cemetery of Thiais, near Paris. No obituaries in the Soviet press marked his passing: the official silence which isolated Zamiatin from Russian readers during his lifetime continuing after his death. It lasted twenty years—but while it is being broken now in some critical circles, the works of this extraordinary and brilliant writer are still banned from his native land.

MARC SLONIM

Bronxville, N.Y.
1959

CONTENTS

Record *Page*

WE

RECORD ONE

An Announcement
The Wisest of Lines
A Poem

This is merely a copy, word for word, of what was published this morning in the State newspaper:

"In another hundred and twenty days the building of the *Integral* will be completed. The great historic hour is near, when the first *Integral* will rise into the limitless space of the universe. One thousand years ago your heroic ancestors subjected the whole earth to the power of the United State. A still more glorious task is before you: the integration of the indefinite equation of the Cosmos by the use of the glass, electric, fire-breathing *Integral.* Your mission is to subjugate to the grateful yoke of reason the unknown beings who live on other planets, and who are perhaps still in the primitive state of freedom. If they will not understand that we are bringing them a mathematically faultless happiness, our duty will be to force them to be happy. But before we take up arms, we shall try the power of words.

"In the name of the Well-Doer, the following is announced herewith to all Numbers of the United State:

"Whoever feels capable must consider it his duty to write treatises, poems, manifestoes, odes, and other compositions on the greatness and the beauty of the United State.

"This will be the first cargo which the *Integral* will carry.

"Long live the United State! Long live the Numbers!! Long live the Well-Doer!!!"

I feel my cheeks burn as I write this. To integrate the colossal, universal equation! To unbend the wild curve, to straighten it out to a tangent—to a straight line! For the United State is a straight line, a great, divine, precise, wise line, the wisest of lines!

I, D-503, the builder of the *Integral,* I am only one of the many mathematicians of the United State. My pen, which is accustomed to figures, is unable to express the march and rhythm of consonance; therefore I shall try to record only the things I see, the things I think, or, to be more exact, the things *we* think. Yes, "we"; that is exactly what I mean, and *We,* therefore, shall be the title of my records. But this will only be a derivative of our life, of our mathematical, perfect life in the United State. If this be so, will not this derivative be a poem in itself, despite my limitations? It will. I believe it, I know it.

My cheeks still burn as I write this. I feel something similar to what a woman probably feels when for the first time she senses within herself the pulse of a tiny, blind, human being. It is I, and at the same time it is not I. And for many long months it will be necessary to feed it with my life, with my blood, and then with a pain at my heart, to tear it from myself and lay it at the feet of the United State.

Yet I am ready, as everyone, or nearly everyone of us, is. I am ready.

RECORD TWO

Ballet
Square Harmony
X

SPRING. From behind the Green Wall, from some unknown plains the wind brings to us the yellow honeyed pollen of flowers. One's lips are dry from this sweet dust. Every moment one passes one's tongue over them. Probably all women whom I meet in the street (and certainly men also) have sweet lips today. This somewhat disturbs my logical thinking. But the sky! The sky is blue. Its limpidness is not marred by a single cloud. (How primitive was the taste of the ancients, since their poets were always inspired by these senseless, formless, stupidly rushing accumulations of vapor!) I love, I am sure it will not be an error if I say *we* love, only such a sky—a sterile, faultless sky. On such days the whole universe seems to be moulded of the same eternal glass, like the Green Wall, and like all our buildings. On such days one sees their wonderful equations, hitherto unknown. One sees these equations in everything, even in the most ordinary, everyday things.

Here is an example: this morning I was on the dock where the *Integral* is being built, and I saw the lathes; blindly, with abandon, the balls of the regulators were rotating; the cranks were swinging from side to side with a glimmer; the working beam proudly swung its shoulder; and the mechanical chisels were dancing to the melody of unheard tarantellas. I suddenly perceived all the music, all the beauty, of this colossal, this mechanical ballet, illumined by light blue rays of sunshine. Then the thought came: why beautiful? Why is the dance beautiful? Answer: because it is an *unfree* movement. Because the deep meaning of the dance is contained in its absolute, ecstatic submission, in the ideal *non-freedom*. If it is true that our ancestors would abandon themselves in dancing at the most inspired moments of their lives (religious mysteries, military parades), then it means only one thing: the instinct of non-freedom has been characteristic of human nature from ancient times, and we in our life of today, we are only consciously—

I was interrupted. The switchboard clicked. I raised my eyes—O-90, of course! In half a minute she will be here to take me for the walk.

Dear O-! She always seems to me to look like her name, O-. She is approximately ten centimeters shorter than the required Maternal Norm. Therefore she appears round all over; the rose-colored O of her lips is open to meet every word of mine. She has a round soft dimple on her wrist. Children have such dimples. As she came in, the logical flywheel was still buzzing in my head, and following its inertia, I began to tell her about my new formula which embraced the machines and the dancers and all of us.

"Wonderful, isn't it?" I asked.

"Yes, wonderful . . . Spring!" she replied, with a rosy smile.

You see? Spring! She talks about Spring! Females! . . . I became silent.

We were down in the street. The avenue was crowded. On days when the weather is so beautiful, the afternoon personal hour is usually the hour of the supplementary walk. As always, the big Musical Tower was playing the

March of the United State with all its pipes. The Numbers, hundreds, thousands of Numbers in light blue unifs (probably a derivative of the ancient uniform) with golden badges on the chest—the State number of each one, male or female—the Numbers were walking slowly, four abreast, exaltedly keeping step. I, we four, were but one of the innumerable waves of a powerful torrent: to my left, O-90 (if one of my long-haired ancestors were writing this a thousand years ago he would probably call her by that funny word, *mine*); to my right, two unknown Numbers, a she-Number and a he-Number.

Blue sky, tiny baby suns in each one of our badges; our faces are unclouded by the insanity of thoughts. Rays. . . . Do you picture it? Everything seems to be made of a kind of smiling, a ray-like matter. And the brass measures: Tra-ta-ta-tam . . . Tra-ta-ta-tam . . . Stamping on the brassy steps that sparkle in the sun, with every step you rise higher and higher into the dizzy blue heights. . . . Then, as this morning on the dock, again I saw, as if for the first time in my life, the impeccably straight streets, the glistening glass of the pavement, the divine parallelepipeds of the transparent dwellings, the square harmony of the grayish-blue rows of Numbers. And it seemed to me that not past generations, but I myself, had won a victory over the old god and the old life, that I myself had created all this. I felt like a tower: I was afraid to move my elbow, lest the walls, the cupola, and the machines should fall to pieces.

Then without warning—a jump through centuries: I remembered (apparently through an association by contrast) a picture in the museum, a picture of an avenue of the twentieth century, a thundering, many-colored confusion of men, wheels, animals, billboards, trees, colors, and birds. . . . They say all this once actually existed!

It seemed to me so incredible, so absurd, that I lost control of myself and laughed aloud. A laugh, as if an echo of mine, reached my ear from the right. I turned. I saw white, very white, sharp teeth, and an unfamiliar female face.

"I beg your pardon," she said, "but you looked about you like an inspired mythological god on the seventh day of creation. You look as though you are sure that I, too, was created by you, by no one but you. It is very flattering."

All this without a smile, even with a certain degree of respect (she may know that I am the builder of the *Integral*). In her eyes, nevertheless, and on her brows, there was a strange irritating X, and I was unable to grasp it, to find an arithmetical expression for it. Somehow I was confused; with a somewhat hazy mind, I tried logically to explain my laughter.

"It was absolutely clear that this contrast, this impassable abyss, between the things of today and of years ago—"

"But why impassable?" (What bright. sharp teeth!) "One might throw a bridge over that abyss. Please imagine: a drum battalion, rows—all this existed before and consequently—"

"Oh, yes, it is clear," I exclaimed.

It was a remarkable intersection of thoughts. She said almost in the same words the things I had written down before the walk! Do you understand? Even the thoughts! It is because nobody is *one*, but *one of*. We are all so much alike—

"Are you sure?" I noticed her brows that rose to the temples in an acute angle—like the sharp corners of an X. Again I was confused, casting a glance to the right, then to the left. To my right—she, slender, abrupt, resistantly flexible like a whip, I-330 (I saw her number now). To my left, O—, totally different, all made of circles with a childlike dimple on her wrist; and at the very end of our row, an unknown he-Number, double-curved like the letter S. We were all so different from one another. . . .

The one to my right, I-330, apparently caught the confusion in my eye, for she said with a sigh, "Yes, alas!"

I don't deny that this exclamation was quite in place,

but again there was something in her face or in her voice . . .

With an abruptness unusual for me, I said, "Why, 'alas'? Science is developing and if not now, then within fifty or one hundred years—"

"Even the noses will—"

"Yes, noses!" This time I almost shouted, "Since there is still a reason, no matter what, for envy. . . . Since my nose is button-like and someone else's is—"

"Well, your nose is rather classic, as they would have said in ancient days, although your hands— No, no, show me your hands!"

I hate to have anyone look at my hands; they are covered with long hair—a stupid atavism. I stretched out my hand and said as indifferently as I could, "Apelike."

She glanced at my hand, then at my face.

"No, a very curious harmony."

She weighed me with her eyes as though with scales. The little horns again appeared at the corners of her brows.

"He is registered in my name," exclaimed O-90 with a rosy smile.

I made a grimace. Strictly speaking, she was out of order. This dear O-, how shall I say it? The speed of her tongue is not correctly calculated; the speed per second of her tongue should be slightly less than the speed per second of her thoughts—at any rate not the reverse.

At the end of the avenue the big bell of the Accumulating Tower resounded seventeen. The personal hour was at an end. I-330 was leaving us with that S-like he-Number. He has such a respectable, and I noticed then, such a familiar, face. I must have met him somewhere, but where I could not remember. Upon leaving me I-330 said with the same X-like smile:

"Drop in day after tomorrow at auditorium 112."

I shrugged my shoulders: "If I am assigned to the auditorium you just named—"

She, with a peculiar, incomprehensible certainty: "You will be."

The woman had a disagreeable effect upon me, like an irrational component of an equation which you cannot eliminate. I was glad to remain alone with dear O-, at least for a short while. Hand in hand with her, I passed four lines of avenues; at the next corner she went to the right, I to the left. O- timidly raised her round blue crystalline eyes.

"I would like so much to come to you today and pull down the curtains, especially today, right now. . . ."

How funny she is. But what could I say to her? She was with me only yesterday and she knows as well as I that our next sexual day is day after tomorrow. It is merely another case in which her thoughts are too far ahead. It sometimes happens that the spark comes too early to the motor.

At parting I kissed her twice—no, I shall be exact, three times, on her wonderful blue eyes, such clear, unclouded eyes.

RECORD THREE

A Coat
A Wall
The Tables

I looked over all that I wrote down yesterday and I find that my descriptions are not sufficiently clear. That is, everything would undoubtedly be clear to one of us, but who knows to whom my *Integral* will someday bring these records? Perhaps you, like our ancestors, have read the great book of civilization only up to the page of nine hundred years ago. Perhaps you don't know even such elementary things as the Hour Tables, Personal Hours, Maternal Norm, Green Wall, Well-Doer. It seems droll to me, and at the same time it is very difficult to explain these things. It is as though, let us say, a writer of the twentieth century should start to explain in his novel such words as coat, apartment, wife. Yet if his novel had been translated for primitive races, how could he have avoided explaining what a coat meant? I am sure that the primitive man would look at a coat and think, "What is this for? It is only a burden, an unnecessary burden." I am sure that you will feel the same, if I tell you that not one of us has ever stepped beyond the Green Wall since the Two Hundred Years' War.

But, dear readers, you must think, at least a little. It helps.

It is clear that the history of mankind, as far as our knowledge goes, is a history of the transition from nomadic forms to more sedentary ones. Does it not follow that the most sedentary form of life (ours) is at the same time the most perfect one? There was a time when people rushed from one end of the earth to another, but this was the prehistoric time when such things as nations, wars, commerce, different discoveries of different Americas still existed. Who has need of these things now?

I admit that humanity acquired this habit of a sedentary form of life not without difficulty and not all at once. When the Two Hundred Years' War had destroyed all the roads, which later were overgrown with grass, it was probably very difficult at first. It must have seemed uncomfortable to live in cities which were cut off from each other by green debris. But what of it? Man soon after he lost his tail probably did not learn at once how to chase away flies without its help. I am almost sure that at first he was even lonesome without his tail; but now, can you imagine yourself with a tail? Or can you imagine yourself walking in the street naked, without clothes? (It is possible you go without clothes still.) Here we have the same case. I cannot imagine a city which is not surrounded by a Green Wall; I cannot imagine a life which is not surrounded by the figures of our Tables.

Tables. . . . Now even, purple figures look at me austerely yet kindly from the golden background of the wall. Involuntarily I am reminded of the thing which was called by the ancients "Sainted Image," and I feel a desire to compose verses, or prayers, which are the same. Oh, why am I not a poet, so as to be able to glorify the Tables properly, the heart and pulse of the United State!

All of us and perhaps all of you read in childhood, while in school, that greatest of all monuments of ancient literature, the Official Railroad Guide. But if you compare this with the Tables, you will see side by side graphite and diamonds. Both are the same, carbon. But how eternal, transparent, how shining the diamond! Who does not lose his breath when he runs through the pages of the Guide? The Tables transformed each one of us, actually, into a six-wheeled steel hero of a great poem. Every morning, with six-wheeled precision, at the same hour, at the same minute, we wake up, millions of us at once. At the very same hour, millions like one, we begin our work, and millions like one, we finish it. United into a single body with a million hands, at the very same second, designated by the Tables, we carry the spoons to our mouths; at the same second we all go out to walk, go to the auditorium, to the halls for the Taylor exercises, and then to bed.

I shall be quite frank: even *we* have not attained the absolute, exact solution of the problem of happiness. Twice a day, from sixteen to seventeen o'clock and from twenty-one to twenty-two, our powerful united organism dissolves into separate cells; these are the *personal* hours designated by the Tables. During these hours you would see the curtains discreetly drawn in the rooms of some; others march slowly over the pavement of the main avenue or sit at their desks as I sit now. But I firmly believe, let them call me an idealist and a dreamer, I believe that sooner or later we shall somehow find a place in the general formula even for these hours. Somehow, all of the 86,400 seconds will be incorporated in the Tables of Hours.

I have had opportunity to read and hear many improbable things about those times when human beings still lived in the state of freedom, that is, in an unorganized primitive state. One thing has always seemed to me most improbable: how could a government, even a primitive government, permit people to live without anything like our Tables—without compulsory walks, without precise regulation of the time to eat, for instance? They would get up and go to bed whenever they liked. Some historians even say that in those days the streets were lighted all night, and all night people went about the streets.

That I cannot understand. True, their minds were rather limited in those days. Yet they should have understood, should they not, that such a life was actually wholesale murder, although slow murder, day after day? The State (humanitarianism) forbade in those days the murder of one person, but it did not forbid the killing of millions slowly and by inches. To kill one person, that is, to reduce the individual span of human life by fifty years, was considered criminal, but to reduce the general sum of human life by fifty million years was not considered criminal! Isn't it droll? Today this simple mathematical moral problem could easily be solved in half a minute's time by any ten-year-old Number, yet *they* couldn't do it! All their Immanuel Kants together couldn't do it! It didn't enter the heads of all their Kants to build a system of scientific ethics, that is, ethics based on adding, subtracting, multiplying, and dividing.

Further, is it not absurd that their State (they called it State!) left sexual life absolutely without control? On the contrary, whenever and as much as they wanted . . . absolutely unscientific, like beasts! And like beasts they blindly gave birth to children! Is it not strange to understand gardening, chicken farming, fishery (we have definite knowledge that they were familiar with all these things), and not to be able to reach the last step in this logical scale, namely, production of children—not to be able to discover such things as Maternal and Paternal Norms?

It is so droll, so improbable, that while I write this I am afraid lest you, my unknown future readers, should think I am merely a poor jester. I feel almost as if you may think I want simply to mock you and with a very serious face try to relate absolute nonsense to you. But first I am incapable of jesting, for in every joke a lie has its hidden function. And second, the science of the United State contends that the life of the ancients was exactly what I am describing, and the science of the United State does not make mistakes! Yet how could they have State logic, since they lived in a condition of freedom like beasts, like apes, like herds? What could one expect of them, since even in our day one hears from time to time, coming from the bottom, the primitive depths, the echo of the apes?

Fortunately it happens only from time to time, very seldom. Happily, it is only a case of small parts breaking; these may easily be repaired without stopping the eternal great march of the whole machine. And in order to eliminate a broken peg we have the skillful heavy hand of the Well-Doer, we have the experienced eyes of the Guardians. . . .

By the way, I just thought of that Number whom I met yesterday, the double-curved one like the letter S; I think I have seen him several times coming out of the Bureau of Guardians. Now I understand why I felt such an instinctive respect for him and a kind of awkwardness when I saw that strange I-330 at his side. . . . I must confess that, that I . . . they ring the bell, time to sleep, it is twenty-two-thirty. Till tomorrow, then.

RECORD FOUR

The Wild Man with a Barometer
Epilepsy
If

Until today everything in life seemed to me clear (that is why, I think, I always had a sort of partiality toward the word "clear"), but today . . . I don't understand. First, I really was assigned to auditorium 112, as she said, although the probability was 500 to 10,000,000 or 1:20,000. (Five hundred is the number of auditoriums and there are 10,000,000 Numbers.) And second . . . But let me relate things in proper order.

The auditorium: an enormous half-globe of glass with the sun piercing through. The circular rows of noble, globelike, closely shaven heads. With joy in my heart I looked around. I believe I was looking in the hope of seeing the rose-colored scythe, the dear lips of O- somewhere among the blue waves of the unifs. Then I saw extraordinarily white, sharp teeth like the . . . But no! Tonight at twenty-one o'clock O- was to come to me; therefore my desire to see her was quite natural. The bell. We stood up, sang the Hymn of the United State, and our clever phono-lecturer appeared on the platform with a sparkling golden loud-speaker.

"Respected Numbers, not so long ago our archaeologists dug up a book written in the twentieth century. In this book the ironical author tells about a Wild Man and a barometer. The Wild Man noticed that every time the barometer's hand stopped on the word 'rain,' it actually rained. And as the Wild Man craved rain, he let out as much mercury as was necessary to put it at the level of the word 'rain' (on the screen a Wild Man with feathers, letting out the mercury. Laughter).

"You are laughing at him, but don't you think the 'European' of that age deserves more to be laughed at? He, like the Wild Man, wanted rain—rain with a little 'r,' an algebraic rain; but he remained standing before the barometer like a wet hen. The Wild Man at least had more courage and energy and logic, although primitive logic. The Wild Man showed the ability to establish a connection between cause and effect: by letting out the mercury he made the first step on the path which . . ."

Here (I repeat, I am not concealing anything, I am setting down everything) I suddenly became impermeable to the quickening currents coming from the loud-speaker. I suddenly felt I had come here in vain (why in vain and how could I not have come here, since I was assigned to come here?). Everything seemed to me empty like a shell. I succeeded with difficulty in tuning my attention in again when the phono-lecturer came to the main theme of the evening—to our music as a mathematical composition (mathematics is the cause, music the effect). The phono-lecturer began the description of the recently invented musicometer.

". . . By merely rotating this handle anyone is enabled to produce about three sonatas per hour. What difficulties our predecessors had in making music! They were able to compose only by bringing themselves to attacks of inspiration, an extinct form of epilepsy. Here you have an amusing illustration of their achievements: the music of Scriabin, twentieth century. This black box"—a curtain parted on the platform, and we saw an ancient instrument —"this box they called the 'Royal Grand.' They attached to this idea of *regality*, which also goes to prove how their music . . ."

And I don't remember anything further. Very possibly because . . . I'll tell you frankly, because she, I-330, came to the "Royal" box. Probably I was simply startled by her unexpected appearance on the platform.

She was dressed in a fantastic dress of the ancient time, a black dress closely fitting the body, sharply delimiting the white of her shoulders and breasts, and that warm shadow waving with her breath between. . . . And the dazzling, almost angry teeth. A smile, a bite, directed downward. She took her seat; she began to play something wild, convulsive, loud like all their life then—not a shadow of rational mechanism. Of course all those around me were right; they were laughing. Only a few . . . But why is it that I, too, I . . .?

Yes, epilepsy, a mental disease, a pain. A slow, sweet pain, bite, and it goes deeper and becomes sharper. And then, slowly, sunshine—not our sunshine, not crystalline, bluish, and soft, coming through the glass bricks. No, a wild sunshine, rushing and burning, tearing everything into small bits. . . .

The Number at my left glanced at me and chuckled. I don't know why but I remember exactly how a microscopic saliva bubble appeared on his lips and burst. That bubble brought me back to myself. I was again I.

Like all the other Numbers I heard now only the senseless, disorderly crackling of the chords. I laughed; I felt so light and simple. The gifted phono-lecturer represented to us only too well that wild epoch. And that was all.

With what a joy I listened afterward to our contemporary music. It was demonstrated to us at the end of the lecture for the sake of contrast. Crystalline, chromatic scales converging and diverging into endless series; and synthetic harmony of the formulae of Taylor and McLauren, wholesome, square, and massive like the "trousers of Pythagoras." Sad melodies dying away in waving movements. The beautiful texture of the spectrum of planets, dissected by Frauenhofer lines . . . what magnificent, what perfect regularity! How pitiful the willful music of the ancients, not limited except by the scope of their wild imaginations!

As usual, in good order, four abreast, all of us left the auditorium. The familiar double-curved figure passed swiftly by. I respectfully bowed.

Dear O- was to come in an hour. I felt agitated, agreeably and usefully. Home at last! I rushed to the house office, handed over to the controller on duty my pink ticket, and received a certificate permitting the use of the curtains. This right exists in our State only for the sexual days. Normally we live surrounded by transparent walls which seem to be knitted of sparkling air; we live beneath the eyes of everyone, always bathed in light. We have nothing to conceal from one another; besides, this mode of living makes the difficult and exalted task of the Guardians much easier. Without it many bad things might happen. It is possible that the strange opaque dwellings of the ancients were responsible for their pitiful cellish psychology. "My (*sic!*) home is my fortress!" How did they manage to think such things?

At twenty-two o'clock I lowered the curtain and at the same second O- came in smiling, slightly out of breath. She extended to me her rosy lips and her pink ticket. I tore off the stub but I could not tear myself away from the rosy lips up to the last moment, twenty-two-fifteen.

Then I showed her my diary and I talked; I think I talked very well on the beauty of a square, a cube, a straight line. At first she listened so charmingly, she was so rosy; then suddenly a tear appeared in her blue eyes, then another, and a third fell straight on the open page (page 7). The ink blurred; well, I shall have to copy it again.

"My dear O-, if only you, if . . ."

"What if? If what?"

Again the old lament about a child or perhaps something new regarding, regarding . . . the other one? Although it seems as though some . . . But that would be too absurd!

RECORD FIVE

The Square
The Rulers of the World
An Agreeable and Useful Function

Again with you, my unknown reader; I talk to you as though you were, let us say, my old comrade, R-13, the poet with the lips of a Negro—well, everyone knows him. Yet you are somewhere on the moon, or on Venus, or on Mars. Who knows you? Where and who are you?

Imagine a square, a living, beautiful square. Imagine that this square is obliged to tell you about itself, about its life. You realize that this square would hardly think it necessary to mention the fact that all its four angles are equal. It knows this too well. This is such an ordinary, obvious thing. I am in exactly the same square position. Take the pink checks, for instance, and all that goes with them: for me they are as natural as the equality of the four angles of the square. But for you they are perhaps more mysterious and hard to understand than Newton's binomial theorem. Let me explain: an ancient sage once said a clever thing (accidentally, beyond doubt). He said, "Love and Hunger rule the world." Consequently, to dominate the world, man had to win a victory over hunger after paying a very high price. I refer to the great Two Hundred Years' War, the war between the city and the land. Probably on account of religious prejudices, the primitive peasants stubbornly held on to their "bread."[1]

[1] This word came down to us for use only as a poetic form, for the chemical constitution of this substance is unknown to us.

In the thirty-fifth year before the foundation of the United State our contemporary petroleum food was invented. True, only about two tenths of the population of the globe did not die out. But how beautifully shining the face of the earth became when it was cleared of its impurities!

Accordingly the 0.2 which survived have enjoyed the greatest happiness in the bosom of the United State. But is it not clear that supreme bliss and envy are only the numerator and the denominator, respectively, of the same fraction, happiness? What sense would the innumerable sacrifices of the Two Hundred Years' War have for us if a reason were left in our life for jealousy? Yet such a reason persisted because there remained buttonlike noses and classical noses (cf: our conversation during the promenade). For there were some whose love was sought by everyone, and others whose love was sought by no one.

Naturally, having conquered hunger (that is, algebraically speaking, having achieved the total of bodily welfare), the United State directed its attack against the second ruler of the world, against love. At last this element also was conquered, that is, organized and put into a mathematical formula. It is already three hundred years since our great historic *Lex Sexualis* was promulgated: "A Number may obtain a license to use any other Number as a sexual product."

The rest is only a matter of technique. You are carefully examined in the laboratory of the Sexual Department where they find the content of the sexual hormones in your blood, and they accordingly make out for you a Table of sexual days. Then you file an application to enjoy the services of Number so and so, or Numbers so and so. You get for that purpose a checkbook (pink). That is all.

It is clear that under such circumstances there is no reason for envy or jealousy. The denominator of the fraction of happiness is reduced to zero and the whole fraction is thus converted into a magnificent infiniteness. The thing which was for the ancients a source of innumerable stupid tragedies has been converted in our time into a harmonious, agreeable, and useful function of the organism, a function like sleep, physical labor, the taking of food, digestion, etc., etc. Hence you see how the great power of logic purifies everything it happens to touch. Oh, if only you unknown readers can conceive this divine power! If you will only learn to follow it to the end!

It is very strange. While I was writing today of the loftiest summit of human history, all the while I breathed the purest mountain air of thought, but within me it was and remains cloudy, cobwebby, and there is a kind of cross-like, four-pawed X. Or perhaps it is my paws and I feel like that only because they are always before my eyes, my hairy paws. I don't like to talk about them. I dislike them. They are a trace of a primitive epoch. Is it possible that there is in me . . . ?

I wanted to strike out all this because it trespasses on the limits of my synopsis. But then I decided: no, I shall not! Let this diary give the curve of the most imperceptible vibrations of my brain, like a precise seismograph, for at times such vibrations serve as forewarnings . . . Certainly this is absurd! This certainly should be stricken out; we have conquered all the elements; catastrophes are not possible any more.

Now everything is clear to me. The peculiar feeling inside is a result of that very same square situation of which I spoke in the beginning. There is no X in me. There can be none. I am simply afraid lest some X will be left in you, my unknown readers. I believe you will understand that it is harder for me to write than it ever was for any author throughout human history. Some of them wrote for contemporaries, some for future generations, but none of them ever wrote for their ancestors, or for beings like their primitive, distant ancestors.

RECORD SIX

An Accident
The Cursed "It's Clear"
Twenty-four Hours

I must repeat, I have made it my duty to write concealing nothing. Therefore I must point out now that, sad as it may be, the process of the hardening and crystallization of life has evidently not been completed even here in our State. A few steps more and we will be within reach of our ideal. The ideal (it's clear) is to be found where nothing *happens*, but here. . . . I will give you an example: in the State paper I read that in two days the holiday of Justice will be celebrated on the Plaza of the Cube. This means that again some Number has impeded the smooth running of the great State machine. Again something that was not foreseen, or forecalculated, *happened*.

Besides, something *happened* to me. True, it occurred during the personal hour, that is during the time specifically assigned to unforeseen circumstances, yet . . .

At about sixteen (to be exact, ten minutes to sixteen), I was at home. Suddenly the telephone:

"D-503?"—a woman's voice.

"Yes."

"Are you free?"

"Yes."

"It is I, I-330. I shall run over to you immediately. We shall go together to the Ancient House. Agreed?"

I-330! . . . This I- irritates me, repels me. She almost frightens me; but just because of that I answered, "Yes."

In five minutes we were in an aero. Blue sky of May. The bright sun in its own golden aero buzzed behind us without catching up and without lagging behind. Ahead of us a white cataract of a cloud. Yes, a white cataract of a cloud, nonsensically fluffy like the cheeks of an ancient cupid. That cloud was disturbing. The front window was open; it was windy; lips were dry. Against one's will one passed the tongue constantly over them and thought about lips.

Already we saw in the distance the hazy green spots on the other side of the Wall. Then a slight involuntary sinking of the heart, down–down–down, as if from a steep mountain, and we were at the Ancient House.

That strange, delicate, blind establishment is covered all around with a glass shell, otherwise it would undoubtedly have fallen to pieces long ago. At the glass door we found an old woman all wrinkles, especially her mouth, which was all made up of folds and pleats. Her lips had disappeared, having folded inward; her mouth seemed grown together. It seemed incredible that she should be able to talk, and yet she did.

"Well, dear, come again to see my little house?"

Her wrinkles shone, that is, her wrinkles diverged like rays, which created the impression of shining.

"Yes, Grandmother," answered I-330.

The wrinkles continued to shine.

"And the sun, eh, do you see it, you rogue, you! I know, I know. It's all right. Go all by yourselves–I shall remain here in the sunshine."

Hmm. . . . Apparently my companion was a frequent guest here. Something disturbed me; probably that unpleasant optical impression, the cloud on the smooth blue surface of the sky.

While we were ascending the wide, dark stairs, I-330 said, "I love her, that old woman."

"Why?"

"I don't know. Perhaps for her mouth—or perhaps for nothing, just so."

I shrugged my shoulders. She continued walking upstairs with a faint smile, or perhaps without a smile at all.

I felt very guilty. It is clear that there must not be "love, just so," but "love because of." For all elements of nature should be . . .

"It's clear . . ." I began, but I stopped at that word and cast a furtive look at I-330. Did she notice it or not? She looked somewhere, down; her eyes were closed like curtains.

It struck me suddenly: evening about twenty-two; you walk on the avenue and among the brightly lighted, transparent, cubic cells are dark spaces, lowered curtains, and there behind the curtains . . . What has she behind her curtains? Why did she phone me today? Why did she bring me here? and all this. . . .

She opened a heavy, squeaking, opaque door and we found ourselves in a somber disorderly space (they called it an "apartment"). The same strange "royal" musical instrument and a wild, unorganized, crazy loudness of colors and forms like their ancient music. A white plane above, dark blue walls, red, green, orange bindings of ancient books, yellow bronze candelabra, a statue of Buddha, furniture with lines distorted by epilepsy, impossible to reduce to any clear equation.

I could hardly bear that chaos. But my companion apparently possessed a stronger constitution.

"This is my most beloved—" she suddenly caught herself (again a smile, bite, and white sharp teeth)—"to be more exact, the most nonsensical of all 'apartments.'"

"Or, to be most exact, of all the States. Thousands of microscopic States, fighting eternal wars, pitiless like—"

"Oh, yes, it's clear," said I-330 with apparent sincerity.

We passed through a room where we found a few small children's beds (children in those days were also private property). Then more rooms, glimmering mirrors, somber closets, unbearably loud-colored divans, an enormous "fireplace," a large mahogany bed. Our contemporary beautiful, transparent, eternal glass was represented here only by pitiful, delicate, tiny squares of windows.

"And to think; here there was love 'just so'; they burned and tortured themselves." (Again the curtain of the eyes was lowered.) "What a stupid, uneconomical spending of human energy. Am I not right?"

She spoke as though reading my thoughts, but in her smile there remained always that irritating X. There behind the curtains something was going on, I don't know what, but something that made me lose my patience. I wanted to quarrel with her, to scream at her (exactly, to scream), but I had to agree. It was impossible not to agree.

We stopped in front of a mirror. At that moment I saw only her eyes. An idea came to me: human beings are built as nonsensically as these stupid "apartments," human heads are opaque, and there are only two very small windows that lead inside, the eyes. She seemed to have guessed my thoughts; she turned around: "Well, here they are, my eyes. . . . Well" (this suddenly, then silence).

There in front of me were two gloomy, dark windows and behind them, inside, such strange hidden life. I saw there only fire, burning like a peculiar "fireplace," and unknown figures resembling . . .

All this was certainly very natural; I saw in her eyes the reflection of my own face. But my feelings were unnatural and not like me. Evidently the depressing influence of the surroundings was beginning to tell on me. I definitely felt fear. I felt as if I were trapped in a strange cage. I felt that I was caught in the wild hurricane of ancient life.

"Do you know . . ." said I-330. "Step for a moment into

the next room." Her voice came from there, from inside, from behind the dark window eyes, where the fireplace was blazing.

I went in, sat down. From a shelf on the wall there looked straight into my face, somewhat smiling, the snub-nosed, asymmetrical physiognomy of one of the ancient poets; I think it was Pushkin.

"Why do I sit here enduring this smile with such resignation, and what is this all about? Why am I here? And why all these strange sensations, this irritating, repellent female, this strange game?"

The door of the closet slammed; there was the rustle of silk. I felt it difficult to restrain myself from getting up and, and . . . I don't remember exactly; probably I wanted to tell her a number of disagreeable things. But she had already appeared.

She was dressed in a short, bright-yellowish dress, black hat, black stockings. The dress was of light silk. I saw clearly very long black stockings above the knees, an uncovered neck, and the shadow between. . . .

"It's clear that you want to seem original. But is it possible that you—?"

"It is clear," interrupted I-330, "that to be original means to stand out among others; consequently, to be original means to violate the law of equality. What was called in the language of the ancients 'to be common' is with us only the fulfilling of one's duty. For—"

"Yes, yes, exactly," I interrupted impatiently, "and there is no use, no use . . ."

She came near the bust of the snub-nosed poet, lowered the curtain on the wild fire of her eyes, and said (this time I think she was really in earnest, or perhaps she merely wanted to soften my impatience with her, but she said a very reasonable thing):

"Don't you think it surprising that once people could stand types like this? Not only stand them, but worship them? What a slavish spirit, don't you think so?"

"It's clear . . . that is . . .!" I wanted . . . (damn that cursed "it's clear!").

"Oh, yes, I understand. But in fact these poets were stronger rulers than the crowned ones. Why were they not isolated and exterminated? In our State–"

"Oh, yes, in our State–" I began.

But suddenly she laughed. I saw the laughter in her eyes. I saw the resounding sharp curve of that laughter, flexible, tense like a whip. I remember my whole body shivered. I thought of grasping her . . . and I don't know what. . . . I had to do something, it mattered little what; automatically I looked at my golden badge, glanced at my watch–ten minutes to seventeen!

"Don't you think it is time to go?" I said in as polite a tone as possible.

"And if I should ask you to stay here with me?"

"What? Do you realize what you are saying? In ten minutes I must be in the auditorium."

"And 'all the Numbers must take the prescribed courses in art and science,' " said I-330 with my voice.

Then she lifted the curtain, opened her eyes–through the dark windows the fire was blazing.

"I have a physician in the Medical Bureau; he is registered to me; if I ask him, he will give you a certificate declaring that you are ill. All right?"

Understood! At last I understood where this game was leading.

"Ah, so! But you know that every honest Number as a matter of course must immediately go to the office of the Guardians and–"

"And as a matter not of course?" (Sharp smile-bite.) "I am very curious to know: will you or will you not go to the Guardians?"

"Are you going to remain here?"

I grasped the knob of the door. It was a brass knob, a cold, brass knob, and I heard, cold like brass, her voice:

"Just a minute, may I?"

She went to the telephone, called a Number (I was so upset it escaped me), and spoke loudly: "I shall be waiting for you in the Ancient House. Yes, yes, alone."

I turned the cold brass knob.

"May I take the aero?"

"Oh, yes, certainly, please!"

In the sunshine at the gate the old woman was dozing like a plant. Again I was surprised to see her grown-together mouth open, and to hear her say:

"And your lady, did she remain alone?"

"Alone."

The mouth of the old woman grew together again; she shook her head; apparently even her weakening brain understood the stupidity and the danger of that woman's behavior.

At seventeen o'clock exactly I was at the lecture. There I suddenly realized that I did not tell the whole truth to the old woman. I-330 was not there alone *now*. Possibly this fact, that I involuntarily told the old woman a lie, was torturing me now and distracting my attention. Yes, not alone—that was the point.

After twenty-one-thirty o'clock I had a free hour; I could therefore have gone to the office of the Guardians to make my report. But after that stupid adventure I was so tired; besides, the law provides two days. I shall have time tomorrow; I have another twenty-four hours.

RECORD SEVEN

An Eyelash
Taylor
Henbane and Lily of the Valley

Night. Green, orange, blue. The red royal instrument. The yellow dress. Then a brass Buddha. Suddenly it lifted the brass eyelids and sap began to flow from it, from Buddha. Sap also from the yellow dress. Even in the mirror, drops of sap, and from the large bed and from the children's bed and soon from myself. . . . It is horror, mortally sweet horror! . . .

I woke up. Soft blue light, the glass of the walls, of the chairs, of the table was glimmering. This calmed me. My heart stopped palpitating. Sap! Buddha! How absurd! I am sick, it is clear; I never saw dreams before. They say that to see dreams was a common normal thing with the ancients. Yes, after all, their life was a whirling carousel: green, orange, Buddha, sap. But we, people of today, we know all too well that dreaming is a serious mental disease. I . . . Is it possible that *my* brain, this precise, clean, glittering mechanism, like a chronometer without a speck of dust on it, is . . . ? Yes, it is, now. I really feel there in the brain some foreign body like an eyelash in the eye. One does not feel one's whole body, but this eye with a hair in it; one cannot forget it for a second. . . .

The cheerful, crystalline sound of the bell at my head. Seven o'clock. Time to get up. To the right and to the left as in mirrors, to the right and to the left through the glass walls I see others like myself, other rooms like my own, other clothes like my own, movements like mine, duplicated thousands of times. This invigorates me; I see myself as a part of an enormous, vigorous, united body; and what precise beauty! Not a single superfluous gesture, or bow, or turn. Yes, this Taylor was undoubtedly the greatest genius of the ancients. True, he did not come to the idea of applying his method to the whole life, to every step throughout the twenty-four hours of the day; he was unable to integrate his system from one o'clock to twenty-four. I cannot understand the ancients. How could they write whole libraries about some Kant and take only slight notice of Taylor, of this prophet who saw ten centuries ahead?

Breakfast was over. The hymn of the United State had been harmoniously sung; rhythmically, four abreast we walked to the elevators, the motors buzzed faintly, and swiftly we went down—down—down, the heart sinking slightly. Again that stupid dream, or some unknown function of that dream. Oh, yes! Yesterday in the aero, then down—down! Well, it is all over, anyhow. Period. It is very fortunate that I was so firm and brusque with her.

The car of the underground railway carried me swiftly to the place where the motionless, beautiful body of the *Integral,* not yet spiritualized by fire, was glittering in the docks in the sunshine. With closed eyes I dreamed in formulae. Again I calculated in my mind what was the initial velocity required to tear the *Integral* away from the earth. Every second the mass of the *Integral* would change because of the expenditure of the explosive fuel. The equation was very complex, with transcendent figures. As in a dream I felt, right here in the firm calculated world, how someone sat down at my side, barely touching me and saying, "Pardon." I opened my eyes.

At first, apparently because of an association with the *Integral,* I saw something impetuously flying into the distance—a head; I saw pink wing ears sticking out on the sides of it, then the curve of the overhanging back of the head, the double-curved letter S.

Through the glass walls of my algebraic world again I felt the eyelash in my eye. I felt something disagreeable, I felt that today I must . . .

"Certainly, please." I smiled at my neighbor and bowed.

I saw Number S-4711 glittering on his golden badge (that is why I associated him with the letter S from the very first moment: an optical impression which remained unregistered by consciousness). His eyes sparkled, two sharp little drills; they were revolving swiftly, drilling in deeper and deeper. It seemed that in a moment they would drill in to the bottom and would see something that I do not even dare to confess to myself. . . .

That bothersome eyelash became wholly clear to me. S- was one of them, one of the Guardians, and it would be the simplest thing immediately, without deferring, to tell him everything!

"I went yesterday to the Ancient House . . ." My voice was strange, husky, flat—I tried to cough.

"That is good. It must have given you material for some instructive deductions."

"Yes . . . but . . . You see, I was not alone; I was in the company of I-330, and then . . ."

"I-330? You are fortunate. She is a very interesting, gifted woman; she has a host of admirers."

But he, too—then during the promenade. . . . Perhaps he is even assigned as her he-Number! No, it is impossible to tell him, unthinkable. This was perfectly clear.

"Yes, yes, certainly, very." I smiled, more and more broadly, more stupidly, and felt as if my smile made me look foolish, naked.

The drills reached the bottom; revolving continually they screwed themselves back into his eyes. S- smiled double-curvedly, nodded, and slid to the exit.

I covered my face with the newspaper (I felt as if

everybody were looking at me), and soon I forgot about the eyelash, about the little drills, about everything, I was so upset by what I read in the paper: "According to authentic information, traces of an organization, which still remains out of reach, have again been discovered. This organization aims at liberation from the beneficial yoke of the State."

Liberation! It is remarkable how persistent human criminal instincts are! I use deliberately the word "criminal," for freedom and crime are as closely related as—well, as the movement of an aero and its speed: if the speed of an aero equals zero, the aero is motionless; if human liberty is equal to zero, man does not commit any crime. That is clear. The way to rid man of criminality is to rid him of freedom. No sooner did we rid ourselves of freedom (in the cosmic sense centuries are only a "no sooner.") than suddenly some unknown pitiful degenerates. . . . No, I cannot understand why I did not go immediately yesterday to the Bureau of Guardians. Today, after sixteen o'clock, I shall go without fail.

At sixteen-ten I was in the street; at once I noticed O-90 at the corner; she was all rosy with delight at the encounter. She has a simple, round mind. A timely meeting; she would understand and lend me support. Or, no, I did not need any support; my decision was firm.

The pipes of the Musical Tower thundered out harmoniously the March—the same daily March. How wonderful the charm of this dailiness, of this constant repetition and mirror-like smoothness!

"Out for a walk?" Her round blue eyes opened toward me widely, blue windows leading inside; I penetrate there unhindered; there is nothing in there, I mean nothing foreign, nothing superfluous.

"No, not for a walk. I must go." I told her where. And to my astonishment I saw her rosy round mouth form a crescent with the horns downward as if she tasted something sour. This angered me.

"You she-Numbers seem to be incurably eaten up by prejudices. You are absolutely unable to think abstractly. Forgive me the word, but this I call bluntness of mind."

"You? . . . to the spies? How ugly! And I went to the Botanical Garden and brought you a branch of lily of the valley . . ."

"Why 'and I'? Why this 'and'? Just like a woman!"

Angrily (this I must confess), I snatched the flowers. "Here they are, your lilies of the valley. Well, smell them! Good? Yes? Why not use a little bit of logic? The lilies of the valley smell good; all right! But you cannot say about an odor, about the conception of an odor, that it *is* good or bad, can you? You can't, can you? There is the smell of lilies of the valley, and there is the disagreeable smell of henbane. Both are odors. The ancient States had their spies; we have ours . . . yes, spies! I am not afraid of words. But is it not clear to you that there the spies were henbane; here they are lilies of the valley? Yes, lilies of the valley. Yes!"

The rosy crescent quivered. Now I understand that it was only my impression, but at that moment I was certain she was going to laugh. I shouted still louder:

"Yes, lilies of the valley! And there is nothing funny about it, nothing funny!"

The smooth round globes of heads passing by were turning toward us. O-90 gently took my hand.

"You are so strange today . . . are you ill?"

My dream. . . . Yellow color. . . . Buddha. . . . It was at once borne clearly upon me that I must go to the Medical Bureau.

"Yes, you are right, I am sick," I said with joy (that seems to me an inexplicable contradiction; there was nothing to be joyful about).

"You must go at once to the doctor. You understand that; you are obliged to be healthy; it seems strange to have to prove it to you."

"My dear O-, of course you are right. Absolutely right."

I did not go to the Bureau of Guardians; I could not; I had to go to the Medical Bureau; they kept me there until seventeen o'clock.

In the evening (incidentally, the Bureau of Guardians is closed evenings)—in the evening O- came to see me. The curtains were not lowered. We busied ourselves with the arithmetical problems of an ancient textbook. This occupation always calms and purifies our thoughts. O- sat over her notebook, her head slightly inclined to the left; she was so assiduous that she poked out her left cheek with the tongue from within. She looked so child-like, so charming. . . . I felt everything in me was pleasant, precise, and simple.

She left. I remained alone. I breathed deeply two times (it is very good exercise before retiring for the night). Suddenly—an unexpected odor reminiscent of something very disagreeable! I soon found out what was the matter: a branch of lily of the valley was hidden in my bed. Immediately everything was aroused again, came up from the bottom. Decidedly, it was tactless on her part to put these lilies of the valley there surreptitiously. Well, true I did not go; I didn't, but was it my fault that I had felt indisposed?

RECORD EIGHT

An Irrational Root
R-13
The Triangle

It was long ago, during my school days, when I first encountered the square root of minus one. I remember it all very clearly: a bright globelike class hall, about a hundred round heads of children, and Plappa—our mathematician. We nicknamed him Plappa; it was a very much used-up mathematician, loosely screwed together; as the member of the class who was on duty that day would put the plug into the socket behind, we would hear at first from the loud-speaker, "Plap-plap-plap-plap—tshshsh. . . ." Only then the lesson would follow. One day Plappa told us about irrational numbers, and I remember I wept and banged the table with my fist and cried, "I do not want that square root of minus one; take that square root of minus one away!" This irrational root grew into me as something strange, foreign, terrible; it tortured me; it could not be thought out. It could not be defeated because it was beyond reason.

Now, that square root of minus one is here again. I read over what I have written and I see clearly that I was insincere with myself, that I lied to myself in order to avoid seeing that square root of minus one. My sickness is all nonsense! I *could go there.* I feel sure that if such a thing had happened a week ago I should have gone without hesitating. Why, then, am I unable to go now? . . . Why?

Today, for instance, at exactly sixteen-ten I stood before the glittering Glass Wall. Above was the shining, golden, sun-like sign: "Bureau of Guardians." Inside, a long queue of bluish-gray unifs awaiting their turns, faces shining like the oil lamps in an ancient temple. They had come to accomplish a great thing: they had come to put on the altar of the United State their beloved ones, their friends, their own selves. My whole being craved to join them, yet . . . I could not; my feet were as though melted into the glass plates of the sidewalk. I simply stood there looking foolish.

"Hey, mathematician! Dreaming?"

I shivered. Black eyes varnished with laughter looked at me—thick Negro lips! It was my old friend the poet, R-13, and with him rosy O-. I turned around angrily (I still believe that if they had not appeared I should have entered the Bureau and have torn the square root of minus one out of my flesh).

"Not dreaming at all. If you will, 'standing in adoration,'" I retorted quite brusquely.

"Oh, certainly, certainly! You, my friend, should never have become a mathematician; you should have become a poet, a great poet! Yes, come over to our trade, to the poets. Eh? If you will, I can arrange it in a jiffy. Eh?"

R-13 usually talks very fast. His words run in torrents, his thick lips sprinkle. Every "p" is a fountain, every "poets" a fountain.

"So far I have served knowledge, and I shall continue to serve knowledge."

I frowned. I do not like, I do not understand jokes, and R-13 has the bad habit of joking.

"Oh, to the deuce with knowledge. Your much-heralded knowledge is but a form of cowardice. It is a fact! Yes, you want to encircle the infinite with a wall, and you fear to cast a glance behind the wall. Yes, sir! And if ever you should glance beyond the wall, you would be dazzled and close your eyes—yes—"

"Walls are the foundation of every human," I began.

R-13 sprinkled his fountain. O- laughed rosily and roundly. I waved my hand. "Well, you may laugh, I don't care." I was busy with something else. I had to find a way of eating up, of crushing down, that square root of minus one. "Suppose," I offered, "we go to my place and do some arithmetical problems." (The quiet hour of yesterday afternoon came to my memory; perhaps today also. . . .)

O- glanced at R-, then serenely and roundly at me; the soft, endearing color of our pink checks came to her cheeks.

"But today I am . . . I have a check to him today." (A glance at R-.) "And tonight he is busy, so . . ."

The moist, varnished lips whispered good-naturedly: "Half an hour is plenty for us, is it not, O-? I am not a great lover of your problems; let us simply go over to my place and chat."

I was afraid to remain alone with myself or, to be more correct, with that strange new self who by some curious coincidence bore my number, D-503. So I went with R-. True, he is not precise, not rhythmic, his logic is jocular and turned inside out, yet we are . . . Three years ago we both chose our dear, rosy O-. This tied our friendship more firmly together than our school days did. In R-'s room everything seems like mine: the Tables, the glass of the chairs, the table, the closet, the bed. But as we entered, R- moved one chair out of place, then another—the room became confused, everything lost the established order and seemed to violate every rule of Euclid's geometry. R- remained the same as always; in Taylor and in mathematics he always lagged at the tail of the class.

We recalled Plappa, how we boys used to paste the whole surface of his glass legs with paper notes expressing our thanks (we all loved Plappa). We recalled our priest (it goes without saying that we were not taught the "law" of ancient religion but the law of the United State). Our priest had a very powerful voice; a real hurricane would come out of the loud-speaker. And we children would yell the prescribed texts after him with all our lung power. We recalled how our scapegrace, R-13, used to stuff the priest with chewed paper; every word was thus accompanied by a paper wad shot out. Naturally, R- was punished, for what he did was undoubtedly wrong, but now we laughed heartily—by we I mean our triangle, R-, O-, and I. I must confess, I, too.

"And what if he had been a living one? Like the ancient ones, eh? We'd have b . . . b . . ." a fountain running from the fat bubbling lips. The sun was shining through the ceiling, the sun above, the sun from the sides, its reflection from below. O- on R-13's lap and minute drops of sunlight in O-'s blue eyes. Somehow my heart warmed up. The square root of minus one became silent and motionless. . . .

"Well, how is your *Integral*? Will you soon hop off to enlighten the inhabitants of the planets? You'd better hurry up, my boy, or we poets will have produced such a devilish lot that even your *Integral* will be unable to lift the cargo. 'Every day from eight to eleven' . . ." R- wagged his head and scratched the back of it. The back of his head is square; it looks like a little valise (I recalled for some reason an ancient painting "In the Cab"). I felt more lively.

"You, too, are writing for the *Integral*? Tell me about it. What are you writing about? What did you write today, for instance?"

"Today I did not write; today I was busy with something else." ("B-b-busy" sprinkled straight into my face.)

"What else?"

R- frowned. "What? What? Well, if you insist I'll tell you. I was busy with the Death Sentence. I was putting the Death Sentence into verse. An idiot—and to be frank, one of our poets. . . . For two years we all lived side by side with him and nothing seemed wrong. Suddenly he went crazy. 'I,' said he, 'am a genius! and I am above the law.' All that sort of nonsense. . . . But it is not a thing to talk about."

The fat lips hung down. The varnish disappeared from the eyes. He jumped up, turned around, and stared through the wall. I looked at his tightly closed little "valise" and thought, "What is he handling in his little valise now?"

A moment of awkward, asymmetric silence. I could not see clearly what was the matter, but I was certain there was something. . . .

"Fortunately the antediluvian time of those Shakespeares and Dostoevskys (or what were their names?) is past," I said in a voice deliberately loud.

R- turned his face to me. Words sprinkled and bubbled out of him as before, but I thought I noticed there was no more joyful varnish to his eyes.

"Yes, dear mathematician, fortunately, fortunately. We are the happy arithmetical mean. As you would put it, the integration from zero to infinity, from imbeciles to Shakespeare. Do I put it right?"

I do not know why (it seemed to me absolutely uncalled for) I recalled suddenly the other one, *her* tone. A thin, invisible thread stretched between her and R- (what thread?). The square root of minus one began to bother me again. I glanced at my badge; sixteen-twenty-five o'clock! They had only thirty-five minutes for the use of the pink check.

"Well, I must go." I kissed O-, shook hands with R-, and went to the elevator.

As I crossed the avenue I turned around. Here and there in the huge mass of glass penetrated by sunshine there were grayish-blue squares, the opaque squares of lowered curtains, the squares of rhythmic, Taylorized happiness. On the seventh floor I found R-13's square. The curtains were already lowered.

Dear O-. . . . Dear R-. . . . He also has (I do not know why I write this "also," but I write as it comes from my pen), he, too, has something which is not entirely clear in him. Yet I, he, and O-, we are a triangle; I confess, not an isosceles triangle, but a triangle nevertheless. We, to speak in the language of our ancestors (perhaps to you, my planetary readers, this is the more comprehensible language), we are a family. And one feels so good at times, when one is able for a short while, at least, to close oneself within a firm triangle, to close oneself away from anything that . . .

RECORD NINE

Liturgy
Iambus
The Cast-iron Hand

A solemn, bright day. On such days one forgets one's weaknesses, inexactitudes, illnesses, and everything is crystalline and imperturbable like our new glass. . . .

The Plaza of the Cube. Sixty-six imposing concentric circles—stands. Sixty-six rows of quiet, serene faces. Eyes reflecting the shining of the sky, or perhaps it is the shining of the United State. Red like blood are the flowers—the lips of the women. Like soft garlands the faces of the children in the first rows, nearest the place of action. Profound, austere, Gothic silence.

To judge by the descriptions that reach us from the ancients, they felt somewhat like this during their "church services." But they served their nonsensical, unknown god; we serve our rational god, whom we know most thoroughly. Their god gave them nothing but eternal, torturing seeking; our god gives us absolute truth—that is, he has rid us of any kind of doubt. Their god did not invent anything cleverer than sacrificing oneself, nobody knows what for; we bring to our god, the United State, a quiet, rational, carefully thought-out sacrifice.

Yes, it was a solemn liturgy for the United State, a reminiscence of the great days, years, of the Two Hundred Years' War—a magnificent celebration of the victory of *all* over *one*, of the *sum* over the *individual!*

That *one* stood on the steps of the Cube which was filled with sunlight. A white, no not even white but already colorless, glass face, lips of glass. And only the eyes—thirsty, swallowing black holes leading into that dreadful world from which he was only a few minutes away. The golden badge with the number already had been taken off. His hands were tied with a red ribbon. (A symbol of ancient custom. The explanation of it is that in the old days, when this sort of thing was not done in the name of the United State, the convicted naturally considered that they had the right to resist, hence their hands were usually bound with chains.)

On the top of the Cube, next to the Machine, the motionless, metallic figure of him whom we call the Well-Doer. One could not see his face from below. All one could see was that it was bounded by austere, magnificent, square lines. And his hands. . . . Did you ever notice how sometimes in a photograph the hands, if they were too near the camera, appear to be enormous? They then compel your attention, overshadow everything else. Those hands of his, heavy hands, quiet for the time being, were stony hands—it seemed the knees on which they rested must have ached in bearing their weight.

Suddenly one of those hands rose slowly. A slow, cast-iron gesture; obeying the will of the lifted hand, a Number came out on the platform. It was one of the State poets, whose fortunate lot it was to crown our celebration with his verses.

Divine, iambic brass verses thundered over the many stands. They dealt with the man who, his reason lost and lips like glass, stood on the steps and waited for the logical consequences of his own insane deeds.

. . . A blaze. . . . Buildings were swaying in those iambic lines, and sprinkling upward their liquefied golden substance, they broke and fell. The green trees were scorched, their sap slowly ran out and they remained standing like black crosses, like skeletons. Then appeared Prometheus (that meant *us*):

> ". . . he harnessed fire
> With machines and steel
> And fettered chaos with Law . . ."

The world was renovated; it became like steel—a sun of steel, trees of steel, men of steel. Suddenly an insane man "unchained the fire and set it free," and again the world had perished. . . . Unfortunately I have a bad memory for poetry, but one thing I am sure of: one could not choose more instructive or more beautiful parables.

Another slow, heavy gesture of the cast-iron hand and another poet appeared on the steps of the Cube. I stood up. Impossible! But . . . thick Negro lips—it *was* he. Why didn't he tell me that he was to be invested with such high . . . His lips trembled; they were gray. Oh, I certainly understood; to be face to face with the Well-Doer, face to face with the hosts of Guardians! Yet one should not allow oneself to be so upset.

Swift, sharp verses like an ax. . . . They told about an unheard-of crime, about sacrilegious poems in which the Well-Doer was called. . . . But no, I do not dare to repeat. . . .

R-13 was pale when he finished, and looking at no one (I did not expect such bashfulness of him) he descended and sat down. For an infinitesimal fraction of a second I saw right beside him somebody's face—a sharp, black triangle—and instantly I lost it; my eyes, thousands of eyes, were directed upward toward the Machine. Then—again the superhuman, cast-iron, gesture of the hand.

Swayed by an unknown wind, the criminal moved; one step . . . one more . . . then the last step in his life. His face was turned to the sky, his head thrown back—he was on his last. . . . Heavy, stony like fate, the Well-Doer went around the machine, put his enormous hand on the lever . . . . Not a whisper, not a breath around; all eyes were upon that hand. . . . What crushing, scorching power one must feel to be the tool, to be the resultant of hundreds of thousands of wills! How great his lot!

Another second. The hand moved down, switching in the current. The lightning-sharp blade of the electric ray. . . . A faint crack like a shiver, in the tubes of the Machine. . . . The prone body, covered with a light phosphorescent smoke; then, suddenly, under the eyes of all, it began to melt—to melt, to dissolve with terrible speed. And then nothing; just a pool of chemically pure water which only a moment ago had been so red and had pulsated in his heart. . . .

All this was simple; all of us were familiar with the phenomenon, dissociation of matter—yes, the splitting of the atoms of the human body! Yet every time we witnessed it, it seemed a miracle; it was a symbol of the superhuman power of the Well-Doer.

Above, in front of Him, the burning faces of the female Numbers, mouths half-open from emotion, flowers swaying in the wind.[1] According to custom, ten women were covering with flowers the unif of the Well-Doer, which was still wet with spray. With the magnificent step of a supreme priest He slowly descended, slowly passed between the rows of stands. Like tender white branches there rose toward Him the arms of the women; and, millions like one, our tempestuous cheers! Then cheers in honor of the Guardians, who all unseen were present among us. . . . Who knows, perhaps the fancy of the an-

[1] These flowers naturally were brought from the Botanical Museum. I, personally, am unable to see anything beautiful in flowers, or in anything else that belongs to the lower kingdom which now exists only beyond the Green Wall. Only rational and useful things are beautiful: machines, boots, formulae, food, etc.

cient man foresaw them centuries ahead, when he created the gentle and formidable "Guardian Angels" assigned to each person from the day of his birth?

Yes, there was in our celebration something of the ancient religions, something purifying like a storm. . . . You whose lot it may be to read this, are you familiar with such emotions? I am sorry for you if you are not.

RECORD TEN

A Letter
A Membrane
Hairy I

Yesterday was for me like the filter paper that chemists use for filtering their solutions (all suspended and superfluous particles remain on the paper). This morning I went downstairs all purified and distilled, transparent.

Downstairs in the hall the controller sat at a small table, constantly looking at her watch and recording the Numbers who were leaving. Her name is U- . . . well, I prefer not to give her Number, for I fear I may not write kindly about her—although, as a matter of fact, she is a very respectable, mature woman. The only thing I do not like in her is that her cheeks fold down a little like the gills of a fish (although I don't see anything wrong in this appearance). She scratched with her pen and I saw on the page "D-503"—and suddenly, splash! an ink blot. No sooner did I open my mouth to call her attention to that than she raised her head and blotted me with an inky smile. "There is a letter for you. You will receive it, dear. Yes, yes, you will."

I knew a letter, after she had read it, must go through the Bureau of Guardians (I think it is unnecessary to explain in detail this natural order of things); I would receive it not later than twelve o'clock. But that tiny smile confused me; the drop of ink clouded the transparency of the distilled solution. At the *Integral's* dock I could not concentrate; I even made a mistake in my calculations, something that had never happened to me before.

At twelve o'clock, again the rosy-brown fish gills' smile, and at last the letter was in my hands. I cannot say why I did not read it right there; instead, I put it in my pocket and ran into my room. I opened it, scanned it quickly, and . . . sat down. It was an official notice to the effect that Number I-330 had had me assigned to her, and that today at twenty-one o'clock I was to go to her. Her address was given.

"No! After all that had happened! After I had shown her frankly my attitude toward her! Besides, how could she know that I did not go to the Bureau of Guardians? She had no way of knowing that I have been ill and could not. . . . And despite all this . . ."

A dynamo was whirling and buzzing in my head. Buddha . . . yellow . . . lilies of the valley . . . rosy crescent. . . . Besides—besides, O- wanted to come to see me today! I was sure she would not believe (how could one believe?) that I had absolutely nothing to do with the matter, that . . . I was also sure that we (O- and I) would have a difficult, foolish, and absolutely illogical conversation. No, anything but that! Let the situation solve itself mechanically; I would send her a copy of the official communication.

While I was hastily putting the paper in my pocket, I noticed my terrible ape-like hand. I remembered how that day, during our walk, she had taken my hand and looked at it. Is it possible that she really . . . that she . . .

A quarter to twenty-one. A white northern night. Everything was glass, greenish. But it was a different kind of glass, not like ours, not genuine but very breakable, a thin glass shell, and within that shell things were flying, whirling, buzzing. I wouldn't have been surprised if suddenly the cupola of the auditorium had risen in slow, rolling clouds of smoke; or if the ripe moon had sent an inky smile, like that one at the little table this morning; or if in every house suddenly all the curtains had been lowered, and behind the curtains . . .

I felt something peculiar; my ribs were like iron bars that interfered, decidedly interfered, with my heart, giving it too little space. I stood at a glass door on which were the golden letters I-330. I-330 sat at the table with her back to me; she was writing something. I stepped in.

"Here"—I held out the pink check—"I received the notice this noon and here I am!"

"How punctual you are! Just a minute, please, may I? Sit down. I shall finish in a minute."

She lowered her eyes to the letter. What had she there, behind her lowered curtains? What would she say? What would she do in a second? How to learn it? How to calculate it, since she comes from beyond, from the wild, ancient land of dreams? I looked at her in silence. My ribs were iron bars. The space for the heart was too small. . . . When she speaks, her face is like a swiftly revolving, glittering wheel; you cannot see the separate bars. But at that moment the wheel was motionless. I saw a strange combination: dark eyebrows running right to the temples —a sharp, mocking triangle; and still another dark triangle with its apex upward—two deep wrinkles from the nose to the angles of the mouth. And these two triangles somehow contradicted each other. They gave the whole face that disagreeable, irritating X, or cross—a face marked obliquely by a cross.

The wheel started to turn; its bars blurred.

"So you did not go to the Bureau of Guardians, after all?"

"I did . . . I did not feel well . . . I could not."

"Yes? I thought so; something *must* have prevented you, it matters little what"—sharp teeth—a smile. "But now you are in my hands. You remember: 'Any Number who within forty-eight hours fails to report to the Bureau is considered . . .'"

My heart banged so forcibly that the iron bars bent. If I were not sitting . . . like a little boy, how stupid! I was caught like a little boy, and stupidly I kept silent. I felt I was in a net; neither my legs nor my arms . . .

She stood up and stretched herself lazily. She pressed the button, and the curtains on all four walls fell with a slight rustle. I was cut off from the rest of the world, alone with her.

She was somewhere behind me, near the closet door. The unif was rustling, falling. I was listening, *all* listening. I remembered—no, it glistened in my mind for one hundredth of a second—I once had to calculate the curve of a new type of street membrane. (These membranes are handsomely decorated and are placed over all the avenues, registering all street conversations for the Bureau of Guardians.) I remembered a rosy, concave, trembling membrane, a strange being consisting of one organ only, an ear. I was at that moment such a membrane.

Now the "click" of the snap at her collar, at her breast, and . . . lower. The glassy silk rustled over her shoulders and knees, over the floor. I heard—and it was clearer than actually seeing—I heard how one foot stepped out of the grayish-blue heap of silk, then the other. . . . Soon I'd hear the creak of the bed, and . . .

The tensely stretched membrane trembled and registered the silence—no, the sharp, hammerlike blows of the heart against the iron bars, and endless pauses between beats. And I heard, saw, how she, behind me, hesitated for a second, thinking. The door of the closet. . . . It slammed; again silk . . . silk . . .

"Well, all right."

I turned around. She was dressed in a saffron-yellow dress of an ancient style. This was a thousand times worse than if she had not been dressed at all. Two sharp points glowing with rosiness through the thin tissue; two burning embers piercing through ashes; two tender, round knees . . .

She was sitting in a low armchair. In front of her on a small square table I noticed a bottle filled with something poisonously green, and two small glasses with thin stems. In the corner of her mouth she had a very thin paper tube; she was ejecting smoke formed by the burning of that ancient smoking substance whose name I do not now remember.

The membrane was still vibrating. Within, the sledge hammer was pounding the red-hot iron bars of my chest. I heard distinctly every blow of the hammer, and . . . What if she, too, heard it?

But she continued to produce smoke very calmly; calmly she looked at me; and nonchalantly she flicked ashes on the pink check!

With as much self-control as possible I asked, "If you still feel that way, why did you have me assigned to you? And why did you make me come here?"

As if she had not heard at all, she poured some of the green liquid from the bottle into one of the small glasses, and sipped it.

"Wonderful liqueur! Want some?"

Then I understood: alcohol! Like lightning there came to memory what I had seen yesterday: the stony hand of the Well-Doer, the unbearable blade of the electric ray; there on the Cube, the head thrown back, the stretched-out body! I shivered.

"Please listen," I said. "You know, do you not, that anyone who poisons himself with nicotine, and more particularly with alcohol, is severely treated by the United State?"

Dark brows raised high to the temples, the sharp mocking triangle.

" 'It is more reasonable to annihilate a few than to allow many to poison themselves. . . . And degeneration,' . . . etc. . . . This is true to the point of indecency."

"Indecency?"

"Yes. To let out into the street such a group of bald-headed, naked little truths. Only imagine, please. Imagine, say, that persistent admirer of mine–S-, well, you know him. Then imagine: if he should discard the deception of clothes and appear in public in his true form. . . . Oh!" She laughed. But I clearly saw her lower, sorrowful triangle: two deep grooves from the nose to the mouth. And for some reason these grooves made me think: that double-curved being, half-hunched, with winglike ears–he embraced her? Her, such . . . Oh!

Naturally, I try now merely to express my abnormal feelings of that moment. Now, as I write, I understand perfectly that all this is as it should be; that he, S-4711, like any other honest Number, has a perfect right to the joys of life, and that it would be unjust . . . But I think the point is quite clear.

I-330 laughed a long, strange laugh. Then she cast a look at me, into me.

"The most curious thing is that I am not in the least afraid of you. You are such a dear, I am sure of it! You would never think of going to the Bureau and reporting that I drink liqueurs and smoke. You will be sick or busy, or I don't know what. . . . Furthermore, I am sure you will drink this charming poison with me."

What an impertinent, mocking tone! I felt definitely that in a moment I would hate her. (Why in a moment? In fact, I hated her all the time.)

I-330 tilted the little glass of green poison straight into her mouth. Then she stood up, and all rosy through the translucent saffron-yellow tissue, she made a few steps and stopped behind my chair. . . . Suddenly her arms were about my neck . . . her lips grew into mine, no, even somewhere much deeper, much more terribly. . . . I swear all this was very unexpected for me. That is why perhaps . . . for I could not–at this moment I see clearly–I could not myself have the desire to . . .

Unbearably sweet lips. (I suppose it was the taste of the liqueur.) It was as though burning poison were being poured into me, and more, and more. . . .

I tore away from the earth and began revolving as an independent planet, down, down, following an incalculable curve. . . .

What happened next I am able to describe only in an approximate way, only by way of more or less suitable analogies.

It never occurred to me before but it is true: we who live on the earth, we are always walking over a seething red sea of fire which is hidden in the womb of the earth. We never think of it. But imagine the ground under our feet suddenly transformed into a thin glass shell; suddenly we should behold . . . !

I became glass-like and saw within myself. There were two selves in me. One, the former D-503, Number D-503; and the other . . . Before, that other used only to show his hairy paws from time to time, but now that whole other self left his shell. That shell was breaking, and in a moment . . .

Grasping the last straw (the arms of the chair) with all my strength, I asked loudly (so as to hear my first self), "Where, where did you get this poison?"

"Oh, this? A physician, one of my . . ."

"'One of my! one of my' what?" And my other self jumped up suddenly and yelled: "I won't allow it! I want no one but me . . . I shall kill anyone who . . . Because I . . . You . . ." I saw my other self grasp her rudely with his hairy paws, tear the silk, and put his teeth in her flesh! . . . I remember exactly, his teeth! . . .

I do not remember how, but I-330 slipped away and I saw her straighten, her head raised high, her eyes overlaid by that cursed, impenetrable curtain. She stood leaning with her back against the closet door and listening to me.

I remember I was on the floor; I embraced her limbs, kissed her knees, and cried supplicatingly, "At once, right away, right away."

Sharp teeth. . . . The sharp, mocking triangle of the brows. . . . She bent over and in silence unbuttoned my badge.

"Yes, yes, dear—dear."

I began hastily to remove my unif. But I-330, silent as before, lifted my badge to my eyes, showing me the clock upon it. It was twenty-two-twenty-five.

I became cold. I knew what it meant to be out in the street after twenty-two-thirty. My insanity disappeared at once. I was again I. I saw clearly one thing: I hated her, hated her, hated . . . Without saying good-by, without looking back, I ran out of the room. Hurriedly trying to fasten the badge back in its place, I ran down the stairs (I was afraid lest someone notice me in the elevator), and tore out into a deserted street.

Everything was in its place; life so simple, ordinary, orderly. Glittering glass houses, pale glass sky, a greenish, motionless night. But under that cool glass something wild, something red and hairy, was silently seething. I was gasping for breath, but I continued to run so as not to be late.

Suddenly I felt that my badge which I had hurriedly pinned on was detaching itself; it came off and fell to the sidewalk. I bent over to pick it up and in the momentary silence I heard somebody's steps. I turned. Someone small and hunched was disappearing around the corner. At least so it seemed. I started to run as fast as I could. The wind whistled in my ears. At the entrance to my house I stopped and looked at the clock; one minute to twenty-two-thirty! I listened; nobody behind. It was my foolish imagination, the effect of the poison.

The night was full of torture. My bed seemed to lift itself under me, then to fall again, then up again! I used autosuggestion: "At night all the Numbers must sleep; sleeping at night is a duty just like working during the day. To sleep at night is necessary for the next day's work. Not to sleep at night is criminal." Yet I could not sleep—I could not. I was perishing! I was unable to fulfill my duties to the United State! I . . .

RECORD ELEVEN

No, I Can't; Let It Be without Headings!

Evening. It is somewhat foggy. The sky is covered with a milky-golden tissue, and one cannot see what is there, beyond, on the heights. The ancients "knew" that the greatest, bored skeptic—their god—lived there. We know that crystalline, blue, naked, indecent Nothing is there. I no longer know what *is* there. I have learned too many things of late. Knowledge, self-confident knowledge, which is sure that it is faultless, is faith. I had firm faith in myself; I believed that I knew all about myself. But then . . . I look in the mirror. And for the first time in my life, yes, *for the first time in my life* I see clearly, precisely, consciously and with surprise, I see myself as some "him"! I am "he." Frowning, black, straight brows; between them, like a scar, there is a vertical wrinkle. (Was that wrinkle there before?) Steel-gray eyes encircled by the shadow of a sleepless night. And behind that steel . . . I understand; I never knew before what there was behind that steel. From there (this "there" is at once so near and so infinitely distant!) I look at myself—at "him." And I know surely that "he" with his straight brows is a stranger, that I meet him here for the first time in my life. The real I is *not* he.

No. Period. All this is nonsense. And all these foolish emotions are only delirium, the result of last night's poisoning. . . . Poisoning with what? With a sip of that green poison, or with her? It matters little. I write all this merely in order to demonstrate how strangely confused our precise and sharp human reason may become. This reason, strong enough to make infinity, which the ancients feared so much, understandable by means of . . . . The switch buzzes. "Number R-13." Well, I am even glad; alone I should . . .

Twenty minutes later:

On the plane of this paper, in a world of two dimensions, these lines follow each other, but in another world they . . . I am losing the sense for figures. . . . Twenty minutes! Perhaps two hundred or two hundred thousand! . . .

It seems so strange, quietly, deliberately, measuring every word, to write down my adventure with R-. Imagine yourself sitting down at your own bed, crossing your legs, watching curiously how you yourself shrivel in the very same bed. My mental state is similar to that.

When R-13 came in I was perfectly quiet and normal. With sincere admiration I began to tell him how wonderfully he succeeded in versifying the death sentence of that insane man, and that his poem, more than anything else, had smothered and annihilated the transgressor of the law.

"More than that," I said, "if I were ordered to prepare a mathematical draft of the Machine of the Well-Doer, I should undoubtedly, undoubtedly, put on that draft some of your verses!" Suddenly I saw R-'s eyes becoming more and more opaque, his lips acquiring a gray tint.

"What's the matter?"

"What? Well . . . Merely that I am dead sick of it. Everybody keeps on: 'The death sentence, the death sentence!' I want to hear no more of it! You understand? I do not want . . ." He became serious, rubbing his neck—that little valise filled with luggage which I cannot understand. A silence. There! He found something in that little valise of his, removed it, unwrapped it, spread it out; his eyes became covered with the varnish of laughter. He began:

"I am writing something for your *Integral*. Yes. . . . I am!" He was himself again: bubbling, sprinkling lips, words splashing like a fountain.

"You see, it is the ancient legend of paradise." ("p" like a fountain.) "That legend referred to us of today, did it not? Yes. Only think of it, think of it a moment! There were two in paradise and the choice was offered to them: happiness without freedom, or freedom without happiness. No other choice. *Tertium non datur*. They, fools that they were, chose freedom. Naturally, for centuries afterward they longed for fetters, for the fetters of yore. This was the meaning of their world weariness, *Weltschmerz*. For centuries! And only we found a way to regain happiness. . . . No, listen, follow me! The ancient god and we, side by side at the same table! Yes, we helped god to defeat the devil definitely and finally. It was he, the devil, who led people to transgression, to taste pernicious freedom—he, the cunning serpent. And we came along, planted a boot on his head, and . . . squash! Done with him! Paradise again! We returned to the simple-mindedness and innocence of Adam and Eve. No more meddling with good and evil and all that; everything is simple again, heavenly, childishly simple! The Well-Doer, the Machine, the Cube, the giant Gas Bell, the Guardians—all these are good. All this is magnificent, beautiful, noble, lofty, crystalline, pure. For all this preserves our non-freedom, that is, our happiness. In our place those ancients would indulge in discussions, deliberations, etc. They would break their heads trying to make out what was moral or unmoral. But we . . . Well, in short, these are the highlights of my little paradise poem. What do you think of it? And above all the style is most solemn, pious. Understand me? Nice little idea, is it not? Do you understand?"

Of course I understood. I remember my thoughts at that moment: "His appearance is nonsensical and lacking in symmetry, yet what an orderly-working mind he has!" This made him dear to me, that is to the real *me*. (I still insist that that I of before is the real one; my I of late is, certainly, only an illness.)

Apparently R- read my thought in my face; he put his hand on my shoulders and laughed: "Oh, you! . . . Adam! By the way, about Eve . . ." He searched for something in his pockets, took out a little book, turned over a few leaves, and said, "For the day after tomorrow—oh, no, two days from now—O-90 has a pink check on you. How about it? . . . As before? . . . You want her to?"

"Of course, of course!"

"All right then, I'll tell her You see she herself is very bashful. . . . What a funny story! You see, for me she has only a pink-check affection, but for you . . . And you, you did not even come to tell us how a fourth member sneaked into our triangle! Who is it? Repent, sinner! Come on!"

A curtain arose inside me; rustle of silk, green bottle, lips . . . For no reason whatsoever I exclaimed (oh, why didn't I restrain myself at that moment?), "Tell me, R-, did you ever have an opportunity to try nicotine or alcohol?"

R- sucked in his lips, looked at me from under his brows. I distinctly heard his thoughts: "Friend though he is, yet . . ." And he answered:

"What shall I say? Strictly speaking, no. But I know a woman . . ."

"I-330?" I cried.

"What! You? You, also?" R- was full of laughter; he chuckled, ready to splash over.

My mirror was hanging in such a way that in order to see R- clearly I had to turn and look across the table. From my armchair I could see now only my own forehead and eyebrows. Then I, the real I, suddenly saw in the mirror a broken, quivering line of brow; I, the real I, heard suddenly a wild, disgusting cry: "What? What does that 'also' mean? What does that 'also' mean? I demand . . ."

Widely parted Negro lips. . . . Eyes bulging, I (the real

I) grasped my other wild, hairy, heavily breathing self forcibly. I (the real I) said to him, to R-, "In the name of the Well-Doer, please forgive me. I am very sick; I don't sleep; I do not know what *is* the matter with me."

A swiftly passing smile appeared on the thick lips.

"Yes, yes, I understand, I understand. I am familiar with all this—theoretically, of course. Good-by."

At the door he turned around like a little black ball, came back to the table and put a book upon it. "This is my latest book. I came to bring it to you. Almost forgot. Good-by." ("b" like a splash.) The little ball rolled out.

I am alone. Or, to be more exact, I am *tête-à-tête* with that other self. I sit in the armchair and, having crossed my legs, I watch curiously from some indefinite "there" how I, myself, am shriveling in my bed!

Why, oh, why is it, that for three years R-, O-, and I were so friendly together and now suddenly—one word only about that other female, about I-330, and . . . Is it possible that that insanity called love and jealousy does exist, and not only in the idiotic books of the ancients? What seems most strange is that I, I! . . . Equations, formulae, figures, and suddenly this! I can't understand it, I can't! Tomorrow I shall go to R- and tell him . . . No, it isn't true; I shall not go; neither tomorrow nor day after tomorrow, nor ever. . . . I can't, I do not want to see him. This is the end. Our triangle is broken up.

I am alone. It is evening. There is a light fog. The sky is covered by a thin, milky-golden tissue. If I only knew what is there—higher. If I only knew who I am. Which I am I?

RECORD TWELVE

The Delimitation of the Infinite
Angel
Meditations on Poetry

I continue to believe that I shall recover, that I may recover. I slept very well. No dreams or any other symptoms of disease. Dear O-90 will come tomorrow. Everything will again be simple, regular, and limited like a circle. I am not afraid of this word "limited." The work of the highest faculty of man, judgment, is always directed toward the constant limiting of the infinite, toward the breaking up of the infinite into comfortably digestible portions, differentials. This is what gives divine beauty to my vocation, mathematics. And it is exactly this beauty that that other female lacks. But this last thought of mine is only an accidental mental association.

These thoughts swarmed in my mind while I was listening to the regular, rhythmic sounds of the underground railway. Silently I followed the rhythm of its wheels and recited to myself R-'s verses (from the book which he gave me yesterday), and I felt that behind me someone was leaning over my shoulder and looking at the open pages. I did not turn around but with the corner of my eye I noticed pink ears, spread like wings, the double-curved . . . like the letter. . . . It was he, but I did not want to disturb him. I feigned not to have noticed him. How he came in, I do not know. I did not see him when I got into the car.

This incident, insignificant in itself, had an especially good effect upon me; it invigorated me, I should say. It is pleasant to feel that somebody's penetrating eye is watching you from behind your shoulder, lovingly guarding you from making the most minute mistake, from the most minute incorrect step. It may seem to you too sentimental, but I do see in all this the materialization of the dream of the ancients about a Guardian Angel. How many things, of which the ancients had only dreams, are materialized in our life!

At the moment when I became aware of the presence of the Guardian Angel behind me, I was enjoying a poem entitled "Happiness." I think I am not mistaken when I say that it is a piece of rare beauty and depth of thought. These are the first four lines:

> Two times two–eternal lovers;
> Inseparable in passion four . . .
> Most flaming lovers in the world,
> Eternally welded, two times two.

And the rest is in the same vein: on the wisdom and the eternal happiness of the multiplication table. Every poet is inevitably a Columbus. America existed before Columbus for ages, but only Columbus found it. The multiplication table existed before R-13 for ages, but only R-13 could find in the virginal forest of figures a new Eldorado. Is it not true? Is there any happiness more wise and cloudless in this wonderful world? Steel may rust. The ancient god created ancient man, i.e., the man capable of mistakes; *ergo*, the ancient god himself made a mistake. The multiplication table is more wise and more absolute than the ancient god, for the multiplication table never (do you understand—*never*) makes mistakes! There are no more fortunate and happy people than those who live according to the correct, eternal laws of the multiplication table. No hesitation! No errors! There is but one truth, and there is but one path to it; and that truth is: four, and that path is: two times two. Would it not seem preposterous for these happily multiplied twos suddenly to begin thinking of some foolish kind of freedom?—i.e. (is it not clear?), of a mistake? It seems undeniable, axiomatic, that R-13 knows how to grasp the most fundamental, the most . . .

At that moment again I felt (first near the back of my head, then on my left ear) the warm, tender breath of the Guardian Angel. He apparently noticed that the book on my lap had long been closed and that my thoughts were somewhere very far. . . . Well, I am ready this minute to spread before him the pages of my brain. This gives one such a feeling of tranquillity and joy. I remember I even turned around and gazed long and questioningly into his eyes; but either he did not understand, or he did not want to understand me. He did not ask me anything. . . . The only thing left for me is to relate everything to you, my unknown readers. You are to me now as dear and as near and as far out of reach as he was at that moment.

This was my way of thinking: from the part to the whole—R-13 is the part, the whole is our Institution of State Poets and Authors. I thought: how was it that the ancients did not notice the utter absurdity of their prose and poetry? The gigantic, magnificent power of the artistic word was spent by them in vain. It is really funny; anybody wrote whatever happened to come into his head! It was as foolish as the fact that in the days of the ancients the ocean blindly splashed on the shore for twenty-four hours a day, without interruption or use. The millions of kilogram meters of energy which were hidden in the waves were used only for the stimulation of sweethearts! We obtained electricity from the amorous whisper of the waves! We made a domestic animal out of that sparkling, foaming, rabid one! And in the same manner, we domesticated and harnessed the wild element of poetry. Now poetry is no longer the unpardonable whistling of nightingales, but a State Service! Poetry is a commodity.

Our famous "Mathematical Norms"! Without them in our schools, how could we love so sincerely and dearly our four rules of arithmetic? And "Thorns"! This is a classical image: the Guardians are thorns about a rose, thorns that guard our tender State Flower from coarse hands. Whose heart could resist, could remain indifferent, when seeing and hearing the lips of our children recite like a prayer: "A bad boy caught the rose with his hand, but the thorn of steel pricked him like a needle; the bad boy cried and ran home," etc., etc. And the "Daily Odes to the Well-Doer!" Who, having read them, will not bow piously before the unselfish service of that Number of all Numbers? And the dreadful red "Flowers of Court Sentences!" And the immortal tragedy, "Those Who Come Late to Work!" And the popular book, *Stanzas on Sex Hygiene!*

Our whole life in all its complexity and beauty is thus stamped forever in the gold of words. Our poets do not soar any longer in the unknown; they have descended to earth and they march with us, keeping step to the accompaniment of our austere and mechanical March of the musical State Tower. Their lyre is the morning rubbing sound of the electric toothbrushes, and the threatening crack of the electric sparks coming from the Machine of the Well-Doer, and the magnificent echo of the Hymn of the United State, and the intimate ringing of the crystalline, shining washbasins, and the stimulating rustle of the falling curtains, and the joyous voices of the newest cookbooks, and the almost imperceptible whisper of the street membranes. . . .

Our gods are here, below. They are with us in the Bureau, in the kitchen, in the shops, in the rest rooms. The gods have become like us, *ergo* we have become like gods. And we shall come to you, my unknown readers on another planet, we shall come to you to make your life as godlike, as rational, and as correct as our own . . .

RECORD THIRTEEN

Fog
Thou
A Decidedly Absurd Adventure

I awoke at dawn. The rose-colored firmament looked into my eyes. Everything was beautiful, round. "O-90 is to come tonight. Surely I am healthy again." I smiled and fell asleep. The Morning Bell! I got up; everything looked different. Through the glass of the ceiling, through the walls, nothing could be seen but fog—fog everywhere, strange clouds, becoming heavier and nearer; the boundary between earth and sky disappeared. Everything seemed to be floating and thawing and falling. . . . Not a thing to hold on to. No houses to be seen; they were all dissolved in the fog like crystals of salt in water. On the sidewalks and inside the houses dark figures, like suspended particles in a strange milky solution, were hanging, below, above, up to the tenth floor. Everything seemed to be covered with smoke, as though a fire were raging somewhere noiselessly.

At eleven-forty-five exactly (I looked at the clock particularly at that time to catch the figures, to save at least the figures), at eleven-forty-five, just before leaving, according to our Table of Hours, to go and occupy myself with physical labor, I dropped into my room for a moment. Suddenly the telephone rang. A voice—a long needle slowly penetrating my heart:

"Oh, you are at home? I am very glad! Wait for me at the corner. We shall go together. . . . Where? Well, you'll see."

"You know perfectly well that I am going to work now."

"You know perfectly well that you'll do as I say! Au revoir. In two minutes! . . ."

I stood at the corner. I had to wait to try to make clear to her that only the United State directs me, not she. "You'll do as I say!" How sure she is! One hears it in her voice. And what if . . .?

Unifs, dull gray as if woven of damp fog, would appear for a second at my side and then soundlessly redissolve. I was unable to turn my eyes away from the clock. . . . I seemed myself to have become that sharp, quivering hand that marked the seconds. Ten, eight minutes . . . three . . . two minutes to twelve. . . . Of course! I was late! Oh, how I hated her. Yet I had to wait to prove that I . . .

A red line in the milky whiteness of the fog—like blood, like a wound made by a sharp knife—her lips.

"I made you wait, I think. And now you are late for your work anyway?"

"How . . .? Well, yes, it is too late now."

I glanced at her lips in silence. All women are lips, lips only. Some are rosy lips, tense and round, a ring, a tender fence separating one from the world. But these! A second ago they were not here, and suddenly . . . the slash of a knife! I seemed even to see the sweet, dripping blood. . . .

She came nearer. She leaned gently against my shoulder; we became one. Something streamed from her into me. I felt, I knew, it *should* be so. Every fiber of my nervous system told me this, every hair on my head, every painfully sweet heartbeat. And what a joy it was to submit to what *should* be. A fragment of iron ore probably feels the same joy of submission to precise, inevitable law when it clings to a lodestone. The same joy is in a stone which, thrown aloft, hesitates a little at the height of its flight and then rushes down to the ground. It is the same with a man when in his final convulsion he takes a last deep breath and dies.

I remember I smiled vaguely and said for no reason at all, "Fog . . . very."

"Thou lovest fog, dost thou?"

This ancient, long-forgotten *thou*—the thou of a master to his slave—penetrated me slowly, sharply. . . . Yes, I was a slave. . . . This, too, was inevitable, was good.

"Yes, good . . ." I said aloud to myself, and then to her, "I hate fog. I am afraid of fog."

"Then you love it. For if you fear it because it is stronger than you, hate it because you fear it, you love it. For you cannot subject it to yourself. One loves only the things one cannot conquer."

"Yes, that is so. That is why . . . that is precisely why I . . ."

We were walking—as one. Somewhere beyond the fog the sun was singing in a faint tone, gradually swelling, filling the air with tension and with pearl and gold and rose and red. . . . The whole world seemed to be one unembraceable woman, and we who were in her body were not yet born; we were ripening in joy. It was clear to me, absolutely clear, that everything existed only for me: the sun, the fog, the gold—for me. I did not ask where we were going; what did it matter? It was a pleasure to walk, to ripen, to become stronger and more tense. . . .

"Here . . ." I-330 stopped at a door. "It so happens that today there is someone on duty who . . . I told you about him in the Ancient House."

Carefully guarding the forces ripening within me, I read the sign: "Medical Bureau." Only automatically I understood.

. . . A glass room, filled with golden fog; shelves of glass, colored bottles, jars, electric wires, bluish sparks in tubes; and a male Number—a very thin flattened man. He might have been cut out of a sheet of paper. Wherever he was, whichever way he turned, he showed only a profile, a sharply pointed, glittering blade of a nose, and lips like scissors.

I could not hear what I-330 told him. I merely saw her lips when she was talking, and I felt that I was smiling, irrepressibly, blissfully. The scissors-like lips glittered and the doctor said, "Yes, yes, I see. A most dangerous disease. I know of nothing more dangerous." And he laughed. With his thin, flat, papery hand he wrote something on a piece of paper and gave it to I-330; he wrote on another piece of paper and handed it over to me. He had given us certificates, testifying that we were ill, that we were unable to go to work. Thus I stole my work from the United State; I was a thief; I deserved to be put beneath the Machine of the Well-Doer. Yet I was indifferent to this thought; it was as distant from me as though it were written in a novel. I took the certificate without an instant's hesitation. I, all my being, my eyes. my lips, my hands, knew it was as it should be.

At the corner, from a half-empty garage, we took an aero. I-330 took the wheel as she had done before, pressed the starter, and we tore away from the earth. We soared. Behind us the golden haze, the sun. The thin, blade-like profile of the doctor seemed to me suddenly so dear, so beloved. Formerly I knew everything revolves around the sun. Now I knew everything was revolving around me. Slowly, blissfully, with half-closed eyes. . . .

At the gate of the Ancient House we found the same old woman. What a dear mouth, with lips grown together and raylike wrinkles around it! Probably those lips have remained grown together all these days; but now they parted and smiled.

"Ah! you mischievous girl, you! Work is too much for you? Well, all right, all right. If anything happens, I'll run up and warn you."

A heavy, squeaky, opaque door. It closed behind us, and at once my heart opened painfully, widely, still wider. . . . My lips . . . hers. . . . I drank and drank from them. I tore myself away; in silence I looked into her widely open eyes, and then again. . . .

The room in half dusk. . . . Blue and saffron-yellow lights, dark green morocco leather, the golden smile of Buddha, a wide mahogany bed, a glimmer of mirrors. . . . And my dream of a few days before became so comprehensible, so clear to me; everything seemed saturated with the golden prime juice of life, and it seemed that I was overflowing with it—one second more and it would splash out. . . . Like iron ore to a lodestone, in sweet submission to the precise and unchangeable law, inevitably, I clung to her. . . . There was no pink check, no counting, no United State; I was myself no more. Only, drawn together, the tenderly sharp teeth were there, only her golden, widely open eyes, and through them I saw deeper within. . . . And silence. . . . Only somewhere in a corner, thousands of miles away it seemed, drops of water were dripping from the faucet of the washstand. I was the Universe! . . . And between drops whole epochs, eras, were elapsing. . . .

I put on my unif and bent over I-330 to draw her into me with my eyes—for the last time.

"I knew it. . . . I knew you," said I-330 in a very low voice. She passed her hand over her face as though brushing something away; then she arose brusquely, put on her unif and her usual sharp, bite-like smile.

"Well, my fallen angel, you perished just now, do you know that? No? You are not afraid? Well, au revoir. You shall go home alone. Well?"

She opened the mirror door of the cupboard and, looking at me over her shoulder, she waited. I left the room obediently. Yet no sooner had I left the room than I felt it was urgent that she touch me with her shoulder—only for one second with her shoulder, nothing more. I ran back into the room, where, I presumed, she was standing before the mirror, busily buttoning up her unif; I rushed in, and stopped abruptly. I saw—I remember it clearly—

I saw the key in the keyhole of the closet, and the ancient ring upon it was still swinging, but I-330 was not there. She could not have left the room as there was but one exit. . . . Yet I-330 was not there! I looked around everywhere. I even opened the cupboard and felt of the different ancient dresses; nobody. . . .

I feel somewhat ridiculous, my dear planetary readers, relating to you this most improbable adventure. But what else can I do since it all happened exactly as I relate it? Was not the whole day, from early morning, full of improbable adventures? Does it not all resemble the ancient disease of dream seeing? If this be so, what does it matter if I relate one absurdity more, or one less? Moreover, I am convinced that sooner or later I shall be able to include all these absurdities in some kind of logical sequence. This thought comforts me as I hope it will comfort you.

. . . How overwhelmed I am! If only you knew how overwhelmed!

RECORD FOURTEEN

"Mine"
Impossible
A Cold Floor

I shall continue to relate my adventures of yesterday. I was busy during the personal hour before retiring to bed, and thus I was unable to record everything last night. But everything is graven in me; especially, for some reason, and apparently forever, I shall remember that unbearably cold floor. . . .

I was expecting O-90 last evening, as it was her regular day. I went downstairs to the controller on duty to get a permit for the lowering of my curtains.

"What is the matter with you?" asked the controller. "You seem so peculiar tonight."

"I . . . I am sick."

Strictly speaking, I told her the truth. I certainly am sick. All this *is* an illness. Presently I remembered; of course, my certificate! I touched it in my pocket. Yes, there it was, rustling. Then all this did happen! It did actually happen!

I held out the paper to the controller. As I did so, I felt the blood rushing to my cheeks. Without looking directly at her, I noticed with what an expression of surprise she gazed at me.

Then at twenty-one-thirty o'clock. . . . In the room to the left the curtains were lowered, and in the room to the right my neighbor was sitting over a book. His head is bald and covered with bulging lumps. His forehead is enormous—a yellow parabola. I was walking up and down the room suffering. How could I meet her, after all that happened? O-90, I mean. I felt plainly, to my right, how the eyes of my neighbor were staring at me. I clearly saw the wrinkles on his forehead like a row of yellow, illegible lines; and for some reason I was certain that those lines dealt with me.

A quarter of an hour before twenty-two the cheerful, rosy whirlwind was in my room; the firm ring of her rosy arms closed about my neck. Then I felt how that ring grew weaker and weaker; and then it broke and her arms dropped. . . .

"You are not the same, not the same man! You are no longer mine!"

"What curious terminology: 'mine.' I never belonged—" I faltered. It suddenly occurred to me: true, I had belonged to no one before, but now . . . Is it not clear that now I no longer live in our rational world but in the ancient delirious world, in a world of the square root of minus one?

The curtains fell. There to my right my neighbor let his book drop at that moment from the table to the floor. And through the last narrow space between the curtain and the floor I saw a yellow hand pick up the book. Within I felt: "Only to seize that hand with all my power."

"I thought . . . I wanted to meet you during the hour for the walk. I wanted . . . I must talk to you about so many things, so many . . ."

Poor, dear O-90. Her rosy mouth was a crescent with its horns downward. But I could not tell her everything, could I, if for no other reason than that it would make her an accomplice to my crimes? I knew that she would not have the courage to report me to the Bureau of Guardians, consequently . . .

"My dear O-, I am sick, I am exhausted. I went again today to the Medical Bureau; but it is nothing, it will pass. But let us not talk about it; let us forget it."

O-90 was lying down. I kissed her gently. I kissed that childish, fluffy fold at her wrist. Her blue eyes were closed. The pink crescent of her lips was slowly blooming, more and more like a flower. I kissed her. . . .

Suddenly I clearly realized how empty I was, how I had given away . . . No, I could not—impossible! I knew I must . . . but no—impossible! I ought . . . but no—impossible! My lips cooled at once. The rosy crescent trembled, darkened, drew together. O-90 covered herself with the bedspread, her face hidden in·the pillow.

I was sitting near the bed, on the floor. What a desperately cold floor! I sat there in silence. The terrible cold from the floor rose higher and higher. There in the blue, silent space among the planets, there probably it is as cold.

"Please understand, dear; I did not mean . . ." I muttered, "With all my heart, I . . ."

It was the truth. I, my real self, did not mean. . . . Yet how could I express it in words? How could I explain to her that the piece of iron did not want to? . . . But that the law is precise, inevitable!

O-90 lifted her face from the pillow and without opening her eyes she said, "Go away." But because she was crying she pronounced it "Oo aaa-ay." For some reason this absurd detail will not leave my memory.

Penetrated by the cold, and torpid, I went out into the hall. I pressed my forehead against the cold glass. Outside a thin, almost imperceptible film of haze was spread. "Toward night," I thought, "it will descend again and drown the world. How sad a night it will be!"

O-90 passed swiftly by, going toward the elevator. The door slammed.

"Wait a minute!" I screamed. I was frightened.

But the elevator was already groaning, going down, down, down. . . .

"She robbed me of R-, she robbed me of O-90, yet, yet . . . nevertheless . . ."

RECORD FIFTEEN

The Bell
The Mirror-like Sea
I Am to Burn Eternally

I was walking on the dock where the *Integral* is being built, when the Second Builder came to meet me. His face, as usual, was round and white, a porcelain plate. When he speaks it seems as if he serves you a plate of something unbearably tasty.

"You chose to be ill, and without the Chief we had sort of an accident yesterday."

"An accident?"

"Yes, sir. We finished the bell and started to let it down, and imagine; the men caught a male without a number. How he got in I can't make out. They took him to the Operation Department. Oh, they'll get the answers out of the fellow there; 'why' and 'how,' etc. . . ." He smiled delightedly.

Our best and most experienced physicians work in the Operation Department under the direct supervision of the Well-Doer himself. They have all kinds of instruments, but the best of all is the Gas Bell. The procedure is taken from an ancient experiment of elementary physics: they used to put a rat under a gas bell and gradually pump out the air; the air becomes more and more rarefied, and . . . you know the rest.

But our Gas Bell is certainly a more perfect apparatus,

and it is used in combination with different gases. Furthermore, we don't torture a defenseless animal as the ancients did. We use it for a higher purpose: to guard the security of the United State—in other words, the happiness of millions. About five centuries ago, when the work of the Operation Department was only beginning, there were yet to be found some fools who compared our Operation Department with the ancient Inquisition. But this is as absurd as to compare a surgeon performing a tracheotomy with a highway cutthroat. Both use a knife, perhaps the same kind of knife, both do the same thing, viz., cut the throat of a living man; yet one is a well-doer, the other is a murderer; one is marked plus, the other minus. . . . All this becomes perfectly clear in one second, in one turn of our wheel of logic, the teeth of which engage that *minus*, turn it upward, and thus change its aspect.

One other matter is somewhat different: the ring in the door was still oscillating, apparently the door had just closed, yet she, I-330, had disappeared, she was not there! The wheel of logic could not turn this fact. A dream? But even now I still feel in my right shoulder that incomprehensibly sweet pain of I-330 near me in the fog, pressing herself against me. "Thou lovest fog?" Yes, I love the fog, too. I love everything, and everything appears to me wonderful, new, tense; everything is so good! . . .

"So good," I said aloud.

"Good?" The porcelain eyes bulged out. "What good do you find in that? If that man without a number contrived to sneak in, it means that there are others around here, everywhere, all the time, here around the *Integral*, they—"

"Whom do you mean by 'they'?"

"How do I know who? But I sense them, all the time."

"Have you heard about the new operation which has been invented? I mean the surgical removal of fancy?" (There really were rumors of late about something of the sort.)

"No, I haven't. What has that to do with it?"

"Merely this: if I were you, I should go and ask to have this operation performed upon me."

The plate distinctly expressed something lemonlike, sour. Poor fellow! He took offense if one even hinted that he might possess imagination. Well, a week ago I, too, would have taken offense at such a hint. Not now though, for I know that I have imagination; that is what my illness consists of. And more than that: I know that it is a wonderful illness—one does not want to be cured, simply does not want to!

We ascended the glass steps; the world spread itself below us like the palm of a hand.

You, readers of these records, whoever you may be, you have the sun above you. And if you ever were ill, as I am now, then you know what kind of sun there is or may be in the morning; you know that pinkish, lucid, warm gold; the air itself looks a little pinkish; everything seems permeated by the tender blood of the sun; everything is alive; the stones seem soft and living, iron living and warm, people full of life and smiles. Perhaps in a short while all this will disappear, in an hour the pinkish blood of the sun will be drained out; but in the meantime everything is alive. And I see how something flows and pulsates in the sides of the *Integral*; I see the *Integral*; I think of its great and lofty future, of the heavy cargo of inevitable happiness which it is to carry up there into the heights, to you, unseen ones, to you who seek eternally and who never find. You shall find! You shall be happy! You must be happy, and now you have not very long to wait!

The body of the *Integral* is almost ready; it is an exquisite, oblong ellipsoid, made of our glass, which is everlasting like gold and flexible like steel. I watched them within, fixing its transverse ribs and its longitudinal stringers; in the stern they were erecting the base of the gigantic motor. Every three seconds the powerful tail of the *Integral* will eject flame and gases into universal space, and the *Integral* will soar higher and higher, like a flaming Tamerlane of happiness! I watched how the workers, true to the Taylor system, would bend down, then unbend and turn around swiftly and rhythmically like levers of an enormous engine. In their hands they held glittering glass pipes which emitted bluish streaks of flame; the glass walls were being cut into with flame; with flame were being welded the angles, the ribs, the bars. I watched the monstrous glass cranes easily rolling over the glass rails; like the workers themselves, they would obediently turn, bend down, and bring their loads inward into the bowels of the *Integral*. All seemed one: humanized machine and mechanized humans. It was the most magnificent, most stirring beauty, harmony, music!

Quick! Down! To them and with them! And I descended and mingled with them, fused with their mass, caught in the rhythm of steel and glass. Their movements were measured, tense and round. Their cheeks were colored with health, their mirrorlike foreheads unclouded by the insanity of thinking. I was floating upon a mirrorlike sea. I was resting. . . . Suddenly one of them turned his carefree face toward me.

"Well, better today?"

"What, better?"

"You were not here yesterday. And we thought something serious . . ." His forehead was shining—a childish and innocent smile.

My blood rushed to my face. No, I could not lie, facing those eyes. I remained silent; I was drowning. . . . Above, a shiny, round, white porcelain face appeared in the hatchway.

"Hey! D-503! Come up here! Something is wrong with a frame and brackets here, and . . ."

Not waiting until he had finished, I rushed to him, upstairs; I was shamefully saving myself by flight. I had not the power to raise my eyes. I was dazed by the sparkling glass steps under my feet, and with every step I felt more and more hopeless. I, a corrupted man, a criminal, was out of place here. No, I shall probably never again be able to fuse myself into this mechanical rhythm, nor float over this mirror-like, untroubled sea. I am to burn eternally from now on, running from place to place, seeking a nook where I may hide my eyes, eternally, until I . . . A spark cold as ice pierced me. "I myself, I matter little, but is it necessary that *she* also . . .? I must see that she . . ."

I crawled through the hatchway to the deck and stood there; where was I to go now? I did not know what I had come for! I looked aloft. The midday sun, exhausted by its march, was fuming dimly. Below was the *Integral*, a gray mass of glass—dead. The pink blood was drained out! It was obvious to me that all this was my imagination and that everything was the same as before; yet it was also clear to me that . . .

"What is the matter with you, D-503? Are you deaf? I call and call you. What is the matter with you?" It was the Second Builder yelling directly into my ear; he must have been yelling that way for quite a while.

What was the matter with me? I had lost my rudder; the motor was groaning as before, the aero was quivering and rushing on, but it had no rudder. I did not even know where I was rushing, down to the earth or up to the sun, to its flame. . . .

RECORD SIXTEEN

Yellow
A Two-dimensional Shadow
An Incurable Soul

I have not written for several days; I don't know how many. All my days are alike. All are of one color, yellow, like dry, overheated sand. Not a patch of shade, not a drop of water, only an infinity of yellow sand. I cannot live without her, but she, since she disappeared that day so mysteriously in the Ancient House . . .

Since that time I have seen her only once, during the hour for the Walk, two, three, four days ago, I do not remember exactly. All my days are alike. She only passed swiftly by and for a second filled up my yellow, empty world. With her, arm in arm, reaching not higher than her shoulder, were the double-curved S- and the thin papery doctor, and a fourth person whose fingers only I remember well; they streamed out, those fingers, from the sleeve of the unif like a bundle of rays, uncommonly thin, white, long. I-330 raised her hand and waved to me, then she bent toward the one with the raylike fingers, over the head of S-. I overheard the word *Integral.* All four turned around to look at me, and then they disappeared in the bluish-gray sea, and my road was once more dry and yellow.

That same evening she had a pink check on me. I stood before the switchboard and with hatred and tenderness I implored it to click and soon show the number I-330. I would rush out into the hall at every sound of the elevator. The door of the latter would open heavily. Pale, tall, blond, and dark they would come out of the elevator, and here and there curtains were falling. . . . But she was not there. She did not come. And it is quite possible that now, at this minute, as I write these lines, at twenty-two o'clock exactly, with her eyes closed she is pressing her shoulder against somebody else *in the same way,* and *in the same way* she may be asking someone: "Do you love me?" Whom? Who is he? That one with raylike fingers, or that thick-lipped, sprinkling R-? Or S-? S-! Why is it that I have heard his steps splashing behind me as though in a ditch all these days? Why has he been following me all these days like a shadow? Ahead of me, to my side, behind me, a grayish-blue, two-dimensional shadow; people cross it, people step on it, but it remains nearby, attached to me by unseen ties. Perhaps that tie is I-330. I do not know. Or perhaps they, the Guardians I mean, already know that I . . .

If someone should tell you your shadow sees you, sees you all the time, would you understand? All at once peculiar sensations arise in you; your arms seem to belong to someone else; they are in the way. That is how I feel; very frequently now I notice how absurdly I wave my hands without any rhythm. I have an irresistible desire to glance behind me, but I am unable to do so; my neck might as well be forged of iron. I flee, I run faster and faster, and even with my back I feel that shadow following me as fast as I can run; and there is no place to hide myself—no place!

At length I reach my room. Alone at last! But here I find another thing, the telephone. I pick up the receiver. "Yes, I-330, please." And again I hear a light noise through the receiver; someone's step in the hall there, passing the door of her room, and—silence. . . . I drop the receiver. I cannot, cannot bear it any longer, and I run to see her!

This happened yesterday. I ran there and for a whole

hour from sixteen to seventeen I wandered near the house in which she lives. Numbers were passing by in rows. Thousands of feet were beating the time like a behemoth with a million legs passing by. I was alone, thrown out by a storm on an uninhabited island, and my eyes were seeking and seeking among the grayish-blue waves. "There, soon," I thought, "will appear from somewhere the sharp mocking angles of the brows lifted to the temples, and the dark window eyes, and there behind them a flaming fireplace and someone's shadow. . . . And I will rush straight in behind those windows and say to her, "Thou"—yes, "thou" without fail. "Thou knowest I cannot live without thee any longer, then why . . .?" But silence reigned.

Suddenly I heard the silence; suddenly I heard the Musical Tower silenced, and I understood! It was after seventeen already; everyone had already left. I was alone. It was too late to return home. Around me—a desert made of glass and bathed with yellow sunshine. I saw, as if in water, the reflection of the walls in the glass smoothness of the street, sparkling walls, hanging upside down. Myself also upside down, hanging absurdly in the glass.

"I must go at once, this very second, to the Medical Bureau, or else . . . Or perhaps *this* would be best: to remain here, to wait quietly until they see me and come and take me into the Operation Department and put an end to everything at once, redeem everything. . . ." A slight rustle—and the double-curved S- was before me. Without looking I felt his two gray steel-drill eyes bore quickly into me. I plucked up all my strength to show a smile and to say (I had to say something), "I . . . I must go to the Medical Bureau."

"Who is detaining you? What are you standing here for?"

I was silent, absurdly hanging upside down.

"Follow me," said S- austerely.

I followed obediently, waving my unnecessary foreign

arms. I could not raise my eyes. I walked through a strange world turned upside down, where people had their feet pasted to the ceilings, and where engines stood with their bases upward, and where, still lower, the sky merged in the heavy glass of the pavement. I remember what pained me most was the fact that looking at the world for the last time in my life I should see it upside down rather than in its natural state; but I could not raise my eyes.

We stopped. Steps. One step . . . and I should see the figures of the doctors in their white aprons, and the enormous, dumb Bell.

With force, with some sort of an inner twist, I succeeded at last in tearing my eyes away from the glass beneath my feet, and I noticed the golden letters, "Medical Bureau." Why did he bring me here rather than to the Operation Department? Why did he spare me? About this I did not even think at the moment. I made all the steps in one jump, firmly closed the door behind me, and took a very deep breath—as if I had not breathed since morning, as if my heart had not beaten for the same length of time, as if only now I started to breathe and only now a sluice opened in my chest. . . .

Inside there were two of them, one a short specimen with heavy legs, his eyes like the horns of a bull tossing the patients up, the other extremely thin with lips like sparkling scissors, a nose like a blade—it was the same man who . . . I ran to him as to a dear friend, straight over close to the blade, and muttered something about insomnia, dreams, shadows, yellow sand. The scissors lips sparkled and smiled.

"Yes, it *is* too bad. Apparently a soul has formed in you."

A soul? That strange, ancient word that was forgotten long ago. . . .

"Is it . . . v-very dangerous?" I stuttered.

"Incurable," was the cut of the scissors.

"But more specifically, what is it? Somehow I cannot imagine—"

"You see . . . how shall I put it? Are you a mathematician?"

"Yes."

"Then you see . . . imagine a plane, let us say this mirror. You and I are on its surface. You see? There we are, squinting our eyes to protect ourselves from the sunlight, or here is the bluish electric spark in that tube, there the shadow of that aero that just passed. All this is on the surface, is momentary only. Now imagine this very same surface softened by a flame so that nothing can glide over it any longer, so everything will instead penetrate into that mirror world which excites such curiosity in children. I assure you, children are not so foolish as we think they are! The surface becomes a volume, a body, a world. And inside the mirror—within you—there is the sunshine, and the whirlwind caused by the aero propeller, and your trembling lips and someone else's lips also. You see, the cold mirror reflects, throws out, while this one absorbs; it keeps forever a trace of everything that touches it. Once you saw an imperceptible wrinkle on someone's face, and this wrinkle is forever preserved within you. You may happen to hear in the silence a drop of water falling—and you will hear it forever!"

"Yes, yes, that is it!" I grasped his hand. I could hear drops of water dripping in the silence from the faucet of a washstand, and I knew at once it was forever.

"But tell me please, why suddenly . . . suddenly, a soul? There was none, yet suddenly . . . Why is it that no one has it, yet I . . ." I pressed the thin hand; I was afraid to loosen the safety belt.

"Why? Well, why don't we grow feathers or wings, but have only shoulder blades, bases for wings? We have aeros; wings would only be in the way. Wings are needed in order to fly, but we don't need to fly anywhere. We have arrived at the terminus. We have found what we wanted. Is that not so?"

I nodded vaguely. He glanced at me and laughed a scalpel-like, metallic laugh. The other doctor overheard us and stamped out of his room on his heavy legs. He picked up the thin doctor with his horn eyes, then picked me up.

"What is the matter—a soul? You say a soul? Oh, damn it! We may soon retrogress even to the cholera epidemics. I told you"—he tossed the thin one on the horns—"I told you the only thing to do is to operate on them all, wholesale! Simply extirpate the center for fancy. Only surgery can help here, only surgery." He put on a pair of enormous X-ray spectacles and remained thus for a long while, looking into my skull, through the bones into my brain, and making notes.

"Very, very curious! Listen." He looked firmly into my eyes. "Wouldn't you consent to have me perform an extirpation on you? It would be invaluable to the United State; it might help us prevent an epidemic. If you have no special reasons, of course . . ."

Some time ago I should probably have said without hesitation, "I am willing," but now—I was silent. I caught the profile of the thin doctor; I implored him!

"You see," he said at last, "Number D-503 is building the *Integral*, and I am sure the operation would interfere. . . ."

"Ah-h!" grumbled the other, and stamped back into his room.

We remained alone. The paper-like hand was put lightly and caressingly upon mine, the profile-like face came nearer, and he said in a very low voice: "I shall tell you a secret. You are not the only one. My colleague is right when he speaks of an epidemic. Try to remember, haven't you noticed yourself, someone with something similar, very similar, identical?"

He looked at me closely. What was he alluding to? To whom? . . . Is it possible? . . .

"Listen." I jumped up from my seat. But he had already changed the subject. In a loud, metallic tone:

". . . As for the insomnia and the dreams you complain of, I advise you to walk a great deal. Tomorrow morning you must begin taking long walks . . . say, as far as the Ancient House."

Again he pierced me with his eyes and he smiled thinly. It seemed to me that I saw enveloped in the tender tissue of that smile a word, a letter, a name, the only name . . . Or was it only my imagination? I waited impatiently while he wrote a certificate of illness for today and tomorrow. Once more I gently and firmly pressed his hand; then I ran out.

My heart now feels light and swift like an aero; it carries me higher and higher. . . . I know joy will come tomorrow. What joy? . . .

RECORD SEVENTEEN

Through Glass
I Died
The Corridor

I am puzzled. Yesterday, at the very moment when I thought everything was untangled, and that all the X's were at last found, new unknowns appeared in my equation. The origin of the coordinates of the whole story is of course the Ancient House. From this center the axes of all the X's, Y's, and Z's radiate, and recently they have entered into the formation of my whole life.

I walked along the X-axis (Avenue 59) toward the center. The whirlwind of yesterday still raged within me: houses and people upside down; my own hands torturingly foreign to me; glimmering scissors; the sharp sound of drops dripping from the faucet; all this existed, all this *existed* once! All these things were revolving wildly, tearing my flesh, rotating wildly beneath the molten surface, there where the "soul" is located.

In order to follow the instructions of the doctor I chose the road that followed not the hypotenuse but the two legs of a triangle. Soon I reached the road running along the Green Wall. From beyond the Wall, from the infinite ocean of green, there arose toward me an immense wave of roots, branches, flowers, leaves. It rose higher and higher; it seemed as though it would splash over me and that from a man, from the finest and most precise mechanism which I am, I would be transformed into . . . But fortunately there was the Green Wall between me and that wild green sea. Oh, how great and divinely limiting is the wisdom of walls and bars! This Green Wall is, I think, the greatest invention ever conceived. Man ceased to be a wild animal the day he built the first wall; man ceased to be a wild man only on the day when the Green Wall was completed, when by this wall we isolated our machine-like, perfect world from the irrational, ugly world of trees, birds, and beasts. . . .

The blunt snout of some unknown beast was to be seen dimly through the glass of the Wall; its yellow eyes kept repeating the same thought which remained incomprehensible to me. We looked into each other's eyes for a long while. Eyes are shafts which lead from the superficial world into a world which is beneath the surface. A thought awoke in me: "What if that yellow-eyed one, sitting there on that absurd dirty heap of leaves, is happier than I, in his life which cannot be calculated in figures!" I waved my hand. The yellow eyes twinkled, moved back, and disappeared in the foliage. What a pitiful being! How absurd the idea that he might be happier! Happier than I he may be, but I am an exception, am I not? I am sick.

I noticed that I was approaching the dark red walls of the Ancient House, and I saw the grown-together lips of the old woman. I ran to her as fast as I could.

"Is she here?"

The grown-together lips opened slowly.

"Who is 'she'?"

"Who? I-330, of course. You remember we came together, she and I, in an aero the other day."

"Oh, yes, yes, yes—yes."

Ray wrinkles around the lips, artful rays radiating from the eyes. They were making their way deeper and deeper into me.

"Well, she is here, all right. Came in a while ago."

"Here!" I noticed at the feet of the old woman a bush of silver—bitter wormwood. (The court of the Ancient

House, being a part of the museum, is carefully kept in its prehistoric state.) A branch of the bush touched the old woman, she caressed that branch; upon her knees lay stripes of sunshine. For a second, I, the sun, the old woman, the wormwood, those yellow eyes, all seemed to be one; we were firmly united by common veins, and one common blood—boisterous, magnificent blood—was running through those veins.

I am ashamed now to write down all this, but I promised to be frank to the end of these records: yes, I bent over and kissed that soft, grown-together mouth of the old woman. She wiped it with her hand and laughed.

Running, I passed through familiar, half-dark, echoing rooms, and for some reason I ran straight to the bedroom. When I had reached the door, a thought flashed: "And if she is in there . . . not alone?" I stopped and listened. But all I heard was the tick-tock of my heart, not within me, but somewhere near, outside me.

I entered. The large bed—untouched. A mirror . . . another mirror in the door of the cupboard, and in the keyhole an ancient key upon an ancient ring. No one was there. I called softly: "I-330, are you here?" And then in a still lower voice, with closed eyes, holding my breath—in a voice as though I were kneeling before her, "I-, dear." Silence. Only the water was dripping fast into the white basin of the washstand. I cannot now explain why, but I disliked that sound. I turned the faucet hard and went out. She was not there, so much was clear. She must be in another "apartment."

I ran down a wide, somber stairway, pulled one door, another, a third—locked. Every room was locked save that of "our" apartment. And she was not there. I went back again to the same apartment, without knowing why. I walked slowly, with difficulty; my shoe soles suddenly became as heavy as cast iron. I remember distinctly my thought, "It is a mistake that the force of gravity is a constant; consequently all my formulae . . ."

Suddenly—an explosion! A door slammed down below; someone stamped quickly over the flagstones. I became lightfooted again, extremely light! I dashed to the railing to bend over, and in one word, one exclamation, expressed everything: "You!"

I became cold. Below, in the square shadow of the window frame, flapping its pink wing ears, the head of S- passed by!

Like lightning I saw only the naked conclusion. Without any premises (I don't recall any premises even now) the conclusion: he must not see me here! And on the tips of my toes, pressing myself against the wall, I sneaked upstairs into the unlocked apartment.

I stopped for a second at the door. He was stamping upward, here. If only the door . . . I prayed to the door, but it was a wooden one; it squeaked, it squealed. Like a wind something red passed my eyes, something green, and the yellow Buddha. In front of the mirror door of the cupboard my pale face; my ears still following those steps, my lips . . . Now *he* was already passing the green and yellow, now he was passing Buddha. Now at the doorsill of the bedroom . . .

I grasped the key of the cupboard; the ring oscillated. This oscillation reminded me of something. Again a conclusion, a naked conclusion without premises; a conclusion, or, to be more exact, a fragment of one: "Now, I-330 is . . ." I brusquely opened the cupboard and, when inside in the darkness, shut the door firmly. One step! The floor shook under my feet. Slowly and softly I floated somewhere downward; my eyes were dimmed—I died!

Later, when I sat down to describe all these adventures, I sought in my memory and consulted some books; and now I understand, of course! I was in a state of temporary death. This state was known to the ancients, but as far as I am informed it is unknown to us. I have no conception of how long I was dead, probably not longer than five or ten seconds, but after a while I arose from the dead and opened my eyes. It was dark. But I felt I was falling down, down, down. I stretched out my hand to attach myself to something, but the rough wall scratched my fingers; it was running away from me, upward. I felt blood on my fingers. It was clear that all this was not merely a play of my sick imagination. But what was it? What?

I heard my own frequent, trembling breaths. (I am not ashamed to confess this, it was all unexpected and incomprehensible.) A minute, two, three passed; I was still going down. Then a soft bump. The thing that had been falling away from under my feet was motionless. I found in the darkness a knob, and turned it; a door opened; there was a dim light. I now noticed behind me a square platform, traveling upward. I tried to run back to it but it was too late. "I am cut off here," I thought. Where "here" might be I did not know.

A corridor. A heavy silence. The small lamps on the vaulted ceiling resembled an endless, twinkling, dotted line. The corridor was similar to the "tube" of our underground railways but it was much narrower, and made not of our glass but of some other, very ancient material. For a moment I thought of the underground caves where they say many tried to save themselves during the Two Hundred Years' War. There was nothing to do but to walk ahead.

I walked, I think, for about twenty minutes. A turn to the right, the corridor became wider, the small lamps brighter. There was a dim droning somewhere . . . Was it a machine or voices? I did not know. I stood before a heavy, opaque door from behind which came the noise. I knocked. Then I knocked again, louder. Now there was silence behind the door. Something clanked; the door opened slowly and heavily.

I don't know which of us was the more dumfounded; the thin, blade-like doctor stood before me!

"You here!" His scissors opened and remained open.

And I, as if I did not know a human word, stood silent,

merely stared, without comprehending that he was talking to me. He must have told me to leave, for with his thin paper stomach he slowly pressed me to the side, to the more brightly lighted end of the corridor, and poked me in the back.

"Beg your pardon . . . I wanted . . . I thought that she, I-330 . . . but behind me . . ."

"Stay where you are," said the doctor brusquely, and he disappeared.

At last! At last she was nearby, here, and what did it matter where "here" was? I saw the familiar saffron-yellow silk, the smile bite, the eyes with their curtains drawn. . . . My lips quivered, so did my hands and knees, and I had a most stupid thought: "Vibrations make sounds. Shivering must make a sound. Why, then, don't I hear it?"

Her eyes opened for me widely. I entered into them.

"I could not . . . any longer! . . . Where have you been? . . . Why? . . ."

I was unable to tear my eyes away from her for a second, and I talked as if in a delirium, fast and incoherently, or perhaps I only thought without speaking out: "A shadow . . . behind me. I died. And from the cupboard . . . Because that doctor of yours . . . speaks with his scissors . . . I have a soul . . . incurable . . . and I must walk . . ."

"An incurable soul? My poor boy!" I-330 laughed. She covered me with the sparkles of her laughter; my delirium left me. Everywhere around her little laughs were sparkling! How good it was!

The doctor reappeared from around the turn, the wonderful, magnificent, thinnest doctor.

"Well?" He was already beside her.

"Oh, nothing, nothing. I shall tell you later. He got here by accident. Tell them that I shall be back in about a quarter of an hour."

The doctor slid around the corner. She lingered. The door closed with a heavy thud. Then slowly, very slowly, piercing my heart with a sharp sweet needle, I-330 pressed against me with her shoulder and then with her arm, with her whole body, and we walked away as if fused into one.

I do not remember now where we turned into darkness; in the darkness we walked up some endless stairway in silence. I did not see but I knew, I knew that she walked as I did, with closed eyes, blind, her head thrown a little backward, biting her lips and listening to the music—that is to say, to my almost audible tremor.

I returned to consciousness in one of the innumerable nooks in the courtyard of the Ancient House. There was a fence of earth with naked stone ribs and yellow teeth of walls half fallen to pieces. She opened her eyes and said, "Day after tomorrow at sixteen." She was gone.

Did all this really happen? I do not know. I shall learn day after tomorrow. One real sign remains: on my right hand the skin has been rubbed from the tips of three fingers. But today, on the *Integral*, the Second Builder assured me that he saw me touch the polishing wheel with those very same fingers. Perhaps I did. It is quite probable. I don't know. I don't know anything.

RECORD EIGHTEEN

Debris of Logic
Wounds and Plaster
Never Again

Last night, as soon as I had gone to bed, I fell momentarily to the bottom of the ocean of sleep like an overloaded ship that has been wrecked. The heavy mass of wavy green water enveloped me. Then, slowly, I floated from the bottom upward, and somewhere in the middle of that course I opened my eyes—my room! The morning was still green and motionless. A fragment of sunshine coming from the mirror on my closet door shone into my eyes. This fragment did not permit me to sleep, being thus an obstacle in the way of fulfilling exactly the rules of the Tables, which prescribe so many hours of sleep. I should have opened the closet but I felt as though I were in a spider web, and cobweb covered my eyes; I had no power to sit up.

Yet I got up and opened the closet door; suddenly, there behind that door, making her way through the mass of garments that hung there, was I-330! I have become so accustomed of late to most improbable things that as far as I remember I was not even surprised; I did not even ask a question. I jumped into the closet, slammed the mirror door behind me, and breathlessly, brusquely, blindly, avidly I clung to her. I remember clearly even now: through the narrow crack of the door a sharp sun ray like lightning broke into the darkness and played on the floor and walls of the closet, and a little higher the cruel ray blade fell upon the naked neck of I-330, and this for some reason seemed to me so terrible that I could not bear it, and I screamed—and again I opened my eyes. My room!

The morning was still green and motionless. On the door of my closet was a fragment of the sunshine. I was in bed. A dream? Yet my heart was still wildly beating, quivering and twitching; there was a dull pain in the tips of my fingers and in my knees. *This* undoubtedly *did* happen! And now I am no longer able to distinguish what is dream from what is actuality; irrational numbers grow through my solid, habitual, tridimensional life; and instead of firm, polished surfaces, there is something shaggy and rough. . . .

I waited long for the Bell to ring. I was lying thinking, untangling a very strange logical chain. In our superficial life, every formula, every equation, corresponds to a curve or a solid. We have never seen any curve or solid corresponding to my square root of minus one. The horrifying part of the situation is that there *exist* such curves or solids. Unseen by us they do exist, they must, inevitably; for in mathematics, as on a screen, strange, sharp shadows appear before us. One must remember that mathematics, like death, never makes mistakes, never plays tricks. If we are unable to see those irrational curves or solids, it means only that they inevitably possess a whole immense world somewhere beneath the surface of our life. . . .

I jumped up without waiting for the waking Bell and began to pace up and down the room. My mathematics, the only firm and immovable island of my shaken life, this, too, was torn from its anchor and was floating, whirling. Then it means that that absurd thing, the "soul," is as real as my unif, as my boots, although I do not see them since they are behind the door of the closet. If boots are not a sickness, why should the "soul" be one? I sought, but I could not find, a way out of the logical confusion. It looked to me like that strange and sad debris beyond the Green Wall; my debris of logic, too, is filled with extraordinary, incomprehensible, wordless, but speaking beings. It occurred to me for a moment that through some strange, thick glass I saw *it*; I saw it at once infinitely large and infinitely small, scorpion-like, with hidden but ever perceptible sting; I *saw* the square root of minus one. Perhaps it was nothing else but my "soul," which, like the legendary scorpion of the ancients, was voluntarily stinging itself with . . .

The Bell! The day began. All I saw and felt neither died nor disappeared; it merely became covered with daylight, as our visible world does not die or disappear at the end of the day but merely becomes covered with the darkness of night. My head was filled with a light, a thin haze. Through that haze I perceived the long glass tables and the globe-like heads busy chewing—slowly, silently, in unison. At a distance, through the haze, the metronome was slowly beating its tick-tock, and to the accompaniment of this customary and caressing music I joined with the others in counting automatically to fifty: fifty is the number of chewing movements required by the law of the State for every piece of food. And automatically then, keeping time, I went downstairs and put my name down in the book for the outgoing Numbers, as everyone did. But I felt I *lived* separately from everybody; I lived by myself separated by a soft wall which absorbed noises; beyond that wall there was my own world.

Here a thought occurred to me. If that world is only my own, why should I tell about it in these records? Why should I recount all these absurd "dreams" about closets, endless corridors? With great sorrow I notice that instead of a correct and strictly mathematical poem in honor of the United State I am writing a fantastic novel. Oh! if only it were a novel and not my actual life, full of X's, square roots of minus one, and downfalls! Yet all may be for the best. Probably you, my unknown readers, are children still as compared with us. We are brought up by the United State; consequently we have reached the highest summits attainable by man. And you, being children, may swallow without crying all the bitter things I am to give you only if they be coated with the syrup of adventures.

The Same Evening

Are you familiar with the following sensation? You are in an aero and you dash upward along a blue spiral line; the window is open and the wind rushes past your face, whistling. There is no earth. The earth is forgotten. The earth is as far from you as Venus, Saturn, or Jupiter. That is how I live now. A hurricane wind beats into my face; I forget the earth, forget rosy, dear O-90. Yet the earth does exist, and sooner or later I must plane down to that earth; only I close my eyes to avoid seeing the date at which the name O-90 is written on my Tables.

This evening the distant earth reminded me of itself. In order to fulfill the recommendation of the doctor (I desire sincerely, most sincerely I desire, to be cured), I wandered for two hours and eight minutes over the straight lines of the deserted avenues. Everybody was in the auditoriums, in accordance with the Table. Only I, cut off from the rest, I was alone. Strictly speaking, it was a very unnatural situation. Imagine a finger cut off from the whole, from the hand; a separate human finger, somewhat hunched, running over the glass sidewalk. I was such a finger. What seemed most strange and unnatural was that the finger had no desire to be with its hand, with its fellows. I want either to be alone or with *her*; to transfuse my whole being into hers through a contact with her shoulder or through our interwoven fingers.

I came home as the sun was setting. The pink dust of evening was covering the glass of the walls, the golden peak of the Accumulating Tower, the voices and smiles of the Numbers. Isn't it strange: the passing rays of the evening sun fall to the earth at the same angle as the awakening rays of the morning, yet they make everything seem so different; the pink tinge is different. At sunset it is so quiet, somewhat melancholy; at sunrise it is resounding, boisterous.

When I entered the hall downstairs I saw U-, the controller. She took a letter from the heaps of envelopes covered with pink dust and handed it to me. I repeat: she is a very respectable woman, and I am sure she has only the very best feelings toward me. . . . Yet, every time I see those cheeks hanging down, which look like the gills of a fish, I . . .

Holding out her dry hand with the letter, U- sighed. But that sigh only very slightly moved in me the curtains which separate me from the rest of the world. I was completely engrossed by the envelope which trembled in my hand. I had no doubt that it was a letter from I-330.

At that moment I heard another sigh, such a deliberate one, underscored with two lines, that I raised my eyes from the envelope and saw a tender, cloudy smile coming from between the gills, through the bashful blinds of lowered eyes. And then:

"You poor, poor dear!" A sigh underscored with three lines, and a glance at the letter, an imperceptible glance. (What was in the letter she naturally knew, *ex officio*.)

"No, really? . . . Why?"

"No, no, dear, I know better than you. For a long time I have watched you, and I see that you need someone with years of experience of life to accompany you."

I felt all pasted around by her smile. It was like a plaster upon the wounds which were to be inflicted upon me by the letter I held in my hand. Finally, through the bashful blinds of her eyes, she said in a very low voice: "I shall think about it, dear. I shall think it over. And be sure that if I feel myself strong enough . . ."

"Great Well-Doer! Is it possible that is my lot? . . . Is it possible that she means to say, that she? . . ."

My eyes were dimmed and filled with thousands of sinusoids; the letter was trembling. I went near the light, to the wall. There the light of the sun was going out; from the sun the dark, sad, pink dust was falling thicker and thicker, covering the floor, my hands, the letter. I opened the envelope and found the signature as fast as I could —the first wound! It was not I-330; it was O-90! And another wound: in the right-hand corner a slovenly splash, a blot! I cannot bear blots. It matters little whether they are made by ink or by . . . Well, it doesn't matter by what. Heretofore, such a blot would have had only a disagreeable effect, disagreeable to the eyes; but now—why did that small gray blot seem like a cloud, and seem to spread about me a leaden, bluish darkness? Or was it again the "soul" at work? Here is a transcript of the letter:

You know, or perhaps you don't . . . I cannot write well. Little it matters! Now you know that without you there is for me not a single day, a single morning, a single spring, for R- is only . . . Well, that is of no importance to you. At any rate, I am very grateful to him, for without him, alone all these days, I don't know what would . . . During these last few days and nights I have lived through ten years, or perhaps twenty years. My room seemed to me not square but round; I walk around without end, round after round, always the same thing, not a door to escape through. I cannot live without you because I love you; and I should not, I cannot be with you any more— because I love you! Because I see and I understand that you need no one now, no one in the world save that other, and you must realize that it is precisely because I love you that I must . . .

I need another two or three days in order to paste together the fragments of myself and thus restore at least something similar to the O-90 of old. Then I shall go myself, and I myself shall state that I take your name from my list, and this will be better for you; you must feel happy now. I shall never again . . .

Good-by, O-.

Never again. Yes, that is better. She is right. But why, then? . . . Why, then? . . .

RECORD NINETEEN

The Infinitesimal of the Third Order
From Under the Forehead
Over the Railing

There in the strange corridor lighted by the dotted line of dim little electric lamps . . . or no, no, later, when we had already reached one of the nooks in the courtyard of the Ancient House, she had said, "Day after tomorrow." That "day after tomorrow" is today. And everything seems to have wings and to fly; the day flies; and our *Integral,* too, already has wings. We finished placing the motor and tried it out today, without switching it in. What magnificent, powerful salvos! To me each of them sounded like a salute in honor of *her*, the only one—in honor of today!

At the time of the first explosion about a dozen loafing Numbers from the docks stood near the main tube—and nothing was left of them save a few crumbs and a little soot. With pride I now write that this occurrence did not disturb the rhythm of our work for even a second. Not a man shrank. We and our lathes continued our rectilinear or curved motions with the same sparkling and polished precision as before, as if nothing had happened. As a matter of fact, what did happen? A dozen Numbers represent scarcely one hundred millionth part of the United State. For practical consideration, that is but an infinitesimal of the third order. *Pity,* a result of arithmetical ignorance, was known to the ancients; to us it seems absurd.

It also seems droll to me, that yesterday I was thinking, even relating in these pages about a gray blot! All that was only the "softening of the surface" which is normally as hard as diamond, like our walls. (There is an ancient saying: "Shooting beans at a stone wall . . .")

Sixteen o'clock. I did not go for the supplementary walk; who knows, she might come now, when the sun is so noisily bright?

I am almost the only one in this room. Through the walls full of sunshine I see for a distance to the right and to the left, and below strings of other rooms, repeating each other as if in a mirror, hanging in the air and empty. Only on the bluish stairway, striped by the golden ink of the sun, a thin, gray shadow is seen rising. Already I hear steps, and I see through the door, and I feel a smile pasted to my face like a plaster. But it passed to another stairway and down. The click of the switchboard! I threw myself to that little white slit and . . . an unfamiliar male Number! (A consonant means a male Number.)

The elevator groaned and stopped. A big, slovenly, slanting forehead stood before me, and the eyes . . . They impressed me strangely; it seemed as if the man talked with his eyes which were deep under the forehead.

"Here is a letter from her, for you." (From under the awning of that forehead.) "She asked that everything . . . as requested in the letter . . . without fail." This, too, from under the forehead, from under the awning, and he turned, looked about.

"No, there is nobody, nobody. Quickly! the letter!"

He put the letter in my hand and went out without a word.

A pink check fell out of the envelope. It was hers, *her* check! Her tender perfume! I felt like running to catch up with that wonderful under-the-forehead one. A tiny note followed the check from the envelope; three lines: "The check . . . Lower the curtains without fail, as if I were actually with you. It is necessary that they should think that I . . . I am very, very sorry."

I tore the note into small bits. A glance at the mirror revealed my distorted, broken eyebrows. I took the check and was ready to do with it as I had done with the note. "She asked that everything . . . as requested in the letter . . . without fail." My arms weakened and the hands loosened. The check was back on the table. She *is* stronger than I, stronger than I. It seemed as if I were going to act as she wished. Besides . . . However, it is a long time before evening.

The check remained on the table. In the mirror—my distorted, broken eyebrows. Oh, why did I not have a doctor's certificate for today? I should like to go and walk, walk without end around the Green Wall and then to fall on my bed . . . to the bottom of . . . Yet I had to go to Auditorium No. 13, and I should have to get hold of myself, so as to bear up for two hours! Two hours without motion, at a time when I wanted to scream and stamp my feet!

The lecture was on. It was very strange to hear from the sparkling tube of the phono-lecturer not the usual metallic voice but a soft, velvety, mossy one. It was a woman's voice, and I seemed to have a vision of the woman: a little, hooklike old woman, like the one at the Ancient House.

The Ancient House! Suddenly from within me a powerful fountain of . . . I had to use all my strength to control myself, so as not to fill the auditorium with screams. The soft, mossy words were piercing me, yet only empty words about children and child production reached my ear. I was like a photographic plate: everything was making its imprint with a strange, senseless precision on me; the golden scythe which was nothing more than the reflection of light from the loud-speaker of the lecture apparatus: under the loud-speaker a child, a living illustration. It was leaning toward the loud-speaker, a fold of its infinitesimal unif in its mouth, its little fist clenched firmly, its thumb squeezed into the fist, a light fluffy pleat of skin at the wrist. Like a photographic plate I was taking in the impression of all this. Now I saw how its naked leg hung over the edge of the platform, the pink fan of its finger waved in the air. . . . One minute more, one second, and the child would be on the floor!

A female's scream, a wave of translucent wings, her unif on the platform! She caught the child, her lips clung to the fluffy pleat of the baby's wrist; she moved the child to the middle of the table and left the platform. The imprints were registering in me: a pink crescent of a mouth, the horns downward! Eyes like small blue saucers filled with liquid! It was O-90. And as if reading a consequential formula, I suddenly felt the necessity, the naturalness of that insignificant occurrence.

She sat down behind me, somewhat to my left. I looked back. She quietly removed her gaze from the table and the child and looked straight into me. Within again: she, I, the table on the platform—three points. And through those three points lines were drawn, a projection of some as-yet-unforeseen events!

Later I went home through the green dusky street, which seemed many-eyed because of the electric lights. I heard myself tick-tocking like a clock. And the hands of that clock seemed to be about to pass a figure: I was going to do something, something that would cut off every avenue of retreat. She wants somebody, whom I do not know, to think she is with me. I want her; what do I care what *she* wants? I do not want to be alone behind the curtains, and that is all there is to it!

From behind came sounds of a familiar gait, like splashing in a ditch. I did not need to look back, I knew it was S-. He would follow me to the very door, probably. Then he would stay below on the sidewalk, and he would try to drill upward into my room with his boring eyes, until the curtains would fall, concealing something criminal.

Was he my Guardian Angel? No! My decision was made.

When I came into my room and turned on the light, I could not believe my eyes! O-90 stood at my table, or, to be more exact, she was hanging like a creased empty dress. She seemed to have no tensity, no spring beneath the dress; her arms and legs were springless, her voice was hanging and springless.

"About my letter, did you receive it? Yes? I must know your answer, I must—today."

I shrugged my shoulders. I enjoyed looking into her blue eyes which were filled with tears as if she were the guilty one. I lingered over my answer. With pleasure I pricked her:

"Answer? Well . . . You are right. Undoubtedly. In everything."

"Then . . ." (She tried to cover the minute tremor with a smile, but it did not escape me.) "Well, all right. I shall . . . I shall leave you at once."

Yet she remained drooping over the table. Drooping eyelids, drooping arms and legs. The pink check of the other was still on the table. I quickly opened this manuscript, *We*, and with its pages I covered the check, trying to hide it from myself, rather than from O-.

"See, here, I am still busy writing. Already 101 pages! Something quite unexpected comes out in this writing."

In a voice, in a shadow of a voice, "And do you remember . . . how the other day I . . . on the *seventh* page . . . and it dropped. . . ."

The tiny blue saucers filled to the borders; silently and rapidly the tears ran down her cheeks. And suddenly, like the dropping of the tears, rushing forth, words:

"I cannot . . . I shall leave you in a moment. I shall never again . . . and I don't care. . . . Only I want, I must have a child! From you! Give me a child and I will leave. I will!"

I saw she was trembling all over beneath her unif, and

I felt . . . I, too, would soon . . . would . . . I put my hands behind my back and smiled.

"What? You desire to go under the Machine of the Well-Doer?"

Like a stream her words ran over the dam.

"I don't care. I shall feel it for a while within me. I want to see, to see only once the little fold of skin here at the wrist, like that one on the table in the Auditorium. Only for one day!"

Three points: she, I, and a little fist with a fluffy fold of skin there on the table!

I remember how once when I was a child they took me up on the Accumulating Tower. At the very top I bent over the glass railing of an opening in the Tower. Below, people seemed like dots; my heart contracted sweetly. "What if . . ." On that occasion I only clenched my hands around the railing; now I jumped over.

"So you desire . . . being perfectly aware that . . ."

Her eyes were closed as if the sun were beating straight into her face. A wet, shining smile!

"Yes, yes! I want it!"

Quickly I took out the pink check of the other from under the manuscript and down I went to the controller on duty. O-90 caught my hand, screamed out something, but what it was I understood only later, when I returned.

She was sitting on the edge of the bed, hands firmly clasped about the knees.

"Is it, is it her check?"

"What does it matter? Well, it is hers, yes."

Something cracked. It must have been the springs of the bed, for O-90 made a slight motion only. She remained sitting, her hands upon her knees.

"Well, quick . . ." I roughly pressed her hand. A red spot was left on her wrist (tomorrow it will become purple), where the fluffy, infantile fold . . . I turned the switch; my thoughts went out with the light. Darkness, a spark, and I had jumped over the railing, down. . . .

RECORD TWENTY

Discharge
The Material of an Idea
The Zero Rock

Discharge is the best word for it. Now I see that it was actually like an electric discharge. The pulse of my last few days had been becoming dryer and dryer, more and more rapid, more intense. The opposite poles had been drawing nearer and nearer, and already I could hear the dry crackling; one millimeter more, and—an explosion! Then silence.

Within me there is quiet now, and emptiness like that of a house after everybody has left, when one lies ill, all alone, and hears so clearly the distinct, metallic tick-tock of thoughts.

Perhaps that "discharge" cured me at last of my torturing "soul." Again I am like all of us. At least at this moment as I write I can see, as it were, without any pain in my mental eye, how O-90 is brought to the steps of the Cube; or I see her in the Gas Bell. And if there in the Operation Department she should give my name, I do not care. Piously and gratefully I would kiss the punishing hand of the Well-Doer at the last moment. I have this right with regard to the United State: to receive my punishment. And I shall not give up this right. No Number ought, or dares, to refuse this one personal, and therefore most precious, privilege.

. . . Quietly, metallically, distinctly, do the thoughts rap in the head. An invisible aero carries me into the blue height of my beloved abstractions. And I see how there in the height, in the purest rarefied air, my judgment about the only "right" bursts with a crack, like a pneumatic tire. I see clearly that only an atavism, the absurd superstition of the ancients, gives me this idea of "right."

There are ideas of moulded clay and ideas moulded of gold, or of our precious glass. In order to know the material of which an idea is made, one needs only to let fall upon it a drop of strong acid. One of these acids was known to the ancients under the name of *reductio ad absurdum*. This was the name for it, I think. But they were afraid of this poison; they preferred to believe that they saw *heaven*, even though it was a toy made of clay, rather than confess to themselves that it was only a blue nothing. We, on the other hand (glory to the Well-Doer!), we are adults, and we have no need of toys. Now if we put a drop of acid on the idea of "right" . . . Even the ancients (the most mature of them) knew that the source of right was—might! Right is a function of might. Here we have our scale: on the one side an ounce, on the other a ton. On one side "I," on the other "we," the United State. Is it not clear? To assume that I may have any "right" as far as the State is concerned is like assuming that an ounce may equilibrate a ton in a scale! Hence the natural distribution: tons—rights, grams—duties. And the natural road from nothingness to greatness is to forget that one is a gram and to feel that one is one millionth of a ton!

You ripe-bodied, bright Venerians; you sooty, blacksmith-like Uranians, I almost hear your protests in this silence. But only think, everything that is great is simple. Remember, only the four rules of arithmetic are unshakable and eternal! And only that mortality will be unshakable and eternal which is built upon those four rules.

This is the superior wisdom, this is the summit of that pyramid around which people, red with sweat, fought and battled for centuries trying to crawl up!

Looking from this summit down to the bottom, where something is still left swarming like worms, from this summit all that is left over in us from the ancients seems alike. Alike are the unlawful coming motherhood of O-90, a murder, and the insanity of that Number who dared to throw verses into the face of the United State; and alike is the judgment for them—premature death. This is that divine justice of which those stone-housed ancients dreamed, lit by the naïve pink rays of the dawn of history. Their "God" punished sacrilege as a capital crime.

You Uranians, morose and as black as the ancient Spaniards, who were wise in knowing so well how to burn at the stake, you are silent; I think you agree with me. But I hear you, pink Venerians, saying something about "tortures, executions, return to barbarism." My dear Venerians, I pity you! You are incapable of philosophical, mathematical thinking. Human history moves upward in circles, like an aero. The circles are at times golden, sometimes they are bloody, but all have 360 degrees. They go from 0° to 10°, 20°, 200°, 360°—and then again 0°. Yes, we have returned to zero. But for a mathematically working mind it is obvious that this zero is different: it is a perfectly new zero. We started from zero to the right and came to zero on the left. Hence instead of plus zero we are at minus zero. Do you understand?

This zero appears to me now as a silent, immense, narrow rock, sharp as a blade. In cruel darkness, holding our breath, we set sail from the black night side of the zero rock. For centuries we, Columbuses, floated and floated; we made the circuit of the whole world and at last! Hurrah! Salute! We climbed up the masts; before us now was a new side of the zero rock, hitherto unknown, bathed in the polar light of the United State—a blue mass covered with rainbow sparkles! Suns!—a hundred suns! A million rainbows! What does it matter if we are separated from the other black side of the zero rock only by the thickness of a blade? A knife is the most solid, the most immortal, the most inspired invention of man. The knife served on the guillotine. The knife is the universal tool for cutting knots. The way of paradoxes follows its sharp edge, the only way becoming to a fearless mind. . . .

RECORD TWENTY-ONE

The Duty of an Author
The Ice Swells
The Most Difficult Love

Yesterday was her day and again she did not come. Again there came her incoherent note, explaining nothing. But I am tranquil, perfectly tranquil. If I act as I am told to in the note, if I go to the controller on duty, produce the pink check, and then, having lowered the curtains, if I sit alone in my room, I do all this not because I have no power to act contrary to her desire. That seems funny? Decidedly not! It is quite simple: separated from all curative, plaster-like smiles I am enabled quietly to write these very lines. This, first. And second: I am afraid to lose in her, in I-330, perhaps the only clue I shall ever have to an understanding of all the unknowns, like the story of the cupboard, or my temporary death, for instance. To understand, to discover these unknowns as the author of these records, I feel to be my simple duty. Moreover, the unknown is naturally the enemy of man. And Homo sapiens only then becomes man in the complete sense of the word, when his punctuation includes no question marks, only exclamation points, commas, and periods.

Thus, guided by what seems to me my simple duty as an author, I took an aero today at sixteen o'clock and went to the Ancient House. A strong wind was blowing against me. The aero advanced with difficulty through the thicket of air, its transparent branches whistling and whipping. The city below seemed a heap of blue blocks of ice. Suddenly—a cloud, a swift, oblique shadow. The ice became leaden; it swelled. As in springtime, when you happen to stand at the shore and wait, in one more minute everything will move and pull and crack! But the minute passes and the ice remains motionless; you feel as though you yourself are swelling, your heart beats more restlessly, more frequently. . . . But why do I write about all this? And whence all these strange sensations? For is there such an iceberg as could ever break the most lucid, solid crystal of our life?

At the entrance of the Ancient House I found no one. I went around it and found the old janitress near the Green Wall. She held her hand above her eyes, looking upward. Beyond the Wall, the sharp black triangles of some birds; they would rush, cawing, in onslaught on the invisible fence of electric waves, and as they felt the electricity against their breasts, they would recoil and soar once more beyond the Wall.

I noticed oblique, swift shadows on the dark, wrinkled face, a quick glance at me.

"Nobody here, nobody, nobody! No! And no use coming here . . ."

In what respect is it "no use," and what a strange idea, to consider me somebody's shadow. Perhaps all of you are only my shadows. Did I not populate these pages, which only recently were white quadrangular deserts, with you? Without me could they whom I shall guide over the narrow paths of my lines, could they ever see you?

Of course I did not say all this to the old woman. From experience I know that the most torturing thing is to inoculate someone with a doubt as to the fact that he or she is a three-dimensional reality and not some other reality. I remarked only, quite dryly, that her business was to open the gate, and she let me into the courtyard.

It was empty. Quiet. The wind remained beyond the walls, distant as on that day when shoulder to shoulder, two like one, we came out from beneath, from the corridors—if it ever really happened. I walked under stone arches; my steps resounded against the damp vaults and fell behind me, sounding as though someone were continually following me. The yellow walls with patches of red brick were watching me through their square spectacles, windows—watching me open the squeaky doors of a barn, look into corners, nooks, and hidden places. . . . A gate in the fence and a lonely spot. The monument of the Two Hundred Years' War. From the ground naked stone ribs were sticking out. The yellow jaws of the Wall. An ancient oven with a chimney like a ship petrified forever among red-brick waves.

It seemed to me that I had seen those yellow teeth once before. I saw them still dimly in my mind, as at the bottom of a barrel, through water. And I began to search. I fell into caves occasionally; I stumbled over stones; rusty jaws caught my unif a few times; salt drops of sweat ran from my forehead into my eyes.

Nowhere could I find that exit from below, from the corridors—nowhere! There was none. Well, perhaps it was better that it happened so. Probably *all* that was only one of my absurd "dreams."

Tired out, covered with cobwebs and dust, I opened the gate to return to the main yard, when suddenly . . . a rustle behind me, splashing steps, and there before me were the pink wing-like ears and the double-curved smile of S-. Half-closing his eyes, he bored his little drills into me and asked:

"Taking a walk?"

I was silent. My arms were heavy.

"Well, do you feel better now?"

"Yes, thank you. I think I am becoming normal again."

He let me go. He lifted his eyes, looked upward, and I noticed his Adam's apple for the first time; it resembles a broken spring sticking out from beneath the upholstery of a couch.

Above us, not very high (about fifty meters), aeros were buzzing. By their low, slow flight and by the observation tubes which hung down I recognized them. They were the aeros of the Guardians. But there were not two or three, as usual, there were about ten or twelve (I regret to have to confine myself to an approximate figure).

"Why are there so many today?" I dared to ask S-.

"Why? Hm. . . . A real physician begins to treat a patient when he is still well but on the way to becoming sick tomorrow, day after tomorrow, or within a week. Prophylaxis! Yes!"

He nodded and went splashing over the stones of the yard. Then he turned his head and said over his shoulder, "Be careful!"

Again I was alone. Silence. Emptiness. Far beyond the Green Wall the birds and the wind. What did he mean? My aero ran very fast with the wind. Light and heavy shadows from the clouds. Below blue cupolas, cubes of glass ice were becoming leaden and swelling. . . .

The Same Evening

I took up my pen just now in order to write upon these pages a few thoughts which, it seems to me, will prove useful to you, my readers. These thoughts are concerned with the great Day of Unanimity which is now not far away. But as I sat down, I discovered that I could not write at present; instead, I sit and listen to the wind beating the glass with its dark wings; all the while I am busy looking about and I am waiting, expecting . . . What? I do not know. So I was very glad when I saw the brownish-pink gills enter my room, heartily glad, I may say. She sat down and innocently smoothed a fold of her unif that fell between her knees, and very soon she pasted upon me, all over me, a host of smiles, a bit of a smile on each crack of my face, and this gave me pleasant sensations, as if I were tightly bound like an infant of the ancients in a swaddling cloth.

"Imagine! Today, when I entered the classroom"—she works in the Child-Educational Refinery—"I suddenly noticed a caricature upon the blackboard. Indeed! I assure you! They had pictured me in the form of a fish! Perhaps I really—"

"No, no! Why do you say that?" I hastily exclaimed. When one was near her, it was clear indeed that she had nothing resembling gills. No. When I referred to gills in these pages I was certainly irreverent.

"Oh, after all it does not matter. But the act as such, think of it! Of course I called the Guardians at once. I love children very much and I think that the most difficult and the most exalted love is—cruelty. You understand me, of course."

"Certainly!" Her sentence so closely resembled my thoughts! I could not refrain from reading to her a passage from my Record No. 20, beginning "Quietly, metallically, distinctly, do the thoughts" . . . etc. I felt her brownish-pink cheeks twitching and coming closer and closer to me. Suddenly I felt in my hands her firm, dry, even slightly prickling fingers.

"Give, give this to me, please. I shall have it transcribed and make the children learn it by heart. Not only your Venerians need all this, but we ourselves right now, tomorrow, day after tomorrow."

She glanced around and said in a very low voice:

"Have you heard? They say that on the Day of Unanimity—"

I sprang to my feet.

"What? What do they say? What—on the Day of Unanimity?"

The coziness of my room, its very walls, seemed to have vanished. I felt myself thrown outside, where the tremendous, shaggy wind was tossing about and where the slanting clouds of dusk were descending lower and lower. . . .

U- boldly and firmly grasped me by the shoulders. I even noticed how her fingers, responding to my emotion, trembled slightly.

"Sit down, dear, and don't be upset. They say many things; must we believe them all? Moreover, if only you need me, I shall be near you on that day. I shall leave the school children with someone else and I shall stay with you, for you, dear, you, too, are a child and you need . . ."

"No, no!" I raised my hands in protest. "Not for anything! You really think then that I am a child and that I cannot do without a . . . Oh, no! Not for anything in the world." (I must confess I had other plans for that day!)

She smiled. The wording of that smile apparently was: "Oh, what a stubborn, what a stubborn boy!" She sat down, eyelids lowered. Her hands modestly busied themselves with fixing the fold of the unif which fell again between her knees, and suddenly, about something entirely different, she said:

"I think I must decide . . . for your sake. . . . But I implore you, do not hurry me. I must think it over."

I did not hurry her, although I realized that I ought to have been delighted, as there is no greater honor than to crown someone's evening years.

. . . All night strange wings were about. I walked and protected my head with my hands from those wings. And a chair, not like ours, but an ancient chair, came in with a horse-like gait; first the right foreleg and left hind leg, then the left foreleg and right hind leg. It rushed to my bed and crawled into it, and I liked that wooden chair, although it made me uncomfortable and caused me some pain.

It is very strange; is it really impossible to find any cure for this dream sickness, or to make it rational, perhaps even useful?

RECORD TWENTY-TWO

The Benumbed Waves
Everything Is Improving
I Am a Microbe

Please imagine that you stand at the seashore. The waves go rhythmically up, down, up. . . . Suddenly, when they have risen, they remain in that position, benumbed, torpid! It was just as weird and unnatural when everything became confused and our regular walk, which is prescribed by the Tables, suddenly came to an end. The last time such a thing happened was one hundred and nineteen years ago, when according to our historians a meteorite fell hissing and fuming into the very midst of the marchers. We were walking yesterday as usual, that is like warriors on the Assyrian monuments, a thousand heads and two composite, integrated legs and two swinging, integrated arms. At the end of the avenue, where the Accumulating Tower was formidably resounding, a quadrangle appeared: on the sides, in front, and behind —guards; in the center—three Numbers. Their unifs were already stripped of the golden State badge; everything was painfully clear. The enormous dial on the top of the Tower looked like a face; it bent down from the clouds and, spitting down its seconds, it waited with indifference. It showed six minutes past thirteen exactly. There was some confusion in the quadrangle. I was very close, and I saw the most minute details. I clearly remember a thin, long neck and on the temple a confused net of small blue veins like rivers on the map of a small unfamiliar world, and that unknown world was apparently still a very young man. He evidently noticed someone in our ranks; he stopped, rose upon his tiptoes, and stretched his neck. One of the guards snapped his back with the bluish spark of the electric whip—he squealed in a thin voice like a puppy. The distinct snaps followed each other at intervals of approximately two seconds; a snap and a squeal, a snap and a squeal. . . . We continued to walk as usual, rhythmically, in our Assyrian manner. I watched the graceful zigzags of the electric sparks and thought: "Human society is constantly improving, as it should. How ugly a tool was the ancient whip and how much beauty there is—"

At that moment, like a nut flying from a wheel revolving at full speed, a female Number, thin, flexible, and tense, tore herself from our rows, and with a cry, "Enough! Don't you dare!" she threw herself straight into the quadrangle. It was like the meteorite of one hundred and nineteen years ago; our march came to a standstill and our rows appeared like the gray crests of waves frozen by sudden cold. For a second I looked at that woman's figure with the eye of a stranger, as all the others did. She was no Number any longer; she was only a human being, and she existed for us only as a substantiation of the insult which she cast upon the United State. But a motion of hers, her bending while twisting to the left upon her hips, revealed to me clearly who she was. I knew, I knew that body, flexible as a whip! My eyes, my lips, my hands knew it; at that moment I was absolutely certain. . . . Two of the guards dashed to catch her. One more moment, and that limpid, mirror-like point on the pavement would have become the point of meeting of their trajectories, and she would have been caught! My heart fell, stopped. Without thinking whether it was permissible or not, whether it was reasonable or absurd, I threw myself straight to that point.

I felt thousands of eyes bulging with horror fixed upon me, but that only added a sort of desperately joyful power to that wild being with hairy paws which arose in me and ran faster and faster. Two more steps—she turned around—

I saw a quivering face covered with freckles, red eyebrows. . . . It was not she! Not I-330!

A rabid, quivering joy took hold of me. I wanted to shout something like: "Catch her! Get her, that—" But I heard only my whisper. A heavy hand was already upon my shoulder; I was caught and led away. I tried to explain to them:

"But listen, you must understand that I thought that . . ."

But could I explain even to myself all the sickness which I have described in these pages? My light went out; I waited obediently. As a leaf that is torn from its branch by a sudden gust of wind falls humbly, but on its way down turns and tries to catch every little branch, every fork, every knot, so I tried to catch every one of the silent, globe-like heads, or the transparent ice of the walls, or the blue needle of the Accumulating Tower which seemed to pierce the clouds.

At that moment, when a heavy curtain was about to separate me from this beautiful world, I noticed not far away a familiar, enormous head gliding over the mirror surface of the pavement and wagging its winglike ears. I heard a familiar, flat voice:

"I deem it my duty to testify that Number D-503 is ill and is unable to regulate his emotions. Moreover, I am sure that he was led by natural indignation—"

"Yes! Yes!" I exclaimed. "I even shouted, 'Catch her!' "

From behind me: "You did not shout anything."

"No, but I wanted to. I swear by the Well-Doer I wanted to!"

For a second I was bored through by the gray, cold, drill eyes. I don't know whether he believed that what I said was the truth (almost!), or whether he had some secret reason for sparing me for a while, but he wrote a short note, handed it to one of those who had held me, and again I was free. That is, I was again included in the orderly, endless Assyrian rows of Numbers.

The quadrangle, the freckled face, and the temple with the map of blue veinlets disappeared forever around the corner. We walked again—a million-headed body; and in each one of us resided that humble joyfulness with which in all probability molecules, atoms, and phagocytes live. In the ancient days the Christians understood this feeling; they are our only, though very imperfect, direct forerunners. The greatness of the "Church of the United Flock" was known to them. They knew that resignation is virtue, and pride a vice; that "We" is from "God," "I," from the devil.

I was walking, keeping step with the others yet separated from them. I was still trembling from the emotion just felt, like a bridge over which a thundering ancient steel train has passed a moment before. I *felt* myself. To feel one's self, to be conscious of one's personality, is the lot of an eye inflamed by a cinder, or an infected finger, or a bad tooth. A healthy eye, or finger, or tooth is not felt; it is nonexistent, as it were. Is it not clear, then, that consciousness of oneself is a sickness?

Apparently I am no longer a phagocyte which quietly, in a businesslike way, devours microbes (microbes with freckled faces and blue temples); apparently I am myself a microbe, and she, too, I-330, is a microbe, a wonderful, diabolic microbe! It is quite possible that there are already thousands of such microbes among us, still pretending to be phagocytes, as I pretend. What if today's accident, although in itself not important, is only a beginning, only the first meteorite of a shower of burning and thundering stones which the infinite may have poured out upon our glass paradise?

RECORD TWENTY-THREE

Flowers
The Dissolution of a Crystal
If Only (?)

They say there are flowers that bloom only once in a hundred years. Why not suppose the existence of flowers that bloom only once in a thousand years? We may have known nothing about them until now only because today is the "once in a thousand years."

Happy and dizzy, I walked downstairs to the controller on duty, and quickly under my gaze, all around me and silently, the thousand-year-old buds burst, and everything was blooming: armchairs, shoes, golden badges, electric bulbs, someone's dark heavy eyes, the polished columns of the banisters, the handkerchief which someone had lost on the stairs, the small, ink-blotted desk of the controller, and the tender, brown, somewhat freckled cheeks of U-, Everything seemed not ordinary, but new, tender, rosy, moist. U- took the pink stub from me while the blue, aromatic moon, hanging from an unseen branch, shone through the glass of the wall and over the head of U-. With a solemn gesture I pointed my finger and said:

"The moon. You see?"

U- glanced at me, then at the number of the stub, and again made that familiar, charmingly innocent movement with which she fixes the fold of the unif between her knees.

"You look abnormal and ill, dear. Abnormality and illness are the same thing. You are killing yourself. And no one would tell you that, no one!"

That "No one" was certainly equivalent to the number on the stub, I-330. This thought was confirmed by an ink blot which fell close to the figure 330. Dear, wonderful U-! You are right, of course. I am not reasonable. I am sick. I have a soul. I am a microbe. But is blooming not a sickness? Is it not painful when the buds are bursting? And don't you think that spermatozoa are the most terrible of all microbes?

Back upstairs to my room. In the widely open cup of the armchair was I-330. I, on the floor, embracing her limbs, my head on her lap. We were silent. Everything was silent. Only the pulse was audible. Like a crystal I was *dissolving* in her, in I-330. I felt most distinctly how the polished facets which limited me in space were slowly thawing, melting away. I was dissolving in her lap, in her, and I became at once smaller and larger, and larger, unembraceable. For she was not she but the whole universe. For a second I and that armchair near the bed, transfixed with joy, we were one. And the wonderfully smiling old woman at the gate of the Ancient House, and the wild debris beyond the Green Wall, and some strange silver wreckage on a black background, dozing like the old woman, and the slam of a door in the distance—all this was within me, was listening to my pulse and soaring through the happiest of seconds.

In absurd, confused, overflowing words I attempted to tell her that I was a crystal and that there was a door in me, and that I felt how happy the armchair was. But something nonsensical came out of the attempt and I stopped. I was ashamed. And suddenly:

"Dear I-! Forgive me! I understand nothing. I talk so foolishly!"

"And why should you think that foolishness is not fine? If we had taken pains to educate human foolishness through centuries, as we have done with our intelligence, it might perhaps have been transformed into something very precious."

And I think she is right! How could she be wrong at that moment?

". . . And for this foolishness of yours and for what you did yesterday during the walk, I love you the more, much more."

"Then why did you torture me? Why would you not come? Why did you send me the pink check and make me—?"

"Perhaps I wanted to test you. Perhaps I must be sure that you will do anything I wish, that you are completely mine."

"Yes, completely."

She took my face, my whole self, between her palms, lifted my head.

"And how about, 'It is the duty of every honest Number'? Eh?"

Sweet, sharp white teeth—a smile. In the open cup of the armchair she was like a bee, sting and honey combined.

Yes, duty. . . . I turned over in my mind the pages of my records; indeed there is not a thought about the fact that strictly speaking I should . . .

I was silent. Exaltedly, and probably stupidly, I smiled, looking into the pupils of her eyes. I followed first one eye and then the other, and in each of them I saw myself, a millimetric self imprisoned in those tiny rainbow cells. Then again the lips and the sweet pain of blooming.

In each Number of the United State there is an unseen metronome that tick-tocks silently; without looking at the clock we know exactly the time of day within five minutes. But now my metronome had stopped, and I did not know how much time had passed. In fright I grasped my badge with its clock from under the pillow. Glory be to the Well-Doer! I had twenty minutes more! But those minutes were such tiny, short ones! They ran! And I wanted to tell her so many things. I wanted to tell her all about myself; about the letter from O- and about that terrible evening when I gave her a child; and for some reason also about my childhood, about our mathematician Plappa, and about the square root of minus one; and how, when I attended the glorification on the Day of Unanimity for the first time in my life, I wept bitterly because there was an inkstain on my unif—on such a holy day!

I-330 lifted her nead. She leaned on her elbow. In the corners of her lips two long, sharp lines and the dark angle of lifted eyebrows—a cross.

"Perhaps on that day . . ." her brow grew darker; she took my hand and pressed it hard. "Tell me, will you ever forget me? Will you always remember me?"

"But why such talk? What is it, I-, dear?"

She was silent. And her eyes were already sliding past me, through me, away into the distance. I suddenly heard the wind beating the glass with its enormous wings. Of course it had been blowing all the while, but I had not noticed it until then. And for some reason those cawing birds over the Green Wall came to my mind.

I-330 shook her head with a gesture of throwing something off. Once more she touched me for a second with her whole body, as an aero before landing touches the ground for a second with all the tension of a recoiling spring.

"Well, give me my stockings, quick!"

The stockings were on the desk, on the open manuscript, on page 124. Being in haste, I caught some of the pages and they were scattered over the floor, so that it was hard to put them back in the proper order. Moreover, even if I put them in that order there will be no real order; there are obstacles to that anyway, some undiscoverable unknowns.

"I can't bear it," I said. "You are here, near me, yet

you seem to be behind an opaque ancient wall; through that wall I hear a rustle and voices; I cannot make out the words, I don't know what is there. I cannot bear it. You seem always to withhold something from me; you have never told me what kind of place it was where I found myself that day beneath the Ancient House. Where did those corridors lead? Why was the doctor there—or perhaps all that never happened?"

I-330 put her hands on my shoulders and slowly entered deeply into my eyes.

"You want to know all?"

"Yes, I do."

"And you would not be afraid to follow me anywhere? Wherever I should lead you?"

"Anywhere!"

"All right then. I promise you, after the holiday, if only . . . Oh, yes, there is your *Integral.* I always forget to ask; will it soon be completed?"

"No. 'If only' what? Again! 'If only' what?"

She, already at the door: "You shall see."

I was alone again. All that she left behind her was a barely perceptible scent, similar to that of a sweet, dry, yellow dust of flowers from behind the Green Wall; also, sunk deeply within me, question marks like small hooks similar to those the ancients used for fishing (*vide* the Prehistoric Museum).

. . . Why did she suddenly ask about the *Integral*?

RECORD TWENTY-FOUR

The Limit of the Function
Easter
To Cross Out Everything

I am like a motor set in motion at a speed of too many revolutions per second; the bearings have become too hot, and in one more minute the molten metal will begin to drip and everything will go to the devil. Cold water! Quick! Some logic! I pour on pailfuls of it, but my logic merely sizzles on the hot metal and disappears into the air in the form of vapor.

Of course it is clear that in order to establish the true meaning of a function one must establish its limit. It is also clear that yesterday's "dissolution in the universe" taken to its limit is death. For death is exactly the most complete dissolution of the self in the universe. Hence: $L=f(D)$, love is the function of death.

Yes, cxactly, exactly! That is why I am afraid of I-330; I struggle against her, I don't want . . . But why is it that within me "I don't want to" and "I want to" stand side by side? That is the chief horror of the matter; I continue to long for that happy death of yesterday. The horror of it is that even now, when I have integrated the logical function, when it becomes evident that that function contains death hidden within it, still I long for it with my lips, my arms, my heart, with every millimeter. . . .

Tomorrow is the Day of Unanimity. She will certainly

be there and I shall see her, though from a distance. That distance will be painful to me, for I must be, I am inevitably drawn, close to her, so that her hands, her shoulder, her hair . . . I long for even that pain. . . . Let it come. . . . Great Well-Doer! How absurd to desire pain! Who is ignorant of the simple fact that pains are negative items that reduce that sum total we call happiness? Consequently . . . Well, no "consequently" . . . Emptiness. . . . Nakedness!

The Same Evening

Through the glass wall of the house I see a disquieting, windy, feverishly pink sunset. I move my armchair to avoid that pinkness and turn over these pages, and I find I am forgetting that I write this not for myself but for you unknown people whom I love and pity, for you who still lag centuries behind, below. Let me tell you about the Day of Unanimity, about that Great Day. I think it is for us what Easter was for the ancients. I remember I used to prepare an hour calendar on the eve of that day; solemnly I would cross out every time the figure of the hour elapsed: nearer by one hour! one hour less to wait! . . . If I were certain that nobody would discover it, I assure you I should now, too, make out such a calendar and carry it with me, and I should watch how many hours remain until tomorrow. . . . When I shall see, at least from a distance . . .

(I was interrupted. They brought me a new unif from the shop. As is customary, new unifs are given to us for tomorrow's celebration. Steps in the hall, exclamations of joy, noises.)

I shall continue; tomorrow I shall see the same spectacle which we see year after year, and which always awakes in us fresh emotions, as if we saw it for the first time: an impressive throng of piously lifted arms. Tomorrow is the day of the yearly election of the Well-Doer.

Tomorrow we shall again hand over to our Well-Doer the keys to the impregnable fortress of our happiness. Certainly this in no way resembles the disorderly, unorganized election days of the ancients, on which (it seems so funny!) they did not even know in advance the result of the election. To build a state on some non-discountable contingencies, to build blindly—what could be more nonsensical? Yet centuries had to pass before this was understood!

Needless to say, in this respect as in all others we have no place for contingencies; nothing unexpected can happen. The elections themselves have rather a symbolic meaning. They remind us that we are a united, powerful organism of millions of cells, that—to use the language of the "gospel" of the ancients—we are a united church. The history of the United State knows not a single case in which upon this solemn day even a solitary voice has dared to violate the magnificent unison.

They say that the ancients used to conduct their elections secretly, stealthily like thieves. Some of our historians even assert that they would come to the electoral celebrations completely masked. Imagine the weird, fantastic spectacle! Night. A plaza. Along the walls the stealthily creeping figures covered with mantles. The red flame of torches dancing in the wind. . . . Why was such secrecy necessary? It has never been satisfactorily explained. Probably it resulted from the fact that elections were associated with some mystic and superstitious, perhaps even criminal, ceremonies. We have nothing to conceal or to be ashamed of; we celebrate our election openly, honestly, in daylight. I see them all vote for the Well-Doer, and everybody sees me vote for the Well-Doer. How could it be otherwise, since "all" and "I" are one "we"? How ennobling, sincere, lofty this is, compared with the cowardly, thievish "secrecy" of the ancients! And how much more expedient! For even admitting for a moment the impossible—that is, the outbreak of some dissonance in our customary unity—our unseen Guardians are always right there among us, are they not, to register the Numbers who might fall into error and save them from any further false steps? The United State is theirs, the Numbers'! And besides . . .

Through the wall to my left a she-Number before the mirror door of the closet; she is hastily unbuttoning her unif. For a second, swiftly—eyes, lips, two sharp, pink . . . the curtains fell. Within me, all that happened yesterday instantly awoke, and now I no longer know what I meant to say by "besides . . ." I no longer wish to—I cannot. I want one thing. I want I-330. I want her every minute, every second, to be with me, with no one else. All that I wrote about Unanimity is of no value; it is not what I want; I have a desire to cross it out, to tear it to pieces and throw it away. For I know (be it a sacrilege, yet it is the truth) that a glorious Day is possible only with her and only when we are side by side, shoulder to shoulder. Without her tomorrow's sun will appear to me only as a little circle cut out of a tin sheet, and the sky a sheet of tin painted blue, and I myself . . . I snatched the telephone receiver.

"I-330, are you there?"

"Yes, it is I. Why so late?"

"Perhaps not too late yet. I want to ask you . . . I want you to be with me tomorrow—dear!"

I said "Dear" in a very low voice. And for some reason a thing I saw this morning at the docks flashed through my mind: just for fun someone had put a watch under the hundred-ton sledge hammer. . . . A swing, a breath of wind in the face, and the silent, hundred-ton, knife-like weight on the breakable watch . . .

A silence. I thought I heard someone's whisper in I-330's room. Then her voice:

"No, I cannot. Of course you understand that I myself . . . No, I cannot. 'Why?' You shall see tomorrow."

Night.

RECORD TWENTY-FIVE

The Descent from Heaven
The Greatest Catastrophe in History
The Known—Is Ended

At the beginning all arose, and the Hymn, like a solemn mantle, slowly waved above our heads. Hundreds of tubes of the Musical Tower, and millions of human voices. For a second I forgot everything; I forgot that alarming something at which I-330 had hinted in connection with today's celebration; I think I even forgot about her. At that moment I was the very same little boy who once wept because of a tiny inkstain on his unif, which no one else could see. Even if nobody else sees that I am covered with black, ineffaceable stains, I know it, don't I? I know that there should be no place for a criminal like me among these frank, open faces. What if I should rush forward and shout out everything about myself all at once! The end might follow. Let it happen! At least for a second I would feel myself clear and clean and senseless like that innocent blue sky. . . .

All eyes were directed upward; in the pure morning blue, still moist with the tears of night, a small dark spot appeared. Now it was dark, now bathed in the rays of the sun. It was He, descending to us from the sky, He—the new Jehovah—in an aero, He, as wise and as lovingly cruel as the Jehovah of the ancients. Nearer and nearer

He came, and higher toward Him were drawn millions of hearts. Already He saw us. And in my mind with Him I looked over everything from the heights: concentric circles of stands marked with dotted blue lines of unifs —like circles of a spiderweb strewn with microscopic suns (the shining badges). And in the center the wise white spider would soon occupy His place—the Well-Doer clad in white, the Well-Doer who wisely tangled our hands and feet in the salutary net of happiness.

His magnificent descent from the sky was accomplished. The brassy Hymn came to silence; all sat down. At once I perceived that everything was really a very thin spiderweb the threads of which were stretched tense and trembling—and it seemed that in a moment those threads might break and something improbable . . .

I half-rose and looked around, and I met many lovingly worried eyes which passed from one face to another. I saw someone lifting his hand and almost imperceptibly waving his fingers—he was making signs to another. The latter replied with a similar finger sign. And a third. . . . I understood; they were the Guardians. I understood; they were alarmed by something—the spiderweb was stretched and trembling. And within me, as if tuned to the same wave-length, within me there was a corresponding quiver.

On the platform a poet was reciting his pre-electoral ode. I could not hear a single word; I only felt the rhythmic swing of the hexametric pendulum, and with its every motion I felt how nearer and nearer there was approaching some hour set for . . . I continued to turn over face after face like pages, but I could not find the one, the only one, I was seeking, the one I needed to find at once, as soon as possible, for one more swing of the pendulum, and . . .

It was he, certainly it was he! Below, past the main platform, gliding over the sparkling glass, the ear wings flapped by, the running body gave a reflection of a double-curved S-, like a noose which was rolling toward some of the intricate passages among the stands. S-, I-330,—there is some thread between them. I have always felt some thread between them. I don't know yet what that thread is, but someday I shall untangle it. I fixed my gaze on him; he was rushing farther away, behind him that invisible thread. . . . There, he stopped . . . there. . . . I was pierced, twisted together into a knot as if by a lightning-like, many-volted electric discharge; in my row, not more than 40° from me, S- stopped and bowed. I saw I-330, and beside her the smiling, repellent, Negro-lipped R-13.

My first thought was to rush to her and cry, "Why with him? Why did you not want . . .?" But the salutary, invisible spiderweb bound fast my hands and feet; so gritting my teeth, I sat stiff as iron, my gaze fixed upon them. A sharp *physical* pain at my heart. I remember my thought: "If non-physical causes produce physical pain, then it is clear that . . ."

I regret that I did not come to any conclusion. I remember only that something about "heart" flashed through my mind; a purely nonsensical ancient expression, "His heart fell into his boots," passed through my head. My heart sank. The hexameter came to an end. It was about to start. What "It"?

The five-minute pre-election recess established by custom. The custom-established, pre-electional silence. But this time it was not that pious, really prayer-like silence that it usually was. This time it was like the ancient days when the sky, still untamed, would roar from time to time with its "storms." It was like the "lull before the storm" of the ancient days. The air seemed to be made of transparent, vaporized cast iron. You wanted to breathe with your mouth wide open. My hearing, intense to the point of pain, registered from behind a mouse-like, gnawing, worried whisper. Without lifting my eyes I saw those two, I-330 and R-13, side by side, shoulder to shoulder—and on my knees my trembling, foreign, hateful, hairy hands. . . .

Everybody was holding a badge with a clock in his

hands. One. . . . Two. . . . Three. . . . Five minutes. From the main platform a cast-iron, slow voice:

"Those in favor shall lift their hands."

If only I dared look straight into his eyes as I always had! If only I could think devotedly: "Here I am, my whole self! Take me!" But now I did not dare. I had to make an effort to raise my hand, as if my joints were rusty.

The whisper of millions of hands. Someone's subdued "Ah," and I felt something was coming, falling heavily, but I could not understand what it was, and I did not have the strength or courage to take a look. . . .

"Those opposed?" . . .

This was always the most magnificent moment of our celebration: all would remain sitting motionless, joyfully bowing their heads under the salutary yoke of that Number of Numbers. But now, to my horror again I heard a rustle—light as a sigh, yet it was even more distinct than the brass tube of the Hymn. Thus the last sigh in a man's life, around him people with their faces pale and with drops of cold sweat upon their foreheads. . . . I lifted my eyes, and . . .

It took one hundredth of a second only; I saw thousands of hands arise "opposed" and fall back. I saw the pale, cross-marked face of I-330 and her lifted hand. Darkness came upon my eyes.

Another hundredth of a second, silence. Quiet. The pulse. Then, as if at the sign of some mad conductor, from all over the stands a rattling, a shouting, a whirlwind of unifs lifted by the rush, the perplexed figures of the Guardians running to and fro. Someone's heels in the air near my eyes, and close to those heels someone's wide-open mouth tearing itself in an inaudible scream. For some reason this picture remains particularly distinct in my memory: thousands of mouths noiselessly yelling as if on the screen of a monstrous cinema. Also, as if on a screen, somewhere below at a distance, for a second, O-90, pressed against the wall in a passage, her lips white, defending her abdomen with her crossed arms. She disappeared as if washed away by a wave, or else I simply forgot her because . . .

This was not on the screen any more but within me, within my compressed heart, within the rapidly pulsating temples. Over my head, somewhat to the left, R-13 suddenly jumped upon a bench, all sprinkling, red, rabid. In his arms was I-330, pale, her unif torn from shoulder to breast, red blood on white. She held him firmly around the neck, and he with huge leaps from bench to bench, repellent and agile, like a gorilla, was carrying her upward, away.

As if it were in a fire of ancient days, everything became red around me. Only one thing in my head: to jump after them, to catch them. At this moment I cannot explain to myself the source of that strength within me, but like a battering-ram I broke through the crowd, over somebody's shoulders, over a bench, and I was there in a moment and caught R-13 by the collar.

"Don't you dare! Don't you dare, I say! Immediately–"

Fortunately no one could hear my voice, as everyone was shouting and running.

"Who is it? What is the matter? What–" R-13 turned around; his sprinkling lips were trembling. He apparently thought it was one of the Guardians.

"I do not want–I won't allow– Put her down at once!"

But he only sprinkled angrily with his lips, shook his head, and ran on. Then I–I am terribly ashamed to write all this down but I believe I must, so that you, my unknown readers, may make a complete study of my disease–then I hit him over the head with all my might. You understand? I hit him. This I remember distinctly. I remember also a feeling of liberation that followed my action, a feeling of lightness in my whole body.

I-330 slid quickly out of his arms.

"Go away!" she shouted to R-. "Don't you see that he–? Go!"

R-13 showed his white Negro teeth, sprinkled into my face some word, dived down, and disappeared. And I picked up I-330, pressed her firmly to myself, and carried her away.

My heart was beating forcibly. It seemed enormous. And with every beat it would splash out such a thundering, such a hot, such a joyful wave! A flash: "Let them, below there, let them toss and rush and yell and fall; what matter if something has fallen, if something has been shattered to dust? Little matter! Only to remain this way and carry her, carry and carry . . ."

The Same Evening, Twenty-two O'clock

I hold my pen with great difficulty. Such an extraordinary fatigue after all the dizzying events of this morning. Is it possible that the strong, salutary, centuries-old walls of the United State have fallen? Is it possible that we are again without a roof over our heads, back in the wild state of freedom like our remote ancestors? Is it possible that we have lost our Well-Doer? "Opposed!" On the Day of Unanimity—opposed! I am ashamed of *them*, painfully, fearfully ashamed. . . . But who are "they"? And who am I? "They," "We" . . .? Do I know?

I shall continue.

She was sitting where I had brought her, on the uppermost glass bench which was hot from the sun. Her right shoulder and the beginning of the wonderful and incalculable curve were uncovered—an exceedingly thin serpent of blood. She seemed not to be aware of the blood, or that her breast was uncovered. No, I will say rather: she seemed to see all that and seemed to feel that it was essential to her, that if her unif had been buttoned she would have torn it open, she would have . . .

"And tomorrow!" She breathed the words through sparkling white clenched teeth. "Tomorrow, nobody knows what . . . do you understand? Neither I nor anyone else knows; it is unknown! Do you realize what a joy it is? Do you realize that all that was certain has come to an end? Now . . . things will be new, improbable, unforeseen!"

Below the human waves were still foaming, tossing, roaring, but they seemed to be very far away, and to be growing more and more distant. For she was looking at me. She slowly drew me into herself through the narrow golden windows of her pupils. We remained like that, silent, for a long while. And for some reason I recalled how once I had watched some queer yellow pupils through the Green Wall, while above the Wall birds were soaring (or was this another time?).

"Listen, if nothing particular happens tomorrow, I shall take you there; do you understand?"

No, I did not understand, but I nodded in silence. I was dissolved, I became infinitesimal, a geometrical point . . .

After all, there is some logic—a peculiar logic of today—in this state of being a point. A point has more unknowns than any other entity. If a point should start to move, it might become thousands of curves, or hundreds of solids.

I was afraid to budge. What might I have become if I had moved? It seemed to me that everybody, like myself, was afraid now of even the most minute of motions.

At this moment, for instance, as I sit and write, everyone is sitting hidden in his glass cell, expecting something. I do not hear the buzzing of the elevators, usual at this hour, or laughter, or steps; from time to time Numbers pass in couples through the hall, whispering, on tiptoe . . .

What will happen tomorrow? What will become of me tomorrow?

RECORD TWENTY-SIX

The World Does Exist
Rash
Forty-one Degrees Centigrade

Morning. Through the ceiling the sky is, as usual, firm, round, red-cheeked. I think I should have been less surprised had I found above some extraordinary quadrangular sun, or people clad in many-colored dresses made of the skins of animals, or opaque walls of stone. Then the world, *our world*, does exist still? Or is it only inertia? Is the generator already switched out, while the armature is still roaring and revolving; two more revolutions, or three, and at the fourth it will die away?

Are you familiar with that strange state in which you wake up in the middle of the night, when you open your eyes into the darkness, and then suddenly feel you are lost in the dark; you quickly, quickly begin to feel around, seeking in the Journal of the United State; quickly, quickly —I found this:

"The celebration of the Day of Unanimity, long awaited by all, took place yesterday. The same Well-Doer who so often has proved his unshakable wisdom was unanimously re-elected for the forty-eighth time. The celebration was clouded by a little confusion, created by the enemies of happiness, who by their action naturally lost the right to be the bricks for the foundation of the renovated United State. It is clear to everyone that to take their votes into account would mean to consider as a part of a magnificent, heroic symphony the accidental cough of a sick person who happened to be in the concert hall."

Oh, great Sage! Is it really true that despite everything we are saved? What objection, indeed, can one find to this most crystalline syllogism? And further on a few more lines:

"Today at twelve o'clock a joint meeting of the Administrative Bureau, Medical Bureau, and Bureau of Guardians will take place. An important State decree is to be expected momentarily."

No, the Walls still stand erect. Here they are! I can feel them. And that strange feeling of being lost somewhere, of not knowing where I am—that feeling is gone. I am no longer surprised to see the sky blue and the sun round and all the Numbers going to work as usual. . . .

I walked along the avenue with a particularly firm, resounding step. It seemed to me that everyone else walked exactly like me. But at the crossing, on turning the corner, I noticed people strangely shying away, going around the corner of a building sidewise, as if a pipe had burst in the wall, as if cold water were spurting like a fountain on the sidewalk and it was impossible to cross it.

Another five or ten steps and I, too, felt a spurt of cold water that struck me and threw me from the sidewalk; at a height of approximately two meters a quadrangular piece of paper was pasted to the wall, and on that sheet of paper, unintelligible, poisonously green letters:

MEPHI

And under the paper—an S-like curved back and wing ears shaking with anger or emotion. With right arm lifted as high as possible, his left arm hopelessly stretched out backward like a hurt wing, he was trying to jump high enough to reach the paper and tear it off, but he was unable to do so. He was a fraction of an inch too short.

Probably every one of the passers-by had the same thought: "If I go to help him, I, only one of the many, will he not think that I am guilty of something and that I am therefore anxious to . . ."

I must confess I had that thought. But remembering how many times he had proved my real Guardian Angel and how often he had saved me, I stepped toward him and with courage and warm assurance I stretched out my hand and tore off the sheet. S- turned around. The little drills sank quickly into me to the bottom and found something there. Then he lifted his left brow, and winked toward the wall where "Mephi" had been hanging a minute ago. The tail of his little smile even twinkled with a certain pleasure, which greatly surprised me. But why should I be surprised? A doctor always prefers a temperature of 40°C. and a rash to the slow, languid rise of the temperature during the incubation period of a disease; it enables him to determine the character of the disease. Today "Mephi" broke out on the walls like a rash. I understood his smile.

In the passage to the underground railway, under our feet on the clean glass of the steps, again a white sheet: "Mephi." And also on the walls of the tunnel, and on the benches, and on the mirror of the car (apparently pasted on in haste as some were hanging on a slant). Everywhere, the same white, gruesome rash.

I must confess that the exact meaning of that smile became clear to me only after many days which were overfilled with the strangest and most unexpected events.

The roaring of the wheels, distinct in the general silence, seemed to be the noise of infected streams of blood. Some Number was inadvertently touched on the shoulder, and he started so that a package of papers fell out of his hands. To my left another Number was reading a paper, his eyes fixed always on the same line; the paper perceptibly trembled in his hands. I felt that everywhere, in the wheels, in the hands, in the newspapers, even in the eyelashes, the pulse was becoming more and more rapid, and I thought it probable that today when I-330 and I found ourselves *there,* the temperature would rise to 39°C., 40°, perhaps 41° and . . .

At the docks—the same silence filled with the buzzing of an invisible propeller. The lathes were silent as if brooding. Only the cranes were moving almost inaudibly as if on tiptoe, gliding, bending over, picking up with their tentacles the lumps of frozen air and loading the tanks of the *Integral.* We are already preparing the *Integral* for a trial flight.

"Well, shall we have her up in a week?" This was my question addressed to the Second Builder. His face is like porcelain, painted with sweet blue and tender little pink flowers (eyes and lips), but today those little flowers looked faded and washed out. We were counting aloud when suddenly I broke off in the midst of a word and stopped, my mouth wide open; above the cupola, above the blue lump lifted by the crane, there was a scarcely noticeable small white square. I felt my whole body trembling—perhaps with laughter. Yes! I *myself heard* my own laughter. (Did you ever hear your own laughter?)

"No, listen," I said. "Imagine you are in an ancient airplane. The altimeter shows 5,000 meters. A wing breaks; you are dashing down like . . . And on the way you calculate: 'Tomorrow from twelve to two . . . from two to six . . . and dinner at five!' Would it not be absurd?"

The little blue flowers began to move and bulge out. What if I were made of glass and he could have seen what was going on within me at that moment? If he knew that some three or four hours later . . .

RECORD TWENTY-SEVEN

No Headings. It Is Impossible!

I was alone in the endless corridors. In those same corridors . . . A mute, concrete sky. Water was dripping somewhere upon a stone. The familiar, heavy, opaque door—and the subdued noise from behind it.

She said she would come out at sixteen sharp. It was already five minutes, then ten, then fifteen past sixteen. No one appeared. For a second I was my former self, horrified at the thought that the door might open.

"Five minutes more, and if she does not come out . . ."

Water was dripping somewhere upon a stone. No one about. With melancholy pleasure I felt: "Saved," and slowly I turned and walked back along the corridor. The trembling dots of the small lamps on the ceiling became dimmer and dimmer. Suddenly a quick rattle of a door behind me. Quick steps, softly echoing from the ceiling and the walls. It was she, light as a bird, panting somewhat from running.

"I knew you would be here, you would come! I knew you—you . . ."

The spears of her eyelashes moved apart to let me in and . . . How can I describe what effect that ancient, absurd, and wonderful rite has upon me when her lips touch mine? Can I find a formula to express that whirlwind which sweeps out of my soul everything, everything save her? Yes, yes, from my *soul*. You may laugh at me if you will.

She made an effort to raise her eyelids, and her slow words, too, came with an effort:

"No. Now we must go."

The door opened. Old, worn steps. An unbearably multicolored noise, whistling and light. . . .

Twenty-four hours have passed since then and everything seems to have settled in me, yet it is most difficult for me to find words for even an approximate description. . . . It is as though a bomb had exploded in my head. . . . Open mouths, wings, shouts, leaves, words, stones, all these one after another in a heap. . . .

I remember my first thought was: "Fast–back!" For it was clear to me that while I was waiting there in the corridors, *they* somehow had blasted and destroyed the Green Wall, and from behind it everything rushed in and splashed over our city which until then had been kept clean of that lower world. I must have said something of this sort to I-330. She laughed.

"No, we have simply come out *beyond the Green Wall*."

Then I opened my eyes, and close to me, actually, I saw those very things which until then not a single living Number had ever seen except depreciated a thousand times, dimmed and hazy through the cloudy glass of the Wall.

The sun–it was no longer our light evenly diffused over the mirror surface of the pavements; it seemed an accumulation of living fragments, of incessantly oscillating, dizzy spots which blinded the eyes. And the trees! Like candles rising into the very sky, or like spiders that squatted upon the earth, supported by their clumsy paws, or like mute green fountains. And all this was moving, jumping, rustling. Under my feet some strange little ball was crawling. . . . I stood as though rooted to the ground.

I was unable to take a step because under my foot there was not an even plane, but (imagine!) something disgustingly soft, yielding, living, springy, green! . . .

I was dazed; I was strangled—yes, strangled; it is the best word to express my state. I stood holding fast with both hands to a swinging branch.

"It is nothing. It is all right. It is natural, the first time. It will pass. Courage!"

At I-330's side, bouncing dizzily on a green net, someone's thinnest profile, cut out of paper. No, not "someone's." I recognized him. I remembered. It was the doctor. I understood everything very clearly. I realized that they both caught me beneath the arms and laughingly dragged me forward. My legs twisted and glided. . . . Terrible noise, cawing, stumps, yelling, branches, tree trunks, wings, leaves, whistling. . . .

The trees drew apart. A bright clearing. In the clearing, people, or perhaps, to be more exact, *beings*. Now comes the most difficult part to describe, for *this* was beyond any bounds of probability. It is clear to me now why I-330 was stubbornly silent about it before; I would not have believed it, would not have believed even her. It is even possible that tomorrow I shall not believe myself, shall not believe my own description in these pages.

In the clearing, around a naked, skull-like rock, a noisy crowd of three or four hundred . . . people. Well, let's call them people. I find it difficult to coin new words. Just as on the stands you recognize in the general accumulation of faces only those which are familiar to you, so at first I recognized only our grayish-blue unifs. But one second later and I saw distinctly and clearly among the unifs dark, red, golden, black, brown, and white humans—apparently they were humans. None of them had any clothes on, and their bodies were covered with short, glistening hair, like that which may be seen on the stuffed horse in the Prehistoric Museum. But their females had faces exactly, yes, exactly, like the faces of our women: tender, rosy, and not overgrown with hair. Also their breasts were free of hair, firm breasts of wonderful geometrical form. As to the males, only a part of their faces were free from hair, like our ancestors', and the organs of reproduction were similar to ours.

All this was so unbelievable, so unexpected, that I stood there quietly (I assert positively that I stood quietly) and looked around. Like a scale: overload one side sufficiently and then you may gently put on the other as much as you will; the arrow will not move.

Suddenly I felt alone. I-330 was no longer with me. I don't know how or where she disappeared. Around me were only *those*, with their hair glistening like silk in the sunlight. I caught someone's warm, strong, dark shoulder.

"Listen, please, in the name of the Well-Doer, could you tell me where she went? A while, a minute ago, she . . ."

Long-haired, austere eyebrows turned to me.

"Sh . . . sh . . . silence!" He made a sign with his head toward the center of the clearing where there stood the yellow skull-like stone.

There above the heads of all I saw her. The sun beat straight into my eyes, and because of that she seemed coal-black, standing out on the blue cloth of the sky—a coal-black silhouette on a blue background. A little higher the clouds were floating. And it seemed that not the clouds but the rock itself, and she herself upon that rock, and the crowd and the clearing—all were silently floating like a ship, and the earth was light and glided away from under the feet. . . .

"Brothers!" (It was she.) "Brothers, you all know that there inside the Wall, in the City, they are building the *Integral*. And you know also that the day has come for us to destroy that Wall and all other walls, so that the green wind may blow over all the earth, from end to end. But the *Integral* is going to take these walls up, up into the heights, to the thousands of other worlds which every evening whisper to us with their lights through the black leaves of night . . ."

Waves and foam and wind were beating the rock:

"Down with the *Integral*! Down!"

"No, brothers, not 'down.' The *Integral* must be ours. And it *shall* be ours. On the day when it first sets sail into the sky *we* shall be on board. For the Builder of the *Integral* is with us. He left the walls, he came with me here in order to be with us. Long live the Builder!"

A second—and I was somewhere above everything. Under me: heads, heads, heads, wide-open, yelling mouths, arms rising and falling. . . . There was something strange and intoxicating in it all. I felt myself *above everybody*; I was, I, a separate world; I ceased to be the usual item; I became unity. . . .

Again I was below, near the rock, my body happy, shaken, and rumpled, as after an embrace of love. Sunlight, voices, and from above—the smiles of I-330. A golden-haired woman, her whole body silky-golden and diffusing an odor of different herbs, was nearby. She held a cup, apparently made of wood. She drank a little from it with her red lips, and then offered the cup to me. I closed my eyes and eagerly drank the sweet, cold, prickly sparks, pouring them down on the fire which burned within me.

Soon afterward my blood and the whole world began to circulate a thousand times faster; the earth seemed to be flying, light as dawn. And within me everything was simple, light, and clear. Only then I noticed on the rock the familiar, enormous letters: MEPHI, and for some reason the inscription seemed to me *necessary*. It seemed to be a simple thread binding everything together. A rather rough picture hewn in the rock—this, too, seemed comprehensible; it represented a youth with wings and a transparent body and, in the place ordinarily occupied by the heart, a blinding, red, blazing coal. Again I understood that coal—or no, I *felt* it as I felt without hearing every word of I-330's (she continued to speak from above, from the rock); and I felt that all of them breathed one breath, and that they were all ready to fly somewhere like the birds over the Wall.

From behind, from the confusion of breathing bodies, a loud voice:

"But this is folly!"

It seems to me it was I—yes, I am certain it was I who then jumped on the rock; from there I saw the sun, the heads, a green sea on a blue background, and I cried:

"Yes, yes, precisely. All must become insane; we must become insane as soon as possible! We must: I know it."

I-330 was at my side. Her smile—two dark lines from the angles of her mouth directed upward. . . . And within me a blazing coal. It was momentary, light, a little painful, beautiful. . . . And later, only stray fragments that remained sticking in me. . . .

. . . Very low and slowly a bird was moving. I saw it was living, like me. It was turning its head now to the right and then to the left like a human being, and its round black eyes drilled themselves into me. . . .

. . . Then: a human back glistening with fur the color of ancient ivory; a mosquito crawling on that back, a mosquito with tiny transparent wings. The back twitched to chase the mosquito away; it twitched again. . . .

. . . And yet another thing: a shadow from the leaves, a woven, net-like shadow. Some humans lay in that shadow, chewing something, something similar to the legendary food of the ancients, a long yellow fruit and a piece of something dark. They put some of it in my hand, and it seemed strange to me for I did not know whether I might eat it or not. . . .

. . . And again: a crowd, heads, legs, arms, mouths, faces appearing for a second and disappearing like bursting bubbles. For a second (or perhaps it was only a hallucination?) the transparent, flying wing ears appeared. . . .

With all my might I pressed the hand of I-330. She turned to me.

"What is the matter?"

"He is here! I thought, I–"

"Who?"

"S-, a second ago, in the crowd."

The ends of the thin, coal-black brows moved to the temples–a smile like a sharp triangle. I could not see clearly why she smiled. How could she smile?

"But you understand, I-330, don't you, you understand what it means if he, or one of them, is here?"

"You are funny! How could it ever enter the heads of those within the Wall that we are here? Remember; take yourself. Did you ever think it was possible? They are busy hunting us *there*–let them! You are delirious!"

Her smile was light and cheerful and I, too, was smiling; the earth was drunken, cheerful, light, floating. . . .

RECORD TWENTY-EIGHT

Both of Them
Entropy and Energy
The Opaque Part of the Body

If your world is similar to the world of the ancients, then you may easily imagine that one day you suddenly come upon a sixth or a seventh continent, upon some Atlantis, and you find there unheard-of cities, labyrinths, people flying through the air without the aid of wings or aeros, stones lifted into the air by the power of a gaze—in brief, imagine that you see things that cannot come to your mind even if you suffer from dream sickness. That is how I feel now. For you must understand that no one has ever gone beyond the Green Wall since the Two Hundred Years' War, as I have already told you.

I know it is my duty to you, my unknown friends, to give more details about that unsuspected, strange world which has opened to me since yesterday. But for the time being I am unable to return to that subject. Everything is so novel, so novel it is like a rainstorm, and I am not big enough to embrace it all. I spread out the folds of my unif, my palms—and yet pailfuls splash past me and only drops can reach these pages. . . .

At first I heard behind me, behind the door, a loud voice. I recognized her voice, the voice of I-330, tense, metallic—and another one, almost inflexible, like a wooden ruler, the voice of U-. Then the door burst open with a crack and both of them shot into the room. *Shot* is the right word.

I-330 put her hand on the back of my armchair and smiled over her shoulder, but only with her teeth, at U-. I should not care to stand before such a smile.

"Listen," she said to me, "this woman seems to have made it her business to guard you from me like a little child. Is it with your permission?"

"But he *is* a child. Yes! That is why he does not notice that you . . . that it is only in order . . . That all this is only a foul game! Yes! And it is my duty . . ."

For a second (in the mirror) the broken, trembling line of brows. I leaped, controlling with difficulty the other self within me, the one with the hairy fists. With difficulty, pushing every word through my teeth, I cried straight into her face, into her very gills:

"Get out of here at once! Out! At once!"

The gills swelled at first into brick-red lumps, then fell and became gray. She opened her mouth to say something, but without a word she slammed it shut and went out.

I threw myself toward I-330.

"Never, never will I forgive myself! She dared! You . . . But you don't think, do you, that you, that she . . . This is all because she wants to register on me, but I . . ."

"Fortunately she will not have time for that now. Besides, even a thousand like her . . . I don't care . . . I know you will not believe that thousand, but only me. For after all that happened yesterday, I am all yours, all, to the very end, as you wanted it. I am in your hands; you can now at any moment . . ."

"What, 'at any moment'?" (But immediately I understood what. The blood rushed to my ears and cheeks.) "Don't speak about that, you must never speak about that! The *other* I, my former self . . . but now . . ."

"How do I know? Man is like a novel: up to the last page one does not know what the end will be. It would not be worth reading otherwise."

She was stroking my head. I could not see her face, but I could tell by her voice that she was looking somewhere far into the distance; she had hooked herself on to that cloud which was floating silently, slowly, no one knows where to.

Suddenly she pushed me away with her hand, firmly but tenderly.

"Listen. I came to tell you that perhaps we are now . . . our last days . . . You know, don't you, that all Auditoriums are to be closed after tonight?"

"Closed?"

"Yes. I passed by and saw that in all Auditoriums preparations are going on: tables, medics all in white . . ."

"But what does it all mean?"

"I don't know. Nobody knows as yet. That's the worst of it. I feel only that the current is on, the spark is jumping, and if not today, then tomorrow. . . . Yet perhaps they will not have time. . . ."

It has been a long while since I ceased to understand who *they* are and who *we* are. I do not understand what *I* want; do I want them to have or not to have enough time? One thing is clear to me: I-330 is now on the very edge, on the very edge, and in one second more . . .

"But it is folly," I said. "You, versus the United State! It's the same as if you were to cover the muzzle of a gun with your hands and expect that way to prevent the shot. . . . It is absolute folly!"

A smile.

" 'We must all go insane—as soon as possible go insane.' It was yesterday, do you remember?"

Yes, she was right; I had even written it down. Consequently, it really had taken place. In silence I looked into her face. At that moment the dark cross was especially distinct.

"I-, dear, before it is too late . . . If you want . . . I'll leave everything, I'll forget everything, and we'll go there beyond the Wall, to *them*. . . . I do not even know who they are. . . ."

She shook her head. Through the dark windows of her eyes I saw within her a flaming oven, sparks, tongues of flame, and above them a heap of dry wood. It was clear to me that it was too late, my words could be of no avail.

She stood up. She would soon leave. Perhaps these were the last days, or the last minutes. . . . I grasped her hand.

"No, stay a little while longer . . . for the sake . . . for the sake . . ."

She slowly lifted my hand toward the light, my hairy paw which I detest. I wanted to withdraw it, but she held it tightly.

"Your hand . . . You undoubtedly don't know, and very few do know, that women from here occasionally used to fall in love with *them*. Probably there are in you a few drops of that blood of the sun and the woods. Perhaps that is why I . . ."

Silence. It was so strange that because of that silence, because of an emptiness, because of a nothing, my heart should beat so wildly. I cried:

"Ah, you shall not go yet! You shall not go until you tell me about *them*, for you love . . . them, and I don't even know who they are, nor where they come from."

"Where are they? The half we have lost. H_2 and O, two halves, but in order to get water—H_2O, creeks, seas, waterfalls, storms—those two halves must be united."

I distinctly remember every movement of hers. I remember she picked up a glass triangle from my table, and while talking she pressed its sharp edge against her cheek; a white scar would appear, then it would fill again and become pink and disappear. And it is strange that I cannot remember her words, especially the beginning of the story. I remember only different images and colors. At first, I remember, she told me about the Two Hundred Years' War. Red color. . . . On the green of the grass, on the dark clay, on the pale blue of the snow—everywhere red ditches that would not become dry. Then, yellow; yellow grass burned by the sun, yellow, naked wild men and wild dogs side by side near swollen cadavers of dogs or perhaps of men. All this certainly beyond the Walls, for the City was already the victor, and it already possessed our present-day petroleum food. And at night . . . down from the sky . . . heavy black folds. The folds would swing over the woods, the villages—blackish-red, slow columns of smoke. A dull moaning; endless strings of people driven into the City to be saved by force and to be whipped into happiness.

". . . You knew almost all this."

"Yes, almost."

"But you did not know, and only a few did, that a small part of them remained together and stayed to live beyond the Wall. Being naked, they went into the woods. They learned there from the trees, beasts, birds, flowers, and sun. Hair soon grew over their bodies, but under that hair they preserved their warm red blood. With you it was worse; numbers covered your bodies; numbers crawled over you like lice. One ought to strip you of everything, and naked you ought to be driven into the woods. You ought to learn how to tremble with fear, with joy, with wild anger, with cold; you should pray to fire! And we Mephi, we want . . ."

"Wait a minute! 'Mephi,' what does it mean?"

"Mephi? It is from Mephisto. You remember, there on the rock, the figure of the youth? Or, no. I shall explain it to you in your own language, and you will understand better. There are two forces in the world, entropy and energy. One leads into blessed quietude, to happy equilibrium, the other to the destruction of equilibrium, to torturingly perpetual motion. Our, or rather your ancestors, the Christians, worshiped entropy like a God. But we are not Christians, we . . ."

At that moment a slight whisper was suddenly heard, a knock at the door, and in rushed that flattened man with the forehead low over his eyes, who several times had brought me notes from I-330. He ran straight to us, stopped, panting like an air pump, and could say not a word, as he must have been running at top speed.

"But tell me! What has happened?" I-330 grasped him by the hand.

"They are coming here," panted the air pump, "with guards. . . . And with them that what's-his-name, the hunchback . . ."

"S-?"

"Yes. They are in the house by this time. They'll soon be here. Quick, quick!"

"Nonsense, we have time!" I-330 was laughing, cheerful sparks in her eyes. It was either absurd, senseless courage, or else there was something I did not understand.

"I-, dear, for the sake of the Well-Doer! You must understand that this . . ."

"For the sake of the Well-Doer!" The sharp, triangle smile.

"Well . . . well, for my sake, I implore you!"

"Oh, yes, I wanted to talk to you about some other matters. . . . Well, never mind. . . . We'll talk about them tomorrow."

And cheerfully (yes, cheerfully) she nodded to me; the other came out for a second from under his forehead's awning and nodded also. I was alone.

Quick! To my desk! I opened this manuscript and took up my pen so that they should find me at this work, which is for the benefit of the United State. Suddenly I felt every hair on my head living, separated, moving. "What if they should read even one page of these most recently written?"

Motionless I sat at the table, but everything around me seemed to be moving, as if the less than microscopic movements of the atoms had suddenly been magnified millions of times; I saw the walls trembling, my pen trembling, and the letters swinging and fusing together. "To hide them! But where?" Glass all around. "To burn them?" But they would notice the fire through the corridor and in the neighboring room. Besides, I felt unable, I felt too weak, to destroy this torturing and perhaps dearest piece of my own self. . . .

Voices from a distance (from the corridor), and steps. I had time only to snatch a handful of pages and put them under me and then, as if soldered to the armchair—every atom of which was quivering—I remained sitting, while the floor under my feet rolled like the deck of a ship, up and down. . . .

All shrunk together and hidden under the awning of my own forehead, like that messenger, I watched them stealthily; they were going from room to room, beginning at the right end of the corridor. Nearer . . . nearer. . . . I saw that some sat in their rooms, torpid like me; others would jump up and open their doors wide—lucky ones! If only I, too, could . . .

"The Well-Doer is the most perfect fumigation humanity needs; consequently, no peristalsis in the organism of the United State could . . ." I was writing this nonsense, pressing my trembling pen hard, and lower and lower my head bent over the table, and within me some sort of crazy forge . . . With my back I was listening . . . and I heard the click of the doorknob. . . . A current of fresh air. . . . My armchair was dancing a mad dance. . . . Only then, and even then with difficulty, I tore myself away from the page and turned my head in the direction of the newcomers (how difficult it is to play a foul game!). In front of all was S-, morose, silent, his eyes swiftly drilling deep shafts within me, within my armchair, and within the pages which were twitching in my hands. Then for a second—familiar, everyday faces at the door; one of them separated itself from the rest with its bulging, pinkish-brown gills. . . .

At once I recalled everything that had happened in the same room half an hour ago, and it was clear to me that they would presently . . .

All my being was shriveling and pulsating in that fortunately opaque part of my body with which I was covering the manuscript. U- came up to S-, gently plucked his sleeve, and said in a low voice:

"This is D-503, the builder of the *Integral*. You have probably heard of him. He is always like that, at his desk —does not spare himself at all!"

. . . And I thought . . . What a dear, wonderful woman! . . .

S- slid up to me, bent over my shoulder toward the table. I covered the lines I had written with my elbow, but he shouted severely:

"Show us at once what you have there, please!"

Dying with shame, I held out the sheet of paper. He read it over, and I noticed a tiny smile jump out of his eyes, scamper down his face, and, slightly wagging its tail, perch upon the right angle of his mouth. . . .

"Somewhat ambiguous, yet. . . . Well, you may continue; we shall not disturb you any further."

He went splashing toward the door as if in a ditch of water. And with every step of his I felt coming back to me my legs, my arms, my fingers—my soul again distributed itself evenly throughout my whole body; I breathed . . . .

The last thing: U- lingered in my room to come back to me and say right in my ear, in a whisper: "It is lucky for you that I . . ."

I did not understand. What did she mean by that? The same evening I learned that they had led away three

Numbers, although nobody speaks aloud about it, or about anything that happened. This ostensible silence is due to the educational influence of the Guardians who are ever present among us. Conversations deal chiefly with the quick fall of the barometer and the forthcoming change in the weather.

RECORD TWENTY-NINE

Threads on the Face
Sprouts
An Unnatural Compression

It is strange: the barometer continues to fall, yet there is no wind. There is quiet. Above, the storm which we do not yet hear has begun. The clouds are rushing with terrific speed. There are few of them as yet, separate fragments; it is as if above us an unknown city were being destroyed and pieces of walls and towers were rushing down, coming nearer and nearer with tremendous speed, but it will take some days of rushing through the blue infinite before they reach the bottom, that is us, below. And below there is silence.

There are thin, incomprehensible, almost invisible threads in the air; every autumn they are brought here from beyond the Wall. They float slowly, and suddenly you feel something foreign and invisible on your face; you want to brush it off, but no, you cannot rid yourself of it. You feel it especially near the Green Wall, where I was this morning. I-330 made an appointment with me to meet her in the Ancient House in that "apartment" of ours.

I was not far from the rust-red, opaque mass of the Ancient House when I heard behind me short, hasty steps and rapid breathing. I turned around and saw O-90 trying to catch up to me. She seemed strangely and perfectly rounded. Her arms and breast, her whole body, so familiar to me, was rounded out, stretching her unif.

It seemed as though it would soon tear the thin cloth and come out into the sun, into the light. I think that there in the green debris, in springtime, the unseen sprouts try thus to tear their way through the ground in order to send forth their branches and leaves and to bloom.

For a few seconds she stared into my face with her blue eyes, in silence.

"I saw you on the Day of Unanimity."

"I saw you, too." I at once remembered; below, in a narrow passage she had stood, pressing herself to the wall, protecting her abdomen with her arms; and automatically I now glanced at her abdomen which rounded the unif. She must have noticed, for she became pink, and with a rosy smile:

"I am so happy . . . so happy! I am so full of . . . you understand, I am . . . I walk and I hear nothing around me. . . . And all the while I listen within, within me. . . ."

I was silent. Something foreign was shadowing my face and I was unable to rid myself of it. Suddenly, all shining, light blue, she caught my hand; I felt her lips upon it. . . . It was the first time in my life. . . . It was some ancient caress as yet unknown to me. . . . And I was so ashamed and it pained me so much that I swiftly, I think even roughly, pulled my hand away.

"Listen, you are crazy, it seems. . . . And anyway you . . . What are you happy about? Is it possible that you forget what is ahead of you? If not now, then within a month or two. . . ."

Her light went out, her roundness sagged and shrank. And in my heart an unpleasant, even a painful compression, mixed with pity. Our heart is nothing else than an ideal pump: a compression, i.e., a shrinking at the moment of pumping, is a technical absurdity. Hence it is clear how essentially absurd, unnatural, and pathological are all these "loves" and "pities," etc., etc., which create that compression. . . .

Silence. To the left the cloudy green glass of the Wall.

And just ahead the dark red mass. Those two colors combined gave me what I thought was a splendid idea.

"Wait! I know how to save you! I shall save you from . . . To see one's own child for a few moments only, and then be sent to death! No! You shall be able to bring it up! You shall watch it and see it grow in your arms, and ripen like a fruit. . . ."

Her body quivered and she seemed to have chained herself to me.

"Do you remember that woman, I-330? That . . . of . . . of long ago? . . . Who during that walk? . . . Well, she is now right here, in the Ancient House. Let us go to her and I assure you that I shall arrange matters at once."

I already pictured us, I-330 and I, leading O-90 through the corridors . . . then how she would be brought amidst flowers, grass, and leaves. . . . But O-90 stepped back, the little horns of her rosy crescent trembling and bending downward.

"Is she *that same one*?" she asked.

"That is . . ." I was confused for some reason. "Yes, of course . . . that very same. . . ."

"And you want me to go to *her*, to ask her . . . to . . . Don't you ever dare to say another word about it!"

Leaning over, she walked away. . . . Then, as if she had remembered something, she turned around and cried:

"I shall die; all right! And it's none of your business . . . What do you care?"

Silence. From above pieces of blue towers and walls were falling downward with terrific speed . . . they will have perhaps hours or days to fly through the infinite. . . . Unseen threads were slowly floating through the air, planting themselves upon my face, and it was impossible to brush them off, impossible to rid myself of them.

I walked slowly toward the Ancient House, and in my heart I felt that absurd, tormenting compression. . . .

RECORD THIRTY

The Last Number
Galileo's Mistake
Would It Not Be Better?

Here is my conversation with I-330, which took place in the Ancient House yesterday in the midst of loud noise, among colors which stifled the logical course of my thoughts, red, green, bronze, saffron yellow, orange colors . . . and all the while under the motionless, marble smile of that snub-nosed ancient poet.

I shall reproduce the conversation word for word, for it seems to me that it may have an enormous and decisive importance for the fate of the United State—more than that, for the fate of the universe. Besides, in reading it, you, my unknown readers, may find some justification for me. I-330, without preliminaries, at once brought everything down upon my head.

"I know that the day after tomorrow the first trial trip of the *Integral* is to take place. On that day we shall take possession of it."

"What! Day after tomorrow?"

"Yes. Sit down and don't be upset. We cannot afford to lose a minute. Among the hundreds who were arrested yesterday there are twenty Mephis. To let two or three days pass means that they will perish."

I was silent.

"As observers on the trial trip they will send electricians, mechanics, physicians, meteorologists, etc. . . . At twelve sharp—you must remember this—when the bell rings for dinner, we shall remain in the passage; lock them all up in the dining hall, and the *Integral* will be ours. You realize that it is essential, happen what may! The *Integral* in our hands will be a tool that will help to put an end to everything at once without pain. . . . Their aeros? . . . Bah! They would be insignificant mosquitoes against a buzzard. And then, if it proves inevitable, we may direct the tubes of the motors downward, and by their work alone . . ."

I jumped up.

"It is inconceivable! It is absurd! Is it not clear to you that what you are planning is a revolution? Absurd, because a revolution is impossible! Because *our*—I speak for myself and for you—our revolution was the last one. No other revolutions may occur. Everybody knows that."

A mocking, sharp triangle of brows.

"My dear, you are a mathematician, are you not? More than that, a philosopher-mathematician? Well, then, name the last number."

"What is . . . I . . . I cannot understand, which *last*?"

"The last one, the highest, the largest."

"But I-330, that's absurd! Since the number of numbers is infinite, how can there be a last one?"

"And why then do you think there is a *last* revolution . . . their number is infinite. . . . The 'last one' is a child's story. Children are afraid of the infinite, and it is necessary that children should not be frightened, so that they may sleep through the night."

"But what is the use, what is the use of it all? For the sake of the Well-Doer! What is the use since all of us are happy already?"

"All right! Even suppose that is so. And then what?"

"How funny! A purely childish question. You tell a story to children, come to the very end, and they will invariably ask you, 'and then what'? and 'what for'? And then nothing! Period. In the whole world, evenly, everywhere, there is distributed . . ."

'Ah, 'evenly'! 'Everywhere!' That is the point, entropy! Psychological entropy. Don't you as a mathematician know that only differences—only differences—in temperature, only thermic contrasts make for life? And if all over the world there are evenly warm or evenly cold bodies, they must be pushed off! . . . in order to get flame, explosions! And we shall push! . . ."

"But I-330, please realize that our ancestors during the Two Hundred Years' War did exactly that!"

"Oh, they were right! A thousand times right! But they did one thing wrong: later they began to believe that they were the *last* number, a number that does not exist in nature. Their mistake was the mistake of Galileo; he was right in that the earth revolves around the sun, but he did not know that our whole solar system revolves around some other center, he did not know that the real, not relative, orbit of the earth is not a naïve circle."

"And you, the Mephi?"

"We? For the time being we know that there is no *last* number. We may forget that, someday. Of course, we shall certainly forget it when we grow old, as everything inevitably grows old. Then we shall inevitably fall like autumn leaves from the trees, like you the day after tomorrow. . . . No, no, dear, not you personally. You are with us, aren't you? You are with us?"

Flaming, stormy, sparkling! I never before had seen her in such a state. She embraced me with her whole self, and my self disappeared.

Her last word, looking steadily, deeply into my eyes:

"Then, do not forget: at twelve o'clock sharp."

And I answered:

"Yes, I remember."

She left. I was alone amidst a rebellious, multivoiced commotion of blue, red, green, saffron-yellow, and orange. . . .

Yes, at twelve! . . . Suddenly a feeling of something foreign on my face, of something implanted, that could not be brushed off. Suddenly, yesterday morning, and U- and all she had shouted into the face of I-330! Why, how absurd!

I hastened to get out of the house and home, home! Somewhere behind me I heard the chattering of the birds beyond the Wall. And ahead of me in the setting sun the balls of cupolas made of red, crystallized fire, enormous flaming cubes—houses—and the sharp point of the Accumulating Tower high in the sky like a paralyzed streak of lightning. And all this, all this impeccable, most geometric beauty, shall I, I myself, with my own hands . . . ? Is there no way out? No path? No trail?

I passed by an auditorium (I do not recall its number). Inside, the benches were stacked along the walls. In the middle, tables covered with snow-white glass sheets, with pink stains of sunny blood on the white. . . . There was foreshadowed in all that some unknown and therefore alarming tomorrow. It is unnatural for a thinking and seeing human being to live among irregularities, unknowns, X's. If suddenly your eyes were covered with a bandage and you were left to feel around, to stumble, ever aware that somewhere very close to you there was a border line, and one step only and nothing but a compressed, smothered piece of flesh would be left of you. . . . I now feel somewhat like that.

. . . And what if, without waiting for anything, I should . . . just head down. . . . Would it not be the only correct thing to do? To disentangle everything at once?

RECORD THIRTY-ONE

The Great Operation
I Forgave Everything
The Collision of Trains

Saved! At the very last moment, when it seemed that there was nothing to hold on to, that it was the end! . . .

It was as if you already ascended the steps toward the threatening machine of the Well-Doer, or as if the great glass Bell with a heavy thud had already covered you, and for the last time in life you looked at the blue sky to devour it with your eyes . . . when suddenly, it was only a dream! The sun is pink and cheerful and the wall . . . What happiness to be able to touch the cold wall! And the pillow! To delight endlessly in the little cavity formed by your own head in the white pillow! . . . This is approximately what I felt, when I read the *State Journal* this morning. It has all been a terrible dream, and the dream is over. And I was so feeble, so unfaithful, that I thought of selfish, voluntary death! I am ashamed now to reread yesterday's last lines. But let them remain as a memory of that incredible what-might-have-happened, which will not happen! On the front page of the *State Journal* the following gleamed:

REJOICE!

For from now on we are *perfect*!

Until today your own creation, engines, were more perfect than you.

WHY?

For every spark from a dynamo is a spark of pure reason; each motion of a piston, a pure syllogism. Is it not true that the same faultless reason is within you?

The philosophy of the cranes, presses, and pumps is complete and clear like a circle. But is your philosophy less circular? The beauty of a mechanism lies in its immutable, precise rhythm, like that of a pendulum. But have you not become as precise as a pendulum, you who are brought up on the system of Taylor?

Yes, but there is one difference:

MECHANISMS HAVE NO FANCY.

Did you ever notice a pump cylinder with a wide, distant, sensuously dreaming smile upon its face while it was working? Did you ever hear cranes that were restless, tossing about and sighing at night during the hours designed for rest?

NO!

Yet on your faces (you may well blush with shame!) the Guardians have more and more frequently seen those smiles, and they have heard your sighs. And (you should hide your eyes for shame!) the historians of the United State have all tendered their resignations so as to be relieved from having to record such shameful occurrences.

It is not your fault; you are ill. And the name of your illness is:

FANCY.

It is a worm that gnaws black wrinkles on one's forehead. It is a fever that drives one to run further and further, even though "further" may begin where happiness ends. It is the last barricade on our road to happiness.

Rejoice! This Barricade Has Been Blasted at Last! The Road Is Open!

The latest discovery of our State science is that there is a center for fancy—a miserable little nervous knot in the lower region of the frontal lobe of the brain. A triple treatment of this knot with X-rays will cure you of fancy,

Forever!

You are perfect; you are mechanized; the road to one-hundred-per-cent happiness is open! Hasten then all of you, young and old, hasten to undergo the Great Operation! Hasten to the auditoriums where the Great Operation is being performed! Long live the Great Operation! Long live the United State! Long live the Well-Doer!

You, had you not read all this in my records—which look like an ancient, strange novel—had you, like me, held in your trembling hands the newspaper, smelling of typographic ink . . . if you knew, as I do, that all this is a most certain reality—if not the reality of today, then that of tomorrow—would you not feel the very things I feel? Would your head not whirl as mine does? Would there not run over your back and arms those strange, sweet, icy needles? Would you not feel that you were a giant, an Atlas?—that if you only stood up and straightened out you would reach the ceiling with your head?

I snatched the telephone receiver.

"I-330. Yes . . . Yes. Yes . . . 330!" And then, swallowing my own words, I shouted, "Are you at home? Yes? Have you read? You are reading now? Isn't it, isn't it stupendous?"

"Yes. . . ." A long, dark silence. The wires buzzed almost imperceptibly. She was thinking.

"I must see you today without fail. Yes, in my room, after sixteen, without fail!"

Dear . . . she is such a dear! . . . "Without fail!" I was smiling, and I could not stop! I felt I would carry that smile with me into the street like a light above my head.

Outside the wind ran over me, whirling, whistling, whipping, but I felt even more cheerful. "All right, go on, go on moaning and groaning! The Walls cannot be torn down." Flying leaden clouds broke over my head . . . well, let them! They could not eclipse the sun! We chained it to the zenith like so many Joshuas, sons of Nun!

At the corner a group of such Joshuas, sons of Nun, were standing with their foreheads pasted to the glass of the wall. Inside, on a dazzling white table, a Number already lay. You could see two naked soles emerging from under the sheet in a yellow angle. . . . White medics bent over his head—a white hand, a stretched-out hand holding a syringe filled with something. . . .

"And you, what are you waiting for?" I asked nobody in particular, or rather all of them.

"And you?" Someone's round head turned to me.

"I? Oh, afterward! I must first . . ." Somewhat confused, I left the place. I really had to see I-330 first. But why first? I could not explain to myself. . . .

The docks. The *Integral*, bluish like ice, was glistening and sparkling. The engine was caressingly grumbling, repeating some one word, as if it were my word, a familiar one. I bent down and stroked the long, cold tube of the motor. "Dear! What a dear tube! Tomorrow it will come to life, tomorrow for the first time it will tremble with burning, flaming streams in its bowels."

With what eyes would I have looked at the glass monster had everything remained as it was yesterday? If I knew that tomorrow at twelve I should betray it, yes, betray. . . . Someone behind cautiously touched my elbow. I turned around. The plate-like, flat face of the Second Builder.

"Do you know already?" he asked.

"What? About the Operation? Yes. How everything, everything . . . suddenly . . ."

"No, not that. The trial flight is put off until day after tomorrow, on account of that Operation. They rushed us for nothing; we hurried . . ."

"On account of that Operation!" Funny, limited man. He could see no further than his own platter! If only he knew that, but for the Operation, tomorrow at twelve he would have been locked up in a glass cage, tossing about, trying to climb the walls!

At twelve-thirty when I came into my room I saw U-. She was sitting at my table, firm, straight, bone-like, resting her right cheek on her hand. She must have been waiting for a long while, because when she rose brusquely to meet me the five white imprints of her fingers remained on her cheek.

For a second that terrible morning came back to me: she beside I-330, indignant. But for a second only. All that was at once washed away by today's sun—as happens sometimes when you enter your room on a bright day and absent-mindedly turn on the light, and the bulb shines but is out of place, comical, unnecessary.

Without hesitation I held out my hand to her; I forgave her everything. She firmly grasped both my hands and pressed them till they hurt. Her cheeks quivering and hanging down like ancient precious ornaments, she said with emotion:

"I was waiting. . . . I want only one moment. . . . I only wanted to say . . . how happy, how joyous I am for you! You realize, of course, that tomorrow or day after tomorrow you will be healthy again, as if born anew."

I noticed my papers on the table; the last two pages of my record of yesterday were in the place where I had left them the night before. If only she knew what I had written there! But I didn't really care. Now it was only history; it was a ridiculously far-off distance, like an image seen through a reversed opera glass.

"Yes," I said. "A while ago, while passing along the avenue, I saw a man walking ahead of me. His shadow stretched along the pavement—and think of it! His shadow was luminous! I think—more than that, I am absolutely certain—that tomorrow all shadows will disappear. Not a shadow from any person or any thing! The sun will be shining through everything."

She, gently and earnestly:

"You are a dreamer! I would not allow my children in school to talk that way."

She told me something about the children: that they were all led in one herd to the Operation; that it was necessary to bind them afterward with ropes; that one must love pitilessly, "yes, pitilessly," and that she thought she might finally decide to . . .

She smoothed out the grayish-blue fold of the unif that fell between her knees, swiftly pasted her smiles all over me, and went out.

Fortunately the sun did not stop today. The sun was running. It was already sixteen o'clock. . . . I was knocking at the door, my heart was knocking. . . .

"Come in!"

I threw myself upon the floor near her chair, to embrace her limbs, to lift my head upward and look into her eyes, first into one, then into the other, and in each of them to see the reflection of myself in wonderful captivity. . . .

There beyond the wall it looked stormy, there the clouds were leaden—let them be! My head was overcrowded with impetuous words, and I was speaking aloud, and flying with the sun I knew not where. . . . No, now we knew where we were flying; planets were following me, planets sparkling with flame and populated with fiery, singing flowers, and mute planets, blue ones where rational stones were unified into one organized society, and planets which like our own earth had already reached the apex of one-hundred-per-cent happiness.

Suddenly, from above:

"And don't you think that at the apex are, precisely, *stones* unified into an organized society?" The triangle grew sharper and sharper, darker and darker.

"Happiness . . . well? . . . Desires are tortures, aren't they? It is clear, therefore, that happiness is when there are no longer any desires, not a single desire any more. What an error, what an absurd prejudice it was, that we used to mark happiness with the sign 'plus'! No, absolute happiness must be marked 'minus'—divine minus!"

I remember I stammered unintelligibly:

"Absolute zero!—minus 273° C."

"Minus 273°—exactly! A somewhat cool temperature. But doesn't it prove that we are at the summit?"

As before she seemed somehow to speak for me and through me, developing my own thoughts to the end. But there was something so morbid in her tone that I could not refrain . . . with an effort I drew out a "No."

"No," I said. "You, you are mocking. . . ."

She burst out laughing loudly, too loudly. Swiftly, in a second, she laughed herself to some unseen edge, stumbled, and fell over. . . . Silence.

She stood up, put her hands upon my shoulders, and looked into me for a long while. Then she pulled me toward her and everything seemed to have disappeared save her sharp, hot lips. . . .

"Good-by."

The words came from afar, from above, and reached me not at once but only after a minute, perhaps two minutes later.

"Why . . . why 'good-by'?"

"You have been ill, have you not? Because of me you have committed crimes. Hasn't all this tormented you? And now you have the Operation to look forward to. You will be cured of me. And that means—good-by."

"No!" I cried.

A pitilessly sharp black triangle on a white background.

"What? Do you mean that you don't want happiness?"

My head was breaking into pieces; two logical trains collided and crawled upon each other, rattling and smothering. . . .

"Well, I am waiting. You must choose; the Operation and one-hundred-per-cent happiness, or . . ."

"I cannot . . . without you. . . . I must not . . . without you . . ." I said, or perhaps I only thought—I am not sure which—but I-330 heard.

"Yes, I know," she said. Then, her hands still on my shoulders and her eyes not letting my eyes go, "Then . . . until tomorrow. Tomorrow at twelve. You remember?"

"No, it was postponed for a day. Day after tomorrow!"

"So much the better for us. At twelve, day after tomorrow!"

I walked alone in the dusky street. The wind was whirling, carrying, driving me like a piece of paper; fragments of the leaden sky were soaring, soaring—they had to soar through the infinite for another day or two. . . .

Unifs of Numbers were brushing my sides—yet I was walking alone. It was clear to me that all were being saved but that there was no salvation for me. For I *do not want* salvation. . . .

RECORD THIRTY-TWO

I Do Not Believe
Tractors
A Little Human Splinter

Do you believe that *you will die*? Oh, yes, "Man is mortal; I am a man; consequently . . ." No, not that; I know that; you know it. But I ask: Has it ever happened that you *actually believed* it? Believed definitely, believed not with your reason but with your *body*, that you actually felt that someday those fingers which now hold this page will become yellow, icy? . . .

No, of course you cannot believe this. That is why you haven't jumped from the tenth floor to the pavement before now; that is why you eat, turn over these pages, shave, smile, write.

This very thing, yes, exactly this is alive in me today. I know that that small black hand on the clock will slide down here toward midnight, then it will again start to ascend, and it will cross some last border and the improbable tomorrow will have arrived. I *know* it, but somehow I do not *believe* it—or perhaps I think that twenty-four hours are twenty-four years. So I am still able to act, to hurry, to answer questions, to climb the rope ladder to the *Integral*. I am still able to feel how the *Integral* shakes the surface of the water and I still understand that I must grasp the railing, and I am still able to feel the cold glass in my hand. I see the transparent, living cranes, bending their long necks, carefully feeding the *Integral* with the terrible explosive food which the motors need. I still see below on the river the blue veins and knots of water swollen by the wind. . . . Yet all this seems very distant from me, foreign, flat, like a draft on a sheet of paper. And it seems to me strange, when the flat draft-like face of the Second Builder suddenly asks:

"Well, then. How much fuel for the motors shall we load on? If we count on three, or say three and a half hours . . ."

I see before me, over a draft, my hand with the counter and the logarithmic dial at the figure 15.

"Fifteen tons. But you'd better take . . . yes, better take a thousand."

I said that because I *know* that tomorrow . . . I noticed that my hands and the dial began to tremble.

"A thousand! What do you need such a lot for? That would last a week! No, more than a week!"

"Well, nobody knows . . ."

I do know. . . .

The wind whistled, the air seemed to be stuffed to the limit with something invisible. I had difficulty in breathing, difficulty in walking, and with difficulty, slowly but without stopping for a second, the hand of the Accumulating Tower was crawling, at the end of the avenue. The peak of the Tower reached into the very clouds—dull, blue, groaning in a subdued way, sucking electricity from the clouds. The tubes of the Musical Tower resounded.

As always—four abreast. But the rows did not seem as firm as usual; they were swinging, bending more and more, perhaps because of the wind. There! They seemed to stumble upon something at the corner; they drew back and stopped, congealed, a close mass, a clot, breathing rapidly; at once all of them stretched their necks like geese.

"Look! No, look, look—there, quick!"

"*They*? Are those *they*?"

"Ah, never! Never! I'd rather put my head straight into the Machine. . . ."

"Silence! Are you crazy?"

On the corner, the doors of the auditorium were ajar, and a wide column of about fifty people—the word "people" is not the right one. These were heavy-wheeled automatons seemingly bound in iron and moved by an invisible mechanism. Not people, but a sort of human-like tractor. Over their heads, floating in the air—a white banner with a golden sun embroidered on it, and the rays of the sun: "We are the first! We have already been operated upon! Follow us, all of you!"

Slowly, unhesitatingly they moved through the crowd, and it was clear that if they had had in their way a wall, a tree, a house, they would have moved on just as unhesitatingly through the wall, the tree, the house. In the middle of the avenue they fused and stretched out into a chain, arm in arm, their faces turned toward us. And we, a human clot, tense, the hair pricking our heads, we waited. Our necks were stretched out goose fashion. Clouds. The wind whistled. Suddenly the wings of the chain from right and left bent quickly around us, and faster, faster, like a heavy engine descending a hill, they closed the ring and pulled us toward the yawning doors and inside. . . .

Somebody's piercing cry: "They are driving us in! Run!"

Everybody ran. Close to the wall there was still an open, living gate of human beings. Everybody dashed through it, heads forward. Their heads became sharp wedges, and with their ribs, shoulders, hips . . . Like a stream of water compressed in a fire hose they spurted out in the form of a fan, and all around me stamping feet, raised arms, unifs. . . . The double curved S- with his transparent wing ears appeared for a moment close before my eyes; he disappeared as suddenly; I was alone among arms and legs appearing for a second and disappearing. I was running. . . .

I dashed to the entrance of a house to stop to catch my breath, my back close to the door—and suddenly, like a splinter borne by the wind, a human being was thrown toward me.

"All the while I . . . I have been following you. I do not want . . . do you see? I do not want . . . I am ready to . . ."

Small round hands on my sleeves, round dark blue eyes—it was O-90. She just slipped along my body like a unif which, its hanger broken, slips along the wall to fall upon the floor. Like a little bundle she crumpled below me on the cold doorstep, and I stood over her, stroking her head, her face. My hands were wet. I felt as if I were very big and she very small, a small part of myself. I felt something quite different from what I feel toward I-330. I think the ancients must have had similar feelings toward their private children.

Below, filtering through her hands with which she was covering her face, a voice came to me:

"Every night I . . . I cannot! If they cure me . . . Every night I sit in the darkness alone and think of *him*, and of what he will look like when I . . . If I am cured I would have nothing to live with—do you understand me? You must . . . you must . . ."

An absurd feeling, yet it was there; I really must! Absurd, because this "duty" of mine was nothing but another crime. Absurd, because white and black cannot be one, duty and crime cannot coincide. Or perhaps there is no black and white in life, but everything depends upon the first logical premise? If the premise is that I unlawfully gave her a child . . .

"It's all right, but don't, only don't . . ." I said, "Of course I understand. . . . I must take you to I-330, as I once offered to, so that she . . ."

"Yes." (This in a low voice, without uncovering her face.)

I helped her rise. Silently we went along the darkening street, each busy with his own thoughts, or perhaps with the same thought. . . . We walked between silent, leaden houses, through the tense, whipping branches of the wind. . . .

All at once, through the whistling of the wind, I heard, as if splashing through ditches, the familiar footsteps coming from some unseen point. At the corner I turned around, and among the clouds, flying upside down in the dim glass reflection of the pavement, I saw S-. Instantly my arms became foreign, swinging out of time, and I began to tell O-90 in a low voice that tomorrow, yes, tomorrow, was the day of the first flight of the *Integral*, and that it was to be something that had never happened before in all history, great, miraculous.

"Think of it! For the first time in life to find myself outside the limits of our city and see—who knows what is beyond the Green Wall?"

O-90 looked at me extremely surprised, her blue eyes trying to penetrate mine; she looked at my senselessly swinging arms. But I did not let her say a word—I kept talking, talking. . . . And within me, apart from what I was saying and audible only to myself, a thought was feverishly buzzing and knocking. "Impossible! You must somehow . . . you must not lead *him* to I-330!"

Instead of turning to the right I turned to the left. The bridge submissively bent its back in a slavish way to all three of us, to me, to O-, to him behind. Lights were falling from the houses across the water, falling and breaking into thousands of sparks which danced feverishly, sprayed with the mad white foam of the water. Somewhere not far away the wind was moaning like the tensely stretched string of a double bass. And through this bass, behind us, all the while . . .

The house where I live. At the entrance O- stopped and began:

"No! You promised, did you not, that . . ."

I did not let her finish. Hastily I pushed her through the entrance and we found ourselves in the lobby. At the controller's desk the familiar, hanging, excitedly quivering cheeks—a group of Numbers around. They were quarreling about something, heads bending over the banisters on the second floor; they were running downstairs one by one. But about that later. I drew O-90 at once into the opposite, unoccupied corner and sat down with my back to the wall. I saw a dark, large-headed shadow gliding back and forth over the sidewalk. I took out my notebook. O-90 in her chair was sinking slowly, as if she were evaporating from under her unif, as if her body were thawing, as if only her empty unif were left, and empty eyes taking one into the blue emptiness. In a tired voice:

"Why did you bring me here? You lied to me."

"No, not so loud! Look here! Do you see? Through the wall?"

"Yes, I see a shadow."

"He is always following me . . . I cannot . . . Do you understand? I cannot, therefore . . . I am going to write a few words to I-330. You take the note and go alone. I know he will remain here."

Her body began again to take form and to move beneath the unif; on her face a faint sunrise, dawn. I put the note between her cold fingers, pressed her hand firmly, and for the last time looked into her blue eyes.

"Good-by. Perhaps someday . . ." She freed her hand. Bending over slightly, she slowly moved away, made two steps, turned around quickly, and again we were side by side. Her lips were moving; with her lips and with her eyes she repeated some inaudible word. What an unbearable smile! What suffering!

Then the bent-over human splinter went to the door; a bent-over little shadow beyond the wall; without turning around she went on faster, still faster. . . .

I went to U-'s desk. With emotion filling her indignant gills, she said to me:

"They have all gone crazy! He, for instance, is trying to assure me that he himself saw a naked man covered with hair near the Ancient House . . ."

A voice from the group of empty raised heads:

"Yes. I repeat it, yes."

"Well, what do you think of that? Oh, what a delirium!" The word "delirium" came out of her mouth so full of conviction, so unbending, that I asked myself: "Perhaps it really was nothing but delirium, all that has been going on around me lately." I glanced at my hairy hand, and I remembered: "There are, undoubtedly, some drops of that blood of the sun and woods in you. That is why perhaps you . . ." No, fortunately it was not delirium; or no, *un*fortunately it was not delirium.

RECORD THIRTY-THREE

This Without a Synopsis, Hastily, the Last

The day.

Quick, to the newspaper! Perhaps there . . . I read the paper with my eyes (exactly; my eyes now are like a pen, or like a counting machine which you hold and feel in your hands like a tool, something foreign, an instrument). In the newspaper, on the first page, in large print:

THE ENEMIES OF HAPPINESS ARE AWAKE! HOLD TO YOUR HAPPINESS WITH BOTH HANDS. TOMORROW ALL WORK WILL STOP AND ALL NUMBERS ARE TO COME TO BE OPERATED UPON. THOSE WHO FAIL TO COME WILL BE SUBMITTED TO THE MACHINE OF THE WELL-DOER.

Tomorrow! How can there be, how can there be any tomorrow?

Following my daily habit, I stretched out my arm (instrument!) to the bookshelf to put today's paper with the rest within a cover ornamented with gold. While doing this: "What for? What does it matter? Never again shall I . . . Within this cover, never . . ." And out of my hands, down to the floor it fell.

I stood looking all around, over all my room; hastily I was taking away, feverishly putting into some unseen valise, everything I regretted leaving here: my desk, my books, my chair. Upon that chair I-330 had sat that day; I was below on the floor . . . My bed . . . Then for a minute or two I stood and waited for some miracle to happen; perhaps the telephone would ring, perhaps she would say that . . . But no, no miracle . . .

I am leaving, going into the unknown. These are my last lines. Farewell you, my unknown beloved ones, with whom I have lived through so many pages, before whom I have bared my diseased soul, my whole self to the last broken little screw, to the last cracked spring . . . I am going . . .

RECORD THIRTY-FOUR

The Forgiven Ones
A Sunny Night
A Radio-Valkyrie

Oh, if only I had actually broken myself to pieces! If only I had actually found myself with her in some place beyond the Wall, among beasts showing their yellow tusks. If only I had never actually returned here! It would be a thousand, a million times easier! But now—what? Now to go and choke that—! But would it help? No, no, no! Take yourself in hand, D-503! Set into yourself the firm hub of logic; at least for a short while weigh heavily with all your might on the lever and, like the ancient slave, turn the millstones of syllogisms until you have written down and understood everything that happened. . . .

When I boarded the *Integral*, everyone was already there and in his place; all the cells of the gigantic hive were filled. Through the decks of glass—tiny, antlike people below, at the telegraph, dynamo, transformers, altimeters, ventilators, indicators, motor, pumps, tubes. . . . In the saloon people were sitting over tables and instruments, probably those commissioned by the Scientific Bureau; near them the Second Builder and his two aides. All three had their heads down between their shoulders like turtles, their faces gray, autumnal, rayless.

"Well?" I asked.

"Well, somewhat uncanny," one of them replied, smiling a gray, rayless smile. "Perhaps we shall have to land in some unknown place. And, generally speaking, nobody knows . . ."

I could hardly bear to look at them, when in an hour or so I was to throw them out with my own hands, to cast them out from the cozy figures of our Table of Hours, to tear them away forever from the mother's breast of the United State. They reminded me of the tragic figures of "The Three Forgiven Ones"—a story known to all of our school children. It tells about three Numbers, who by way of experiment were exempted for a whole month from any work.[1] "Go wherever you will, do what you will," they were told. The unhappy three spent their whole time wandering around their usual place of work and gazing within with hungry eyes. They would stop on the plazas and busy themselves for hours repeating the motions which they had been used to making during certain hours of the day; it became a bodily necessity for them to do so. They would saw and plane the air; with unseen sledge hammers they would bang upon unseen stakes. Finally, on the tenth day, they could bear it no longer; they took one another by the hand, entered the river, and to the accompaniment of the March they waded deeper and deeper until the water ended their sufferings forever.

I repeat, it was hard for me to look at them, and I was anxious to leave them.

"I just want to take a glance into the engine room, and then off!" I said.

They were asking me questions: "What voltage should be used for the initial spark, how much ballast water was needed in the tank aft?" As if a phonograph were somewhere within me, I was giving quick and precise answers, but I, my inner self, was busy with my own thoughts.

[1] It happened long ago, in the third century A. T. (After the Tables).

In the narrow passage gray unifs were passing, gray faces, and, for a second, one face with its hair low over the forehead, eyes gazing from deep beneath it—it was *that same man.* I understood: *they* had come, and there was no escape from it for me; only minutes remained, a few dozen minutes. . . . An infinitesimal, molecular quiver of my whole body. This quivering did not stop to the very end—it was as if an enormous motor had been placed under the very foundation of my body, which was so light that the walls, partitions, cables, beams, lights—everything was quivering. . . .

I did not yet know whether *she* was there. But I had no time . . . They were calling me: quick! To the commander's bridge; time to go . . . where?

Gray, rayless faces. Below in the water—tense blue veins. Heavy, cast-iron patches of sky. It was so difficult to lift my cast-iron hand and take up the receiver of the commander's telephone! . . . "Up! Forty-five degrees!"

A heavy explosion—a jerk—a rabid, greenish-white mountain of water aft—the deck beneath my feet began to move, soft as rubber; and everything below, my whole life, forever . . . For a second, falling deeper and deeper into a sort of funnel, becoming more and more compressed—the icy-blue relief map of the City, the round bubbles of cupolas, the lonely leaden finger of the Accumulating Tower. . . . Then, instantaneously, a cotton curtain of cloud . . . We pierced it, and there was the sun and the blue sky! Seconds, minutes, miles—the blue was hardening, fast filling with darkness; like drops of cold, silver sweat the stars appeared. . . .

A sad, unbearably bright, black, starry, sunny night. . . . As if one had become deaf, one still saw that the pipes were roaring, but one only *saw*; dead silence all about. The sun was mute. It was natural, of course. One might have expected it; we were beyond the terrestrial atmosphere. The transition was so quick, so sudden, that everyone became timid and silent. Yet I . . . I thought I felt easier under that fantastic, mute sun. I had bounded over the inevitable border, having left my body somewhere there below, and I was soaring bodiless to a new world, where everything was to be different, upside down.

"Keep the same course!" I shouted into the engine room, or perhaps it was not I but a phonograph in me, and the same machine that I was, with a mechanical, hinge-like movement, handed the commander's trumpet to the Second Builder. Permeated by that most delicate, molecular quiver known only to me, I ran down the companionway, to seek . . .

The door of the saloon. . . . An hour later it was to latch and lock itself. . . . At the door stood an unfamiliar Number. He was small, with a face like a hundred or a thousand others which are usually lost in a crowd, but his arms were exceptionally long—they reached down to his knees, as if they had been taken by mistake from another set of human organs and fastened to his shoulders.

The long arm stretched out and barred the way.

"Where do you want to go?"

It was obvious that he was not aware that I knew everything. All right! Perhaps it had to be that way. From above him, in a deliberately significant tone, I said:

"I am the Builder of the *Integral*, and I am directing the test flight. Do you understand?"

The arm drew away.

The saloon. Heads covered with bristles, gray iron bristles, and yellow heads, and bald, ripe heads were bent over the instruments and maps. Swiftly, with a glance, I gathered them in with my eyes; off I ran, back down the long passage, then through the hatch into the engine room. It was hot there from the red tubes, overheated by the explosions: a constant roar—the levers were dancing their desperate, drunken dance, moving ceaselessly with a barely noticeable quiver; the arrows on the dials . . . There! At last! Near the tachometer, a notebook in his hand, was that man with the low forehead.

"Listen," I shouted straight into his ear (because of the roar). "Is she here? Where is she?"

"She? There, at the radio."

I dashed over. There were three of them, all with receiving helmets on. And she seemed a head taller than usual, wingy, sparkling, flying like an ancient Valkyrie; the bluish sparks from the radio seemed to emanate from her—from her also that ethereal, lightning-like odor of ozone.

"Someone—well, you, for instance," I said to her, panting from having run, "I must send a message down to earth, to the docks. Come, I shall dictate it to you."

Close to the apparatus there was a small, box-like cabin. We sat at the table side by side. I found her hand and pressed it hard.

"Well, what is going to happen?"

"I don't know. Do you realize how wonderful it is? To fly without knowing where . . . no matter where? It will soon be twelve o'clock and nobody knows what . . . And when night . . . Where shall you and I be tonight? Perhaps somewhere on the grass, on dry leaves . . ."

Blue sparks emanated from her, and the odor of lightning, and the vibration within me became more and more frequent.

"Write down," I said loudly, panting (from having run). "Time: eleven-twenty; speed, 5,800 . . ."

"Last night she came to me with your note. I know . . . I know everything; don't talk. . . . But the child is yours. I sent her over; she is already beyond the Wall. She will live. . . ."

I was back on the commander's bridge, back in the delirious night with its black starry sky and its dazzling sun. The hands of the clock on the table were slowly moving from minute to minute. Everything was permeated by a thin, hardly perceptible quivering (only I noticed it). For some reason a thought passed through my head: it would be better if all this took place not here but somewhere below, nearer to earth.

"Stop!" I commanded.

We kept moving by inertia, but more and more slowly. Now the *Integral* was caught for a second by an imperceptible little hair, for a second it hung motionless, then the little hair broke and the *Integral*, like a stone, dashed downward with increasing speed. That way minutes, tens of minutes passed in silence. My pulse was audible; the hand of the clock before my eyes came closer and closer to twelve. It was clear to me that I was a stone, I-330 the earth, and the stone was under irresistible compulsion to fall downward, to strike the earth and break into small particles. What if . . .? Already the hard, blue smoke of clouds appeared below. . . . What if . . .? But the phonograph within me, with a hinge-like motion and precision, took the telephone and commanded: "Low speed!" The stone ceased falling. Now only the four lower tubes were growling, two ahead and two aft, only enough to hold the *Integral* motionless; and the *Integral*, only slightly trembling, stopped in the air as if anchored, about one kilometer from the earth.

Everybody came out on deck (it was shortly before twelve, before the sounding of the dinner gong) and leaned over the glass railing; hastily, in huge gulps, they devoured the unknown world which lay below, beyond the Green Wall. Amber, blue, green, the autumnal woods, prairies, a lake. At the edge of a little blue saucer some lone yellow debris, a threatening, dried-out yellow finger—it must have been the tower of an ancient "church" saved by a miracle. . . .

"Look, there! Look! There to the right!"

There—over the green desert—a brown blot was rapidly moving. I held a telescope in my hands and automatically I brought it to my eyes: the grass reaching their chests, a herd of brown horses was galloping, and on their backs—*they*, black, white, and dark . . .

Behind me:

"I assure you, I saw a face!"

"Go away! Tell it to someone else!"

"Well, look for yourself! Here is the telescope."

They had already disappeared. Endless green desert—and in that desert, dominating it completely and dominating me, and everybody, the piercing vibrations of the gong; dinnertime, one minute to twelve.

For a second the little world around me became incoherent, dispersed. Someone's brass badge fell to the floor. It mattered little. Soon it was under my heel. A voice: "And I tell you, it was a face!" A black square, the open door of the main saloon. White teeth pressed together, smiling . . . And at that moment, when the clock began slowly to strike, holding its breath between beats, and when the front rows began to move toward the dining saloon, the rectangle of the door was suddenly crossed by the two familiar, unnaturally long arms.

"STOP!"

Someone's fingers sank piercing into my palm. It was I-330. She was beside me.

"Who is it? Do you know him?"

"Is he not? . . . Is he not? . . ."

He was already lifted upon somebody's shoulders. Above a hundred other faces, his face like hundreds, like thousands of other faces, yet unique among them all. . . .

"In the name of the Guardians! You, to whom I talk, *they* hear me, every one of them hears me. I talk to you: *we know*! We don't know your numbers yet, but we know everything else. The *Integral* shall not be yours! The test flight will be carried out to the end and you, you will not dare to make another move! You, with your own hands, will help to go on with the test and afterward . . . well, I have finished!"

Silence. The glass plates under my feet seemed soft, cotton-like. My feet, too—soft, cotton-like. Beside me—she with a dead-white smile, angry blue sparks. Through her teeth to me:

"Ah! It is your work! You did your 'duty'! Well . . ." She tore her hand from mine; the Valkyrie helmet with indignant wings was soon to be seen some distance in front of me. I was alone, torpid, silent. Like everyone else I followed into the dining saloon.

But it was not I, not I! I told nobody, save these white, mute pages. . . I cried this to her within me, inaudibly, desperately, loudly. She was across the table, directly opposite me, and not once did she even touch me with her gaze. Beside her someone's ripe, yellow, bald head. I heard (it was I-330's voice):

" 'Nobility' of character! But my dear professor, even a superficial etymological analysis of the word shows that it is a superstition, a remnant of the ancient feudal epoch. We . . ."

I felt I was growing pale, and that they would soon notice it. But the phonograph within me performed the prescribed fifty chewing movements for every bite. I locked myself into myself as though into an opaque house; I threw up a heap of rocks before my door and lowered the window blinds. . . .

Afterward, the telephone of the commander was again in my hands, and again we made the flight through the clouds with icy, supreme anxiety into the icy, starry, sunny night. Minutes, hours passed. . . . Apparently all that time the motor of logic within me was working feverishly at full speed. For suddenly somewhere, at a distant point of the dark blue space, I saw my desk, and the gill-like cheeks of U- bent over it, and the forgotten pages of my records! It became clear to me; nobody but her . . . everything was clear to me!

If only I could reach the radio room soon . . . wing-like helmets, the odor of blue lightning . . . I remember telling her something in a low voice, and I remember how she looked *through* me, and how her voice seemed to come from a distance:

"I am busy. I am receiving a message from below. You may dictate yours to her."

The small, box-like little cabin . . . I thought for a second and then dictated in a firm voice:

"Time fourteen-forty. Going down. Motors stopped. The end of all."

The commander's bridge. The machine heart of the *Integral* stopped; we were falling; my heart could not catch up and would remain behind and rise higher and higher into my throat. . . . Clouds. . . . And then a distant green spot—everything green, more and more distinct, running like a storm toward us. "Soon the end."

The porcelain-like distorted white face of the Second Builder! It was he who struck me with all his strength; I hurt my head on something; and through the approaching darkness, I heard while falling:

"Full speed—aft!"

A brusque jolt upward. . . .

RECORD THIRTY-FIVE

In a Ring
A Carrot
A Murder

I did not sleep all night. But one thought the whole night . . . As a result of yesterday's mishap my head is tightly bandaged—it seems to me not a bandage but a ring, a pitiless ring of glass iron, riveted about my head. And I am busy with the same thought, always the same thought in my riveted circle: to kill U-. To kill U- and then go to *her* and say: "Now do you believe?" What is most disquieting is that to kill is dirty, primitive. To break her head with something—the thought of it gives me a peculiar sensation of something disgustingly sweet in my mouth, and I am unable to swallow my saliva; I am always spitting into my handkerchief, yet my mouth feels dry.

I had in my closet a heavy piston rod which had cracked during the casting, and which I had brought home in order to find out with a microscope the cause of the cracking. I made my manuscript into a tube (let her read me to the last letter!), pushed the broken piston into that tube, and went downstairs. The stairway seemed endless, the steps disgustingly slippery, liquid. I had to wipe moisture from off my mouth very frequently. Downstairs . . . my heart dropped. I took the piston out and went to the controller's table. But she was not there; instead, an empty, icy desk with ink blots. And then I remembered that today all work had stopped; everyone was to go to be operated on. There was no need for her to stay here. There was nobody to be registered. . . .

The street. It was windy. The sky seemed to be composed of soaring panels of cast iron. And exactly as it had seemed for one moment yesterday, the whole world was broken up into separate, sharp, independent fragments, and each of these fragments was falling at full speed; each would stop for a second, hang before me in the air, and disappear without a trace. It was as if the precise, black letters on this page should suddenly move apart and begin to jump hither and thither in fright, so that there was not a word on the page, only nonsensical "ap," "jum," "wor." The crowd seemed just as nonsensical, dispersed (not in rows), going forward, backward, diagonally, transversely. . . .

Then nobody. For a second, suddenly stopping in my mad dashing, I saw on the second floor, in the glass cage of a room hanging in the air, a man and a woman—a kiss; she, standing with her whole body bent backward, brokenly: "This is for the last time, forever. . . ."

At a corner a thorny, moving bush of heads. Above the heads separate, floating in the air, a banner: "Down with the machines! Down with the Operation!" And, distinct from my own self, I thought: "Is it possible that each one of us bears such a pain, that it can be removed only with his heart? . . . . That something must be done to each one, before he . . ." For a second everything disappeared for me from the world, except my beast-like hand with the heavy, cast-iron package it held. . . .

A boy appeared. He was running, a shadow under his lower lip. The lower lip turned out like the cuff of a rolled-up sleeve. His face was distorted; he wept loudly; he was running away from someone. The stamping of feet was heard behind him. . . .

The boy reminded me: "U- must be in school. I must hurry!" I ran to the nearest opening of the Underground

Railway. At the entrance someone passed me and said, "Not running. No trains today . . . there!" I descended. A sort of general delirium was reigning. The glitter of cut-crystal suns; the platform packed closely with heads. An empty, torpid train.

In the silence—a voice. I could not see her but I knew, I knew that intense, living, flexible, whip-like, flogging voice! I felt there that sharp triangle of brows drawn to the temples. . . .

"Let me! Let me reach her! I must! . . ."

Someone's tentacles caught my arm, my shoulders. I was nailed. In the silence I heard:

"No. Go up to them. There they will cure you; there they will overfeed you with that leavened happiness. Satiated, you will slumber peacefully, organized, keeping time, and snoring sweetly. Is it possible that you do not hear yet that great symphony of snoring? Foolish people! Don't you realize that they want to liberate you from these gnawing, worm-like, torturing question marks? And you remain standing here and listening to me? Quick! Up! To the Great Operation! What is your concern, if I remain here alone? What does it matter to you if I want to struggle, hopelessly struggle? So much the better! What does it matter to you that I do not want others to desire for me? I want to desire for myself. If I desire the impossible . . ."

Another voice, slow, heavy:

"Ah, the impossible! Which means to run after your stupid fancies; those fancies would whirl from under your very noses like a tail. No, we shall catch that tail, and then . . ."

"And then—swallow it and fall snoring; a new tail will become necessary. They say the ancients had a certain animal which they called 'ass.' In order to make it go forward they would attach a carrot to a bow held in front of its nose, so that it could not reach it. . . . If it had caught and swallowed it . . ."

The tentacles suddenly let me go; I threw myself toward the place she was speaking from; but at that very moment everything was brought down in confusion. Shouts from behind: "They are coming here! Coming here!" The lights twinkled and went out—someone had cut the cable—and everything was like a lava of cries, groaning, heads, fingers. . . .

I do not know how long we were rolled about that way in the underground tube. I only remember that underneath my feet steps were felt, dusk appeared, becoming brighter and brighter, and again we were in the street, dispersing fan wise in different directions.

Again I was alone. Wind. Gray, low twilight crawling over my head. In the damp glass of the sidewalk, somewhere very deep, there were light, topsy-turvy walls and figures moving along, feet upward. And that terribly heavy package in my hands pulled me down into that depth, to the bottom.

At the desk again. U- was not yet there; her room was dark and empty. I went up to my room and turned on the light. My temples, tightly bound by the iron ring, were pulsating. I paced and paced, always in the same circle: my table, the white package on the table, the bed, my table, the white package on the table . . . In the room to my left the curtains were lowered. To my right, the knotty bald head bent over a book, the enormous, parabolic forehead. Wrinkles on the forehead like a series of yellow, illegible lines. At times our eyes met, and then I felt that those lines were about me.

. . . It happened at twenty-one o'clock exactly. U- came in on her own initiative. I remember that my breathing was so loud that I could hear it, and that I wanted to breathe less noisily but was unable to.

She sat down and arranged the fold of her unif on her knees. The pinkish-brown gills were waving.

"Oh, dear, is it true that you are wounded? I just learned about it, and at once I ran . . ."

The piston was before me on the table. I jumped up, breathing even louder. She heard, and stopped halfway through a word and rose. Already I had located the place on her head; something disgustingly sweet was in my mouth. . . . My handkerchief! I could not find it. I spat on the floor.

The fellow with the yellow, fixed wrinkles which think of me! He must not see. It would be even more disgusting if he could . . . I pressed the button (I had no right to, but who cared about rights at that moment?). The curtains fell.

Evidently she felt and understood what was coming, for she rushed to the door. But I was quicker than she, and I locked the door with the key, breathing loudly and not for a second taking my eyes from that place on her head. . . .

"You . . . you are mad! How dare you . . ." She moved backward toward the bed, put her trembling hands between her knees. . . . Like a tense spring, holding her firmly with my gaze, I slowly stretched out my arm toward the table (only one arm could move), and I snatched the piston.

"I implore you! One day—only one day! Tomorrow I shall go and attend to the formalities . . ."

What was she talking about? I swung my arm . . . And I consider I killed her. Yes, you my unknown readers, you have the right to call me murderer. I know that I should have dealt the blow on her head had she not screamed:

"For . . . for the sake . . . I agree. . . . I . . . one moment . . ." With trembling hands she tore off her unif—a large, yellow, drooping body, she fell upon the bed. . . .

Then I understood; she thought that I pulled the curtains . . . in order to . . . that I wanted . . .

This was so unexpected and so stupid that I burst out laughing. Immediately the tense spring within me broke, and my hand weakened, and the piston fell to the floor.

Here I learned from personal experience that laughter

is the most terrible of weapons; you can kill anything with laughter, even murder. I sat at my table and laughed desperately; I saw no way out of that absurd situation. I don't know what would have been the end if things had run their natural course, but suddenly a new factor in the arithmetical chain: the telephone rang.

I hurried, grasped the receiver. Perhaps she . . . I heard an unfamiliar voice:

"Wait a minute."

Annoying, infinite buzzing. Heavy steps from afar, nearer and louder like cast iron, and . . .

"D-503? The Well-Doer speaking. Come at once to me."

Ding! He hung up the receiver. Ding! like a key in a keyhole.

U- was still in bed, eyes closed, gills apart in the form of a smile. I picked up her clothes, threw them on her, and said through clenched teeth:

"Well. Quick! Quick!"

She raised her body on her elbow, her breasts hanging down to one side, eyes round. She became a figure of wax.

"What?"

"Get dressed, that is what!"

Face distorted, she firmly snatched her clothes and said in a flat voice, "Turn away . . ."

I turned away, pressed my forehead against the glass. Light, figures, sparks were trembling in the black, wet mirror. . . . No, all this was I, myself—within me. . . . What did HE call me for? Is it possible that HE knows already about her, about me, about everything?

U-, already dressed, was at the door. I made a step toward her and pressed her hand as hard as though I hoped to squeeze out of it, drop by drop, what I needed.

"Listen . . . Her name, you know whom I am talking of, did you report her name? No? Tell the truth, I must . . . I don't care what happens, but tell the truth!"

"No."

"No? But why not, since you . . ."

Her lower lip turned out like the lip of that boy and her face . . . tears were running down her cheeks.

"Because I . . . I was afraid that if I did you might . . . you would stop lov– Oh, I cannot, I could not!"

I understood. It was the truth. Absurd, ridiculous, human truth. I opened the door.

RECORD THIRTY-SIX

Empty Pages
The Christian God
About My Mother

It is very strange that a kind of empty white page should be left in my hand. How I walked there, how I waited (I remember I had to wait), I know nothing about it; I remember not a sound, not a face, not a gesture, as if all communicating wires between me and the world were cut.

When I came to, I found myself standing before Him. I was afraid to raise my eyes; I saw only the enormous cast-iron hands upon His knees. Those hands weighed upon Him, bending His knees with their weight. He was slowly moving His fingers. His face was somewhere above, as if in fog. And, only because His voice came to my ears from such a height, it did not roar like thunder, it did not deafen me but appeared to be an ordinary, human voice.

"Then you, too, you, the Builder of the *Integral*! You, whose lot it was to become the greatest of all *conquistadores*! You, whose name was to have been at the head of a glorious new chapter in the history of the United State! You . . ."

Blood ran to my head, to my cheeks—and here again a white page; only the pulsation in my temples and the heavy voice from above; but I remember not a word. Only when He became silent, I came to and noticed how His hand moved heavily like a thousand pounds, and crawled slowly—His finger threatened me.

"Well? Why are you silent? Is it true, or not? Executioner? So!"

"So," I repeated submissively. And then I heard clearly every one of His words.

"Well, then? Do you think I am afraid of the Word? Did you ever try to take off its shell and look into its inner meaning? I shall tell you. . . . Remember a blue hill, a crowd, a cross? Some up on the hill, sprinkled with blood, are busy nailing a body to the cross; others below, sprinkled with tears, are gazing upward. Does it not occur to you that the part which those above must play is the more difficult, the more important part? If it were not for them, how could that magnificent tragedy ever have been staged? True, they were hissed by the dark crowd, but for that the author of the tragedy, God, should have remunerated them the more liberally, should He not? And the most clement, Christian God himself, who burned all the infidels on a slow fire, is He not an executioner? Was the number of those burned by the Christians less than the number of burned Christians? Yet (you must understand this!), yet this God was for centuries glorified as the God of love! Absurd? Oh, no. Just the contrary. It is instead a testament to the imperishable wisdom of man, written in blood. Even at the time when he still was wild and hairy, man knew that real, algebraic love for humanity must inevitably be inhuman, and that the inevitable mark of truth is cruelty—just as the inevitable mark of fire is its property of causing the sensation of burning. Could you show me a fire that would not hurt? Well, now prove your point! Proceed! Argue!"

How could I argue? How could I argue when those thoughts were once mine, though I was never able to dress them in such a splendid, tempered armor? I remained silent.

"If your silence is intended to mean that you agree with

me, then let us talk as adults do after the children have gone to bed; let us talk to the logical end. I ask: what was it that man from his diaper age dreamed of, tormented himself for, prayed for? He longed for that day when someone would tell him what happiness is, and then would chain him to it. What else are we doing now? The ancient dream about a paradise . . . Remember: there in paradise they know no desires any more, no pity, no love; there they are all—blessed. An operation has been performed upon their center of fancy; that is why they are blessed, angels, servants of God. . . . And now, at the very moment when we have caught up with that dream, when we hold it like this" (He clenched his hand so hard, that if he had held a stone in it sap would have run out!) ". . . . At the moment when all that was left for us was to adorn our prize and distribute it among all in equal pieces, at that very moment you, you . . ."

The cast-iron roar was suddenly broken off. I was as red as a piece of iron on an anvil under the moulding sledge hammer. The hammer seemed to have stopped for a second, hanging in the air, and I waited, waited . . . until suddenly:

"How old are you?"

"Thirty-two."

"Just double the age, and as simple as at sixteen! Listen. Is it possible that it really never occurred to you that *they* (we do not yet know their names, but I am certain you will disclose them to us), that *they* were interested in you only as the Builder of the *Integral*? Only in order to be able, through the use of you—"

"Don't! Don't!" I cried. But it was like protecting yourself with your hands and crying to a bullet: you may still be hearing your own "don't," but meanwhile the bullet has burned you through, and writhing with pain you are prostrated on the ground.

Yes, yes: the Builder of the *Integral* . . . Yes, yes. . . . At once there came back to me the angry face of U- with twitching, brick-red gills, on that morning when both of them . . .

I remember now, clearly, how I raised my eyes and laughed. A Socrates-like, bald-headed man was sitting before me; and small drops of sweat dotted the bald surface of his head.

How simple, how magnificently trivial everything was! How simple . . . almost to the point of being ridiculous! Laughter was choking me and bursting forth in puffs; I covered my mouth with my hand and rushed wildly out. . . .

Steps. Wind. Damp, leaping fragments of lights and faces . . . And while running: "No! Only to see her! To see her once more!"

Here again an empty white page. All I remember is feet: not people, just feet, hundreds of feet, confusedly stamping feet, falling from somewhere in the pavement, a heavy rain of feet . . . And some cheerful, daring voice, and a shout that was probably for me: "Hey, hey! Come here! Come along with us!"

Afterward—a deserted square heavily overloaded with tense wind. In the middle of the square a dim, heavy, threatening mass—the Machine of the Well-Doer. And a seemingly unexpected image arose within me in response to the sight of the Machine: a snow-white pillow, and on the pillow a head thrown back, and half-closed eyes, and a sharp, sweet line of teeth. . . All this seemed so absurdly, so terribly connected with the Machine. I know *how* this connection has come about, but I do not yet want to see it nor to say it aloud—I don't want to! I don't!

I closed my eyes and sat down on the steps which led upward to the Machine. I must have been running hard, for my face was wet. From somewhere far away cries were coming. But nobody heard them; nobody heard me crying: "Save me from it—save me!"

If only I had a mother as the ancients had—my mother, *mine*, for whom I should be not the Builder of the *Integral*, and not D-530, not a molecule of the United State, but merely a living human piece, a piece of herself, a trampled, smothered, cast-off piece . . . And though I were driving the nails into the cross, or being nailed to it (perhaps it is the same), she would hear what no one else could hear, her old, grown-together, wrinkled lips. . . .

RECORD THIRTY-SEVEN

Infusorian
Doomsday
Her Room

This morning while we were in the refectory my neighbor to my left whispered to me in a frightened tone:

"But why don't you eat? Don't you see, they are looking at you!"

I had to pluck up all my strength to show a smile. I felt it—like a crack in my face; I smiled, and the borders of the crack drew apart wider and wider; it was quite painful.

And then: no sooner had I lifted the small cube of paste upon my fork, than the fork jerked from my hand and tinkled against the plate. And at once the tables, the walls, the plates, even the air, trembled and rang; outside, too, an enormous, iron, round roar reaching the sky—floating over heads and houses, it died away in the distance in small, hardly perceptible circles like those upon water.

I saw faces instantaneously grow faded and bleached; I saw mouths filled with food suddenly motionless, and forks hanging in air. Then everything became confused, jumped off the centuries-old tracks; everybody jumped up from his place (without singing the Hymn!) and confusedly, in disorder, hastily finishing chewing, choking, grasping one another.... They were asking: "What? What happened? What? . . ." And the disorderly fragments of the Machine, which was once perfect and great, fell down in all directions—down the elevators, down the stairs. . . . Stamping of feet . . . Pieces of words like pieces of torn letters carried by the wind. . . .

The same outpour from the neighboring houses. A minute later the avenue seemed like a drop of water seen under a microscope: the infusoria locked up in the transparent, glass-like drop of water were tossing around, from side to side, up and down.

"Ah!" Someone's triumphant voice. I saw the back of a neck, and a finger pointing to the sky. I remember very distinctly a yellowish-pinkish nail, and under the nail a crescent crawling out as if from under the horizon. The finger was like a compass; all eyes were raised to the sky.

There, running away from invisible pursuit, masses of cloud were rushing upon each other; colored by the clouds, the aeros of the Guardians were floating with their tube-like antennae. And farther to the west—something like . . . At first nobody could understand what it was, even I, who knew (unfortunately) more than the others. It was like a great hive of black aeros swarming somewhere at an extraordinary height—they looked like hardly noticeable, swiftly moving points . . . Nearer and nearer . . . Hoarse, guttural sounds began to reach the earth, and finally we saw *birds* just over our heads! They filled the sky with their sharp, black, descending triangles. The furious wind drove them down, and they began to land on the cupolas, on the roofs, poles, and balconies.

"Ah—ah!" and the triumphant back of the neck turned; again I saw that man with the protruding forehead, but it seemed that the name, so to speak, was all that was left of him: he seemed to have crawled out from under his forehead, and on his face, around the eyes and lips, bunches of rays were growing. Through the noise of the wind and the wings and the cawing he cried to me:

"Do you realize? Do you realize! They have blown up the Wall! The Wall has been blown up! Do you *understand*?"

Somewhere in the background figures with their heads drawn in were hastily rushing by and into the houses. In the middle of the pavements was a mass of those who had already been operated upon; they moved toward the west . . .

. . . Hairy bunches of rays around the lips and eyes . . . I grasped his hands:

"Tell me. Where is she? Where is I-330? There? Beyond the Wall, or . . . ? I must . . . Do you hear me? At once . . . I cannot . . ."

"Here!" he shouted in a happy, drunken voice, showing strong yellow teeth, "here in town, and she is acting! Oh, we are doing great work!"

Who are those "we"? Who am I?

There were about fifty around him. Like him, they seemed to have crawled out from under their foreheads. They were loud, cheerful, strong-toothed, swallowing the stormy wind. With their simple not at all terrible-looking electrocutors (where did they get them?), they started to the west, toward the operated ones, encircling them, keeping parallel to avenue Forty-eight . . .

Stumbling against the tightly drawn ropes woven by the wind, I was running to her. What for? I did not know. I was stumbling . . . Empty streets . . . The city seemed foreign, wild, filled with the ceaseless, triumphant hubbub of the birds. It seemed like the end of the world, *Doomsday*.

Through the glass of the walls in quite a few houses (this cut into my mind), I saw male and female Numbers in shameless embraces—without curtains lowered, without pink checks, in the middle of the day! . . .

The house—her house; the door ajar. The lobby, the

control desk, all were empty. The elevator had stopped in the middle of its shaft. I ran panting up the endless stairs. The corridor. Like the spokes of a wheel figures on the doors dashed past my eyes: 320, 326, 330—I-330! Through the glass wall I could see everything in her room upside down, confused, creased: the table overturned, its legs in the air like a beast; the bed absurdly placed away from the wall, obliquely; strewn over the floor—fallen, trodden petals of pink checks.

I bent over and picked up one, two, three of them; all bore the name D-503. I was on all of them, drops of myself, of my molten, poured-out self. And that was all—that was left . . .

Somehow I felt they should not lie there on the floor and be trodden upon. I gathered a handful of them, put them on the table, and carefully smoothed them out, glanced at them, and . . . laughed aloud! I never knew it before but now I know—and you, too, know—that laughter may be of different colors. Laughter is but a distant echo of an explosion within us; it may be the echo of a holiday —red, blue, and golden fireworks—or at times it may represent pieces of human flesh exploded into the air. . . .

I noticed an unfamiliar name on some of the pink checks. I do not remember the figures but I do remember the letter—F. I brushed the stubs from the table to the floor, stepped on them, on myself, stamped on them with my heels—and went out . . .

In the corridor I sat on the window sill in front of her door and waited long and stupidly. An old man appeared. His face was like a pierced, empty bladder with folds; from beneath the puncture something transparent was still slowly dripping. Slowly, vaguely, I realized—tears. And only when the old man was quite far off I came to and exclaimed:

"Please . . . listen. . . . Do you know . . . Number I-330?"

The old man turned around, waved his hand in despair, and stumbled farther away. . . .

I returned home at dusk. On the west side the sky was twitching every second in a pale blue, electric convulsion; a subdued, heavy roar could be heard from that direction. The roofs were covered with black, charred sticks—birds.

I lay down; and instantly, like a heavy beast, sleep came and stifled me. . . .

RECORD THIRTY-EIGHT

I Don't Know What Title—Perhaps the Whole Synopsis May Be Called a Castoff Cigarette Butt

I awoke. A bright glare painful to look at. I half-closed my eyes. My head seemed filled with some caustic blue smoke. Everything was enveloped in fog, and through the fog:

"But I did not turn on the light . . . then how is it . . ."

I jumped up. At the table, leaning her chin on her hand and smiling, sat I-330, looking at me.

She was at the very table at which I am now writing. Those ten or fifteen minutes are already well behind me, cruelly twisted into a very firm spring. Yet it seems to me that the door closed after her only a second ago, and that I could still overtake her and grasp her hand, and that she might laugh out and say . . .

I-330 was at the table. I rushed toward her.

"You? You! I have been . . . I saw your room. . . . I thought you . . ." But midway I hurt myself upon the sharp, motionless spears of her eyelashes, and I stopped. I remembered: she had looked at me in the same way before, in the *Integral*. I felt I had to tell her everything in one split second, and in such a way that she would surely believe, or she would never . . .

"Listen, I-330, I must . . . I must . . . everything! No, no, one moment—let me have a glass of water first."

My mouth was as dry as if it were lined with blotting paper. I poured a glass of water but I couldn't . . . I put the glass back upon the table, and with both hands firmly grasped the carafe.

Now I noticed that the blue smoke came from a cigarette. She brought the cigarette to her lips, and eagerly drew in and swallowed the smoke as I did water; then she said:

"Don't. Be silent. Don't you see it matters very little? I came, anyway. They are waiting for me below. . . . Do you want these minutes, which are our last . . . ?"

Abruptly she threw the cigarette on the floor and bent backward, over the side of the chair, to reach the button in the wall (it was quite difficult to do), and I remember how the chair swayed slightly, how two of its legs were lifted. Then the curtains fell.

She came close to me and embraced me. Her knees, through her dress, were like a slow, gentle, warm, enveloping, and permeating poison . . .

Suddenly (it happens at times) you plunge into sweet, warm sleep—when all at once, as if something pricks you, you tremble and your eyes are again widely open. So it was now; there on the floor in her room were the pink checks stamped with traces of footsteps, some of them bore the letter F- and some figures . . . Plus and minus fused within my mind into one lump . . . I could not say even now what sort of feeling it was, but I crushed her so that she cried out with pain . . .

One more minute out of those ten or fifteen; her head thrown back, lying on the bright white pillow, her eyes half-closed, a sharp, sweet line of teeth . . . And all this reminded me in an irresistible, absurd, torturing way about something forbidden, something not permissible at that moment. More tenderly, more cruelly, I pressed her to myself, brighter grew the blue traces of my fingers . . .

She said, without opening her eyes (I noticed this), "They say you went to see the Well-Doer yesterday; is it true?"

"Yes."

Then her eyes opened widely and with delight I looked at her and saw that her face grew quickly paler and paler, that it effaced itself, disappearing—only the eyes remained.

I told her everything. Only for some reason, why I don't know (no, that's not true, I know the reason), I was silent about one thing: His assertion at the end that they needed me only in order . . .

Like the image on a photographic plate in a developing fluid, her face gradually reappeared: the cheeks, the white line of teeth, the lips. She stood up and went to the mirror door of the closet. My mouth was dry again. I poured water but it was revolting to drink it; I put the glass back on the table and asked:

"Did you come to see me because you wanted to inquire . . . ?"

A sharp, mocking triangle of brows drawn to the temples looked at me from the mirror. She turned around to say something, but said nothing.

It was not necessary; I knew.

To bid her good-by, I moved my foreign limbs, struck the chair with them. It fell upside down, dead, like the table in her room. Her lips were cold . . . just as cold was once the floor, here, near my bed . . .

When she left I sat down on the floor, bent over the cigarette butt . . .

I cannot write any more—I no longer want to!

RECORD THIRTY-NINE

The End

All this was like the last crystal of salt thrown into a saturated solution; quickly, needle-like crystals began to appear, to grow more substantial and solid. It was all clear to me; the decision was made, and tomorrow morning *I shall do it*! It amounts to suicide, but perhaps then I shall be reborn. For only what is killed can be reborn.

Every second the sky twitched convulsively there in the west. My head was burning and pulsating inside; I was up all night, and I fell asleep only at about seven o'clock in the morning, when the darkness of the night was already dispelled and becoming gray, and the roofs crowded with birds became visible . . .

I woke up; ten o'clock. Evidently the bell did not ring today. On the table—left from yesterday—stood the glass of water. I gulped the water eagerly and I ran; I had to do it quickly, as quickly as possible.

The sky was deserted, blue, all eaten up by the storm. Sharp corners of shadows . . . Everything seemed to be cut out of blue autumnal air—thin, dangerous to touch; it seemed so brittle, ready to disperse into glass dust. Within me something similar; I must not think; it was dangerous to think, for . . .

And I did not think, perhaps I did not even see properly; I only registered impressions. There on the pavement, thrown from somewhere, branches were strewn; their leaves were green, amber, and cherry-red. Above, crossing each other, birds and aeros were tossing about. Here below heads, open mouths, hands waving branches . . . All this must have been shouting, buzzing, chirping . . .

Then—streets empty as if swept by a plague. I remember I stumbled over something disgustingly soft, yielding yet motionless. I bent down—a corpse. It was lying flat, the legs apart. The face . . . I recognized the thick Negro lips, which even now seemed to sprinkle with laughter. His eyes, firmly screwed in, laughed into my face. One second . . . I stepped over him and ran: I could no longer . . . I had to have everything done as soon as possible, or else I felt I would snap, I would break in two like an overloaded sail . . .

Luckily it was not more than twenty steps away; I already saw the sign with the golden letters: "The Bureau of Guardians." At the door I stopped for a moment to gulp down as much air as I could, and I stepped in.

Inside, in the corridor, stood an endless chain of Numbers, holding small sheets of paper and heavy notebooks. They moved slowly, advancing a step or two and stopping again. I began to be tossed about along the chain; my head was breaking to pieces. I pulled them by the sleeves, I implored them as a sick man implores to be given something that would, even at the price of sharpest pain, end everything forever.

A woman with a belt tightly clasped around her waist and with two distinctly protruding, squatty hemispheres tossing about as if she had eyes on them, chuckled at me:

"He has a bellyache! Show him to the room second door to the right!"

Everybody laughed, and because of that laughter something rose in my throat; I felt I would either scream or . . . or . . .

Suddenly from behind me someone touched my elbow. I turned around. Transparent wing ears! But they were not pink as usual; they were purplish red; his Adam's apple was tossing about as though ready to tear the covering . . .

Quickly boring into me: "What are you here for?"

I seized him.

"Quickly! Please! Quickly! . . . into your office . . . I must tell everything . . . right away . . . I am glad that you . . . It may be terrible that it should be you to whom . . . But it is good, it is good. . . ."

He, too, knew *her*; this made it even more tormenting for me. But perhaps he, too, would tremble when he heard . . . And we would both be killing . . . And I would not be alone at that, my supreme second . . .

The door closed with a slam. I remember a piece of paper was caught beneath the door, and it rustled on the floor when the door closed. And then a strange, airless silence covered us as if a glass bell had been put over us. If only he had uttered a single, most insignificant word, no matter what, I would have told him everything at once. But he was silent. So keyed up that I heard a noise in my cars, I said without looking at him:

"I think I always hated her from the very beginning . . . I struggled . . . Or, no, no, don't believe me; I could have, but I did not want to save myself. I wanted to perish; this was dearer to me than anything else . . . and even now, even this minute, when I already know everything . . . Do you know that I was summoned to the Well-Doer?"

"Yes, I do."

"But what he told me! Please realize that it was equivalent to . . . it was as if someone should remove the floor from under you this minute, and you and everything here on the desk, the papers, the ink . . . the ink would splash out and cover everything with blots . . ."

"What else? What further? Hurry up, others are waiting!"

Then, stumbling, muttering, I told him everything that is recorded in these pages . . . About my real self, and about my hairy self, and about my hands . . . yes . . . exactly, that was the beginning . . . And how I lied to myself, and how she obtained false certificates for me, and how I grew worse and worse, every day, and about the long corridors underground, and there beyond the Wall . . .

All this I threw out in formless pieces and lumps. I would stutter and fail to find words. The lips double-curved in a smile would prompt me with the word I needed, and I would nod gratefully: "Yes, yes!" . . . Suddenly, what was it? He was talking for me, and I only listened and nodded: "Yes, yes," and then, "Yes, exactly so, . . . yes, yes . . ."

I felt cold around my mouth as though it were wet with ether, and I asked with difficulty:

"But how is it . . . You could not learn anywhere . . ."

He smiled a smile growing more and more curved; then:

"But I see that you do want to conceal something from me. For example, you enumerated everything you saw beyond the Wall, but you failed to mention one thing. You deny it? But don't you remember that once, just in passing, just for a second, you saw me there? Yes, yes, *me*!"

Silence.

Suddenly, like a flash of lightning, it became shamelessly clear to me: he—he, too— And everything about myself, my torment, all that I had brought here, crushed by the burden, plucking up my last strength as if performing a great feat, all appeared to me only funny—like the ancient anecdote about Abraham and Isaac: Abraham all in a cold sweat, with the knife already raised over his son, over himself, and suddenly a voice from above: "Never mind . . . I was only joking."

Without taking my eyes from the smile that grew more and more curved, I put my hands on the edge of the desk and slowly, very slowly pushed myself with my chair away from him. Then instantly gathering myself into my own hands, I dashed madly out, past loud voices, past steps and mouths . . .

I do not remember how I got into one of the public rest rooms, in a station of the Underground Railway. Above, everything was perishing; the greatest civilization, the most rational in human history was crumbling, but here, by some irony, everything remained as before, beautiful. The walls shone; water murmured cozily; and like the water, the unseen, transparent music . . . Only think of it! All this is doomed; all this will be covered with grass someday; only myths will remain . . .

I moaned aloud. At the same instant I felt someone gently patting my knee. It was from the left; it was my neighbor who occupied a seat on my left—an enormous forehead, a bald parabola, yellow, unintelligible lines of wrinkles on his forehead, those lines about me.

"I understand you. I understand completely," he said. "Yet you must calm yourself. You must. It will return. It will inevitably return. It is only important that everybody should learn of my discovery. You are the first to whom I talk about it. I have calculated that there is *no infinity*! No!"

I looked at him wildly.

"Yes, yes, I tell you so. There is no infinity. If the universe is infinite, then the average density of matter must equal zero; but since we know it is not zero, therefore the universe is finite; it is spherical in form, and the square of its radius—R^2—is equal to the average density multiplied by . . .The only thing left is to calculate the numerical coefficient and then . . . Do you realize what it means? It means that everything is final, everything is simple . . . But you, my honored sir, you disturb me, you prevent my finishing my calculations by your yelling!"

I do not know which shattered me more, his discovery, or his positiveness at that apocalyptic hour. Only then did I notice that he had a notebook in his hands, and a logarithmic dial. I understood then that even if everything was perishing it was my duty (before you, my unknown and beloved) to leave these records in a finished form.

I asked him to give me some paper, and here in the rest room, to the accompaniment of the quiet music, transparent like water, I wrote down these last lines.

I was about to put down a period as the ancients would put a cross over the caves into which they used to throw their dead, when all of a sudden my pencil trembled and fell from between my fingers . . .

"Listen!" I pulled my neighbor. "Yes, listen, I say. There, where your finite universe ends, what is there? What?"

He had no time to answer. From above, down the steps stamping . . .

RECORD FORTY

Facts
The Bell
I Am Certain

Daylight. It is clear. The barometer—760 mm. Is it possible that I, D-503, really wrote these—pages? Is it possible that I ever felt, or imagined I felt, all this?

The handwriting is mine. And what follows is all in my handwriting. Fortunately, only the handwriting. No more delirium, no absurd metaphors, no feelings—only facts. For I am healthy—perfectly, absolutely healthy . . I am smiling; I cannot help smiling; a splinter has been taken out of my head, and I feel so light, so empty! To be more exact, not empty, but there is nothing foreign, nothing that prevents me from smiling. (Smiling is the normal state for a normal human being.)

The facts are as follows: That evening my neighbor who discovered the finiteness of the universe, and I, and all others who did not have a certificate showing that we had been operated on, all of us were taken to the nearest auditorium. (For some reason the number of the auditorium, 112, seemed familiar to me.) There they tied us to the tables and performed the great operation. Next day, I, D-503, appeared before the Well-Doer and told him everything known to me about the enemies of happiness. Why, before, it had seemed hard for me to go, I cannot understand. The only explanation seems to be my illness—my soul.

That same evening, sitting at the same table with Him, with the Well-Doer, I saw for the first time in my life the famous Gas Chamber. They brought in that woman. She was to testify in my presence. She remained stubbornly silent and smiling. I noticed that she had sharp and very white teeth which were very pretty.

Then she was brought under the Bell. Her face became very white, and as her eyes were large and dark, all was very pretty. When they began pumping the air from under the Bell she threw her head back and half-closed her eyes; her lips were pressed together. This reminded me of something. She looked at me, holding the arms of the chair firmly. She continued to look until her eyes closed. Then she was taken out and brought back to consciousness by means of electrodes, and again she was put under the Bell. The procedure was repeated three times, yet she did not utter a word.

The others who were brought in with that woman proved to be more honest; many of them began to speak after the first trial. Tomorrow they will all ascend the steps to the Machine of the Well-Doer. No postponement is possible, for there still is chaos, groaning, cadavers, beasts in the western section; and to our regret there are still quantities of Numbers who have betrayed Reason.

But on the transverse avenue Forty we have succeeded in establishing a temporary Wall of high-voltage waves. And I hope we win. More than that; I am certain we shall win. For Reason must prevail.